THE CRUCIFIXION OF ESMERELDA SWEETWATER

A PARABLE FOR ALL AGES

DON ELKINS AND CARLA L. RUECKERT

ISBN: 978-0-945007-06-7

L/L Research
P.O. Box 5195
Louisville, KY 40255-0195

Cover artwork by Don Elkins with assistance from Mary Ann Bowman

In grateful memory of my Beloved Companion,
Lt. Phineas T. Pinkham

Soli Deo Gloria

Donald Tully Elkins

Carla Lisbeth Rueckert

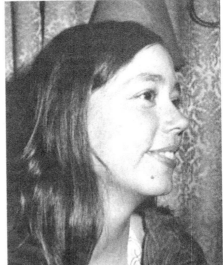

Photographs by Doug Lewis

Table Of Contents

Proem   6

Introduction And Reminiscence   7

Prologue   20

Chapter One   23

Chapter Two   36

Chapter Three   46

Chapter Four   50

Chapter Five   65

Chapter Six   72

Chapter Seven   79

Chapter Eight   89

Chapter Nine   106

Chapter Ten   115

Chapter Eleven   130

Chapter Twelve   152

Chapter Thirteen   163

Chapter Fourteen   178

Chapter Fifteen   185

Chapter Sixteen   198

Chapter Seventeen   212

Chapter Eighteen   215

Postlogue   222

Appendix:
The Prophetic Qualities of *The Crucifixion of Esmerelda Sweetwater*   225

Proem

This novel is the first fruit of L/L Research, written in 1968, refined in 1969, and, because of rejections from many of the major publishers, destined to sit in file drawers until private donations made it possible for us to offer this volume to those for whom it may have some value. That it has some value is of little doubt to me, even though I was the co-author of it. The writing of it was like nothing that I have experienced before or since. Concepts and characters flowed with a clarity and precision onto the paper that I would have thought impossible. It was as if I were watching and reporting on an unfolding situation rather than making up a story.

In the years following, right up through 1984, many things that were written as fiction in THE CRUCIFIXION OF ESMERELDA SWEETWATER seem to be echoed, sometimes quite closely, in the life of Don's and my relationship, our partnership, and the work with our group. Some of the details are synchronistic enough to warrant comment; hence this introduction. But before we touch upon similarities, I would like to sketch the story that unfolded in Don's and my private life which came to parallel so closely many of the events in this book.

Introduction And Reminiscence

Donald Tully Elkins, whom many of his friends called "Phineas" and others "Ichabod" due to his six foot five inch height and slenderness, was a remarkable man. Born in 1930, he was brought up during the Depression by a father who was often absent, due to the difficulty of finding work which would have allowed him to be home more, his mother and her family, devout Christian Scientists. They put heart and soul into raising him, and he was much beloved by all of his family. He was always a silent and independent person, even as a child, and at an early age decided that, even though his mother was a reader for the church, he would elect not to attend church services. With quiet persistence he maneuvered his way through childhood and adolescence going his own way, keeping the extent of his creative and analytical intelligence a secret known only to his mother and, as he put it, accomplishing this anonymity by "sitting behind the fat kid" so that he wouldn't get called on in school, which bored him as much as church did. However, being a person of caution and extreme common sense, Don came to the realization as a senior in high school that he did not wish to work at the kind of job that he could get with a high school education, so he straightened up behind the fat kid, got decent grades, and eventually collected three degrees in engineering from the Speed Scientific School at the University of Louisville.

Faced again with the choice of engineering jobs available, a somewhat disillusioned Phineas turned to graduate degrees and teaching. He became a masterful and magnetic teacher of engineering physics and mechanical engineering, as well as civil engineering, and in 1960-61, during a school year spent at the University of Alaska in Fairbanks, he created the mechanical engineering program and curriculum at that university.

However, Louisville was his favorite city and to Louisville he returned after a year away, regaining his position as Associate Professor at the University of Louisville. He taught his students with a mixture of firmness and liberality. It is difficult to describe what a good teacher Don was. His personality was unflappable. His keen intellect found a mode of expression in sharing knowledge with his students, and his sense of drama was given free reign. As a physics teacher he was a favorite with students, not only because he taught physics so well, but also because he enjoyed the inevitable practical jokes that came his way. An example: one of his students once placed a deceased cat on Don's desk. Don wrote on the chalkboard, "Next time, bring money." He immediately began the day's teaching. The students conferred and, at their next class, when Don came through the classroom door he was pelted with pennies, which Don carefully collected and pocketed before turning to the day's work. The students were daunted, but rallied, and recruited one of the student's girl friends to serve Don a martini at the beginning of the next class. In she came, bunny suit and all. Don lifted the napkin covering the drink and noted, "Too much vermouth." After a stunned moment, the girl fled, and Don got an ovation.

In the army, during the Korean War, he became the youngest man ever to become a Master Sergeant. He was given the job two months before his twenty-first birthday although it was not made official until he become of age. His rise to this high noncommissioned office was meteoric and was the product of his life-long love affair with firearms and his ability to deal dispassionately, fairly, and with a sense of humor, with his troops. A perfect illustration of this skill was his response to an aggrieved general's order that a two-hour lecture be given on the necessity of proper army saluting. Master Sgt. Elkins prepared a two-hour vaudeville show about saluting under farcical and fanciful conditions, enlisting his fellow noncoms for the production. While the rest of the camp's morale dropped like mercury in a blizzard, Elkins had his men whooping with laughter.

He first became noticed by the Army when his guard unit was activated in 1950-51. He was invited by a personal friend who was an officer to come to the officer's shooting range for some target practice. Don shot a perfect score: the target paper showed all shots in the bulls-eye. The leader of the firing range asked to "pull the card" for Don, as he thought such a high score suspicious. Don repeated his perfect score, and the now-convinced leader had Don give an impromptu lesson to every man, all of whom outranked him, on the range. Promotions began at once, and because men liked being led by Don, his longing for the Master Sergeant's private room was quickly fulfilled.

Much of Don's childhood was spent in the small towns of Kentucky, although he was born in Louisville and went to high school there. Many a weekend while he was in high school was spent tramping the wild areas south and west of Louisville with his buddies, Charles P. Sutt and William Rue, friends whom he considered among his best until his life's end.

In 1955, Don began seriously to investigate the world of the paranormal. He flew all over the country, usually assisted by either Jim Crunkleton or D. K. Meador, long-time pilot friends. Chicago, Ohio, Pennsylvania, and California saw him visiting contactee groups, and he spoke with everyone from J. B. Rhine to George Van Tassel. Not all of the groups and individuals Don met were able to offer Don information immediately useful, but Don just collected the "puzzle pieces" as carefully as he could, and spent much time looking at how these puzzle pieces could fit together. In 1962, acting on information which he had received from a UFO contactee group in Detroit, he began what became a long-term and extensive investigation into UFO contact. I was a member of the original group of meditators in that investigation, but it was not until 1968 that Don began to work with me.

Trained as a librarian, I had been very happy at my job as a school librarian for an excellent private school for girls. It was a dream job for a librarian. I was solely in charge of thirteen grades of school children, so that I was able to do everything from choosing books, to cataloging them and working with teachers, to working with each individual child as she came through the study hall, which was in the library. However, when Don asked me to join him in his work, there was no hesitation on my part. And so began our story together.

Don's and my story together was a story of love and a story of work, both of which were highly unusual and unconventional and yet most profound. When I first met Don in 1962, I looked into the deep blue eyes which gazed upon me as he sat across the table, stooped as he habitually was, and I saw a great deal of loneliness. This impression was at variance with most people's first impression of Don, which was that he was a person of whom to be in awe. The usual comment from people who saw Don for the first time was "He can see right through me." This often engendered a certain kind of fear in people which was difficult to overcome until one had spent some time with Don.

After my husband, Jim DeWitt, a wonderful man who married too young, divorced me in 1968, Don spent more and more time in my apartment and eventually took lodgings himself and offered me a room in his dwelling. Since I was receiving a very small monthly stipend, this was of the greatest help to me. Although our relationship was platonic, this arrangement continued until Don's death in November of 1984. He required from me nothing but my presence. I have never known a more unselfish man, nor one capable of purer affection. This affection was entirely unspoken, for Don felt that words were cheap, and the words "I love you" especially had been misused to the point where they had virtually no meaning. Compliments were something to be given to less intimate friends; he thought them to be a hindrance to my maturing process. I called it "the School of No" since Don, though loath to praise, was happy to correct! Nevertheless, his treatment of me was as tender as that of a father towards a child; indeed, he was overprotective often to the point of my own rebellion.

The relationship that developed between us was one of the strongest and certainly the most positive that I have ever experienced. It endured for sixteen years, getting better every year. We shared thousands of jokes both small and large, talked earnestly into the night many nights, shared Don's often impossible dreams, and tried to bring them into reality. We were two different creatures, Don being the archetypical male who would have no truck with anything sentimental; I, on the other hand, being a born romantic, a mystical Christian, and one much involved with music-which Don said hurt his ears. My favorite composer, Johann Sebastian Bach, might have agreed with him had he heard me practicing his magnificent cantatas in my small, boy soprano voice!

In 1965, Don had left his tenured position at the University of Louisville to seek the higher salary and the favorable work schedule of a major airline. Don had been a pilot since his teenage years and had amassed an enormous amount of hours flying people here and there on charters that no one else would take because of bad weather. He was fearless and developed such a reputation at the local private air field that he obtained work from all of the flying services there in his spare time instead of working for only one.

With my aid, Don was able to maximize his research efforts. However, during the middle 70's I became more and more disabled until I was unable to do my work any longer and had to apply for Social Security Disability. Don became interested, due to my ill health, in investigating the field of alternative forms of healing. During this period, we investigated psychic surgery in the Philippines and in Mexico, charismatic healing, the laying on of hands, polarity therapy, crystal healing, color healing, and healing by hypnosis.

In 1974, Don had conducted intensive meditations until he had developed a new batch of channels, the ones developed in the 60's having gradually moved away and disbanded. He, himself, remained aloof from these meditations for the most part and allowed me to conduct them once I had become a channel. In 1978, Jim McCarty began to come to our group meditations and in 1980, realizing that Jim's talents could enhance our practical ability to be of service, Don asked Jim to join us. In the Christmastide of 1980, Jim joined us in our work. Three weeks later, the Ra Contact began.

We had a burst of Ra sessions that began slowing when my many physical ailments began getting in the way of the contacts, which were also somewhat draining to me. Strange and unfortunate incidents began happening to me, unexplainable in any logical sense unless one could diagnose me as an hysteric, a dubious proposition. The "psychic greeting" influence was apparently a significant portion of these events. For instance, at one point, during a walk through the neighborhood I found myself unable to breathe. This lasted for approximately 30 seconds, not long enough to cause physical death, but it certainly was traumatic. This sort of thing began to occur increasingly. It troubled Don a great deal and he slowed the sessions down in order to let me recuperate in between sessions. Typically, I would lose between one and three pounds after a session.

By 1983, it seemed to be obvious to us that we needed to move to be nearer Don's job-as a pilot based in Atlanta-so that he could spend more time at home. The worsening airline situation had Don in Atlanta flying almost non-stop, which caused the Ra Contact to be an ever more infrequent occasion, since Don's work and the necessary commuting were tiring him greatly.

The move to Atlanta signaled a change in Don. In Atlanta Don began to weaken physically and began taking sick leave. We all decided that the Atlanta experiment had been a disaster and after only five months moved back to Louisville. However, with this move, Don's illness seemed to take seat in his mind. Mental illness is not understood because there seems to be a stigma against it. Information about physical illnesses is taught to the virtual exclusion of information regarding mental distress. I have regretted this truth profoundly because without understanding Don's predicament, I was virtually unable to aid him. After a year or so of gradual worsening of the depressed condition which would accept no verdict other than his own death—which he saw occurring in the near future—he died of a gunshot wound to his head. It was listed by the police not as a suicide, though he shot himself, but as a homicide, as the far more enlightened view should be. This was no self-inflicted wound. This was the end of a frame of mind mysterious to me and tinged, we all felt, with an evil we could neither grasp nor confront. The impact of Don's life on those around him cannot be overestimated. His brilliant intellect and deep intuition, his sweetness of character, his clarity of observation, his long and discriminating experience in the field of the paranormal, and his love of telling a good story all conspired to make him a veritable fount of information for thousands of people, not only those he taught during his professorial career but also any of those with whom he came in contact at any time during his life. As he was never one for self-revelation, he lived and died a somewhat mysterious man but one greatly beloved, not only by Jim and me and by his uncle and aunt, Marion and Martha Johnson, but by all those who knew him.

Because Don's and my relationship was never put into words, it is impossible for me to put it into words for you, the reader, but perhaps each of you has known of a couple whose words were calm and affectionate to each other, whose goals in life were such a good match that there was a closeness beyond that of man and woman, and whose house could always be trusted to have peaceful and harmonious vibrations. That was the enviable position that I was in as Don's companion. Don believed in marriage as little as he believed in the outward expression of inward affection, and so we remained happily unmarried for sixteen years. The last year of his life was very difficult for both of us, but on the night he died he asked me for the last time, "Are we still us?" "Yes," I replied, my heart full of sixteen years of the giving and taking of a love which I will never forget, in any part.

ESMERELDA was written in the first flush of our discovery of each other as friends and spiritual mates. Don was a wonderful plot-maker although he could not write. This worked out very well because I was terrible at making up a story but I could "see" each character in detail and was able to write about them as if I were writing about friends. Because lion was then gone about half the time flying, he would put his ideas on tape while he was in Louisville, and when he went off to work, I would get to work at the typewriter. The first draft took about six months and thereafter the re-writes were due to Don's desire to create an impeccable plot. We would rewrite characters and do such things as move a house from New York state to just outside of Washington, D.C. so that a trip could be made to Miami by one of the characters in the appropriate amount of time scheduled in the plot. These painstaking corrections continued for about another six months, and after another year or so of sending the book out and receiving very kind but negative responses from publishers, the book was put on the shelf.

The channelings that begin and end this novel were channeled in the Louisville group in 1968 and are the only portion of the book that was not written at the typewriter in the same manner as was the rest of the novel. We intended it as a parable for all ages, looking back, sometimes half-consciously, at the tremendous story of the Passion of Christ. Until 1974, we had no idea that the book had any prophetic quality in our private lives. However, in 1974, Andrija Puharich's book, URI, was published and when we read the book we realized that the author, Dr. Puharich, had an amazing similarity to Pablo Padeyevsky, one of the characters in our book. Dr. Puharich invited us to visit him at his estate in Westchester County, New York and before we even met the "good doctor," as he is called both by his friends and is called as Padeyevsky in the book, we suffered some amazement pulling into his driveway. His house was virtually a carbon copy of Padeyevsky's house in our novel, which we had also originally located in New York state, before moving it to Washington, D. C. There was one main difference: peonies. When I had seen the house in my mind's eye I had seen a circle driveway ringed with blooming peonies, but there was not a peony to be seen. When we questioned him about the peonies he laughed and said that he had had those removed a couple of years before. So in 1968, when the book was written, the peonies were accurate!

Six years later, in 1980, when Don asked Jim to join the group, there was further resonance with the novel. Don and I had put a good deal of himself into the character of Theodore. However, we had described Theodore's facial features very carefully and that description in the book was very similar to Jim's actual appearance. Although Jim is four inches shorter than six feet and has brown hair rather than blond, there was that same feeling of almost-recognition between Don and Jim and between Jim and me. And after the Ra Contact began, more similarities began to unfold.

As is often the case with authors, Don and I had projected a good many of our feelings, ideas, and perceptions onto the characters about which we wrote. Theodore was described in the book as a person alienated from the human race, with a feeling that he did not belong. He was described as a genius and possessed of an attitude 180° opposite from that of most people. These traits were Don's. Joshua, who partook far more of Don's deeper character, expressed himself in the book as a lonely person and a mysterious one. The way Joshua and Esmerelda treated each other in the novel mirrored the way Don and I were to treat each other, both of us being protective of the other almost to the point sometimes of treating each other as children.

Both Don in real life and Joshua in the novel shouldered responsibility. In the book Joshua said:

"In truth, am I not responsible for all that is to come in that my will was the leading one?"

In real life Don felt a continuing financial responsibility for our group and, during the period of his mental illness, perhaps his chief occasion for woe was his feeling that he had "fumbled the ball" in that regard, although, needless to say, neither Jim nor I wished Don to go on working at a job that had become too strenuous for him. The nature of mental illness is such that it is almost impossible to communicate clearly, and we were never able to convince Don that all was truly well. Before his illness ended the possibility of Ra sessions, Ra had mentioned metaphysical initiation and mental/emotional dysfunction as probabilities concerning Don.

Josh was the embodiment of Don's detachment from the world and his ability to manipulate it successfully without intruding upon it. We gave to Josh Don's ability as a master communicator and, lastly, but certainly not least, there is the offer Josh makes towards the end of the novel of his mind for the space girl's:

"You have a girl trapped outside of her physical body. You have the power to bring her back to it. I ask you to do so. I am willing to repay you by taking her place, my mind for hers."

Don may have accomplished something of a similar nature, according to a channeling that we received from those of Hatonn and Latwii on November 11, 1984, only four days after Don's death.

(Hatonn) "In this instance, which is extreme and extraordinary, the one known as Don exhibited a courage most difficult to express. This entity had a wish to protect those about him, and so he did. Many things that you do will also be misunderstood, though less drastic."

(Latwii) "The one known as Don saw what has been described this evening as the dark carnival and saw the difficulties that awaited should this experience be continued, which had begun in the recent of your times, as you measure experience. There were those images of destruction which filled the mind of the one known as Don, and this entity wished in his deeper self to reserve as much of that difficulty for himself as possible, so that those of his comrades might be spared the added difficulties. The conscious mind made use of this decision, in its own distorted fashion, and leapt first from the precipice in order that the others might avoid it."

We gave to Esmerelda much of my personality. I had been in a protected and sheltered atmosphere all of my life, sheltered in part by my own untested but substantial mystical faith and in part by the desire of all of those around me to keep my naiveté intact. When Esmerelda discovered negativity in Padeyevsky it was a terrible shock.

"All right, so it is there, all this negativity. And my own uncle, the safest man in the world, has it too. But no matter how long I face it I won't get used to it. You can make me face the darkness, but you can't make me turn from the light just because darkness exists."

For me, the full discovery of negativity burst upon me as the bullet burst upon Don's brain. Esmerelda said bravely in the book that she would face negativity and understand it. It has been over a year since Don died and with help from friends, healers, and my spiritual director I have struggled to accept, understand, and praise that which seems so tragic and unnecessary. That understanding has yet to come. But, like Esmerelda, I shall persist seeking grace until my mind and my faith are large enough to encompass the events that have occurred.

On January 15, 1981, the Ra Contact began and the synchronicities between the novel and our life began to compound. The Ra Contact blazed into being as a complete surprise to our group. We had never worked in trance before because, as far as we knew, I was not capable of a trance state. After I had done my usual challenging of the contact in the name of Christ, and worked until I was satisfied enough with my own tuning to receive the contact clearly, I accepted this new contact, having no idea that it was any different from any other. However, shortly after the contact began I seemingly went to sleep and woke up to discover Don as elated as I had ever seen him. It took him no time at all to determine that this contact was different.

Ra asked us to provide for my Christian distortions by the placement of an altar at my head upon which stood a candle and an open Bible on top of a handmade cloth. This was quite similar to the table in Joshua's octagonal house of magical workings, or temple.

The Banishing Ritual of the Lesser Pentagram, found in the Appendix of THE MAGICIAN: HIS TRAINING AND WORK by W. E. Butler, was used in THE CRUCIFIXION OF ESMERELDA SWEETWATER and serendipitously began to be used again when we three who were involved in the Ra Contact discovered that there was a need to keep the room of our working cleansed and sanctified. However, we made one addition. In our version of the banishing ritual, to "Yod He Vau Heh," the ancient name of God, Yahweh, we added "Shin," vibrating "Yod He Shin Vau Heh," due to the fact that this addition spells the name of the Christ, Jesus, and was, we felt, a better vibration for me since I was, and am, a Christian. In the personal portion of Session #67, Don queried Ra about this ritual:

"QUESTIONER: Are you familiar with a book that the instrument and I wrote approximately twelve years ago called THE CRUCIFIXION OF ESMERELDA SWEETWATER, in particular the banishing ritual that we used to bring the entities to Earth?

RA: I am Ra. This is correct.

QUESTIONER: Were there any incorrectnesses in our writing with respect to the way this was performed?

RA: I am Ra. The incorrectnesses occurred only due to the difficulty an author would have in describing the length of training necessary to enable the ones known in that particular writing as Theodore and Pablo in the necessary disciplines. QUESTIONER: It has seemed to me that that book has somehow, in its entirety, been a link to many of those whom we have met since we wrote it and to many of the activities we have experienced. Is this correct?

RA: I am Ra. This is quite so."

As the plot thickened in our novel, a true villain was discovered, capable of energizing thought-forms, especially violent ones:

"It took a great deal of magical skill to be able to put up that sort of barricade; only a few people could have done it. And the trail of violence of the past twenty four hours: the deputy sheriff's wife who had, without any need, shot and killed a man. And the presumably trustworthy Sgt. Armstrong, whose judgment had been terribly bad; who had shot to kill a man, when there were a dozen other completely non-lethal ways of stopping him. None of it had made any sense, unless these acts of negativity and violence were being—say—encouraged, or prompted, by the magic of one as practiced in black rituals as he, himself, was in white magic."

As the Ra Contact unfolded we began to have increasing attacks, or greetings as we preferred to call them, from a friend of negative polarity who, although discarnate, seemed capable of effecting the same energizing of any inborn distortion or freely chosen thoughts or behaviors that were less than balanced within one's being:

(From Ra Session #67) "The normal gambit of such fourth-density attack is the tempting of the entity or group of entities away from total polarization towards service to others and towards the aggrandizement of self or of social organizations with which the self identifies.

"In the case of this particular group each was given a full range of temptations to cease being of service to each other and to the One Infinite Creator. Each entity declined these choices and instead continued with no significant deviation from the desire for a purely other-self service orientation. At this point one of the fifth-density entities overseeing such detuning processes determined that it would be necessary to terminate the group by what you might call magical means, as you understand ritual magic. We have previously discussed the potential for the removal of one of the group by such attack and have noted that by far the most vulnerable is the instrument due to its preincarnative physical complex distortions."

What with kidney disease, rheumatoid arthritis, and lupus, there were so many things about my body that did not work that Don once described it as a Rolls Royce that was also a lemon.

Perhaps the single most skewed perception in the novel as a book of prophesy was that in the novel both Theodore and Esmerelda, the equivalent of Jim and me, were to give their lives in the service of the light. It never occurred to Don or to me that, of the two of us, Don, tall, strapping, healthy, dependably stable, and super-confident, would die instead.

Neither Don nor Josh seemed in any way to be lacking in care for the world. Indeed, both wished to save or rescue all mankind from what each perceived to be the limitations of the mundane world. However, in Don's last year he, himself, said that it was possible that the greatest lesson of his incarnation was the learning of personal compassion as opposed to impersonal compassion.

As the Ra Contact unfolded in 1981 and 1982, we discovered that our fifth-density, negatively-oriented friend wished to stop the contact by separating my true self, my spirit, from my physical body. This was foreshadowed by the events in THE CRUCIFIXION OF ESMERELDA SWEETWATER. Sessions #68 through #70 of Book Three of THE LAW OF ONE describe the concepts involved in both cases. The similarity between them was immediately noticed by Don and in the personal portion of Session #68 Don queried Ra about it:

"QUESTIONER: We have been speaking almost precisely of a portion of the ESMERELDA SWEETWATER book which we wrote having to do with the character Trostrick's misplacement of the space girl's mind/body/spirit complex. What is the significance of that work which we did with respect to our lives? It has been confusing to me for some time as to how it meshes in. Can you tell me that?

RA: I am Ra. We scan each and find we may speak. QUESTIONER: Would you please do so now?

RA: I am Ra. We confirm the following which is already, shall we say, supposed or hypothesized.

"When the commitment was made between the two of this group to work for the betterment of the planetary sphere, this commitment activated a possibility/probability vortex of some strength. The experience of generating this volume was unusual in that it was visualized as if watching the moving picture.

"Time had become available in its present-moment form. The scenario of the volume went smoothly until the ending of the volume. You could not end the volume and the ending was not visualized as the entire body of the material, but was written or authored. This is due to the action of free will in all of the creation. However, the volume contains a view of significant events, both symbolically and specifically, which you saw under the influence of the magnetic attraction which was released when the commitment was made and full memory of the dedication of this, what you may call, mission restored."

Several of our friends, when reading through the manuscript of our book, have protested at the harsh ending of the story itself. Indeed, neither Don nor I was subjectively happy with the ending. However, all attempts to rewrite the ending so that THE CRUCIFIXION OF ESMERELDA SWEETWATER would be an incorrect title were complete failures. After ten tries at rewriting, all of which ended up yielding much the same material as the ending you now see, we decided that the source moving through us to show this point of view was attempting to include within that point of view the acting out of the answer to the question, "What would happen if two perfectly "good" beings were brought down to this complex and dualistic planet?"

In the saddest correspondence of all between Don's and my book and our life together, Don's death seemed inevitable to Don himself for many months before he actually died. Jim and I, as well as his beloved relatives and friends, all tried to rewrite the last chapter of Don's life. We all gave the effort everything we had. And yet, we were unable to affect any change in the ending of Don's earthly story.

In the time since Don's death, we have turned our faith each day to what we know to be the truth: all of us, including Don, are doing what seems to us to be the correct thing to do. We are assured by our metaphysical studies that there are no mistakes, and I have spent much time in prayer enlarging my Christian faith and allowing my God to become larger and more powerful in my life, so that I can see the larger view that Christ always saw. The word "tragedy" is a good word for describing the outer events surrounding Don's passage from this world into larger life, and yet it becomes increasingly clear to us as time goes on that there was a rightness and symmetry to all that occurred. This sometimes extremely fervent search for peace and new joy will continue to be the best way we know to live our lives and to honor the memory of a man who gave his life, day by day, for so many years, to the search for truth.

This book is the beginning of a long series of wonderful dreams which Don Elkins and I shared. We used our research and book-knowledge of the rigorous training of the Magician to attempt to put forth, in novel form, the nature of the world as we perceive it; that is, the world of good and evil. In no way do we wish to suggest by this book that the story ends there, metaphysically speaking, nor do we wish it to be thought that we have joined the hordes of those who cry "doom." Though many of the events in this book and in our own experiences seem to reflect difficulty and disharmony, it is our opinion that this is only the nature of our mundane illusion. We feel that there is no difficulty which does not contain the love of the One Creator, whole, perfect, and balanced. We offer this book to you now in hopes that its time has come and that the information and evoked emotions found therein will be of some small aid to those who seek the truth.

Snow lies on the ground as 1985 draws to a close. Christmas presents are being exchanged, and Christmas trees shine and glitter with their delightful burdens of lights and decorations. An old year is ending and another beginning. May you find strength, promise, and joy in your growing resonance with all the cycles of life and Spirit.

Peace to each of you from Kentucky.

Carla L. Rueckert
December 21, 1985

Prologue

The night comes upon him, standing without movement in the ocean of wheat. The planet under him stiffens in the cold, and he becomes very quiet, welcoming the cold, the wind, the light of the stars.

The heavenly constellations ride past very slowly, but he is unaware of time, for he has cleansed his mind of concept and knows only his pure, original mind, bathing itself in the Creator's light. Into this mind comes the voice of his teacher:

"Picture with me now, if you will, a sphere that is called a planet. What is the color of this planet?

"The eye of the fish gazes upon this planet, and it sees life, and it is glad of life. For out of the planet grow living things. For what constitutes life? They are perfect, and they radiate energy.

"And the eye of the fish looks on.

"Out of the planet come living things, and they move about on its surface, and they swim in its waters, and they fly in its atmosphere, and they do various and many things. And each seeks food. "And the eye of the fish looks on.

"And all of the life interacts with life, and evolves to great consciousness and intellect and knowing. Then rises from the surface that being known in the universe as man, with his awareness of being.

"And the eye of the fish looks on.

"Man goes forth upon his planet, and acts, and thinks, and thinks of his actions, and acts with his fellow creatures. And they learn from each other as they interact with each other.

"And the eye of the fish looks on.

"And man dresses himself in fine garments, and bows down his head to that which he holds holy, and shows great emotion and sense of being.

"And the eye of the fish looks on.

"And man dwells in great wisdom, and his power is great. He knows that he thinks the thoughts of wisdom itself, for he is wise. He knows that he gives forth love, for he is love, and he acts with dignity and grace, for he is divine and full of grace.

"And the eye of the fish looks on.

"Throughout the heavens, the multitudes bow down. And they bow down to the fish. For all that he does is look. And if all that he does is look, then he is wise. The multitudes bow down to wisdom, for they know that it is love.

"And the eye of the fish looks on.

"His wisdom permeates the heavens, and is the heavens, for the heavens are love."

He who seeks stands alone in the field of wheat. As the meditation ends he begins to become aware of the fatigue in his body. The light that has sustained his mind leaves him, and he becomes aware of the cold. He is glad of the cold, and glad of his body. He becomes aware of the convenience of his body, of the changing attitudes of his feet, balancing against the changing wind. Of the arms so ready to use, the hands so ready to serve. Of the neck, supporting the head, cushioning the brain. Of the skin, so sensitive to its environment, telling the mind of the soft, scraping brush of the wheat against him, of the brilliant cold that is affecting him. Of his eyes that can see at his will all that dwells in his world, the moonlit color of the wheat, the velvet black of the winter sky.

And he who seeks, standing alone, accepts himself as part of the creation, and sees that he and his body and his will are part of the all, and are the all.

Stiffly beginning to move, he embarks upon the journey to which he has been summoned, from one planet to another planet, from the service of the Creator to the service of the same Creator.

He prepares his mind and loosens his body to an inner heat, and disappears from the field, summoned to the place of departure. A great hall of white marble stands before him. Birdsong filters through the vaults of the high-domed ceiling, and the sound of the wind chants in the windows. The great hall is totally empty, save for the supporting pillars standing upon its floor.

Through the pillars, walking upon the white floor yellowed by the yellow light sunning *its windows, walks a delft white girl with golden hair. She walks towards him, the golden-haired boy with skin of palest stone. They are twins in coloring, in height, in delicacy of feature, in purity of thought, in strength of will.*

There are no words needed; only the simple mouths of touching speak. They clasp hands and wait, for they know they are to serve together, and they know of their suitability to serve.

The mind of this temple speaks in thunder, and they see in each others' eyes the subtly changing colors of the thought:

"In the creation of the Father there dwells a planet of sorrow. This planet approaches its harvest, and yet in its heart there dwells no joy, for its harvest shall be poor. And as it approaches its harvest, it cries out in its heart for all of those that will fall and be swept away. Few there are on this planet who may stem the tide of sadness, and build a high place for those who would have fallen before the harvest reaper came. These need your aid, to serve in their love as you serve in yours."

The youth and the girl stand for some time, hands and eyes touching, until their will is perfectly as one. Then they speak: "We will go, and we will serve."

They walk in silence from the temple of their fathers and from the time of their joyful, slender innocence. What had been separate is now joined; what had been unthought is now begun. And even as they have been beloved in the garden of their childhood, now they open like flowers, to give forth the scent of their thoughts, and the crystal colors of their ripened souls. For this planet of their childhood is not Earth, with its legacy of sadness, but another, brighter star's planet, with another and brighter legacy, where their souls have been let loose to grow naturally and in joy. And their readiness to serve is as inevitable as the turning of the leaf to the golden, silent sun.

CHAPTER ONE

There was a battered desk in one corner of the large office, and a chair that went behind the desk, and another chair that sat beside the desk. There were also about three thousand books in the room: books lining the walls, books piled in precariously high stacks on the floor, books holding other books open. The window showed its pale morning light to the books, and to the portly, curly-haired little man who sat at the desk, his bright black eyes twinkling merrily across the disarray, watching the door.

Dr. Pablo Padeyevsky was too short, too round-bellied, too reminiscent of the organ grinder without monkey to have the reputation that he had. But he managed to make people forget his rotundity, make them recognize him for the researcher, educator, and consultant that he was. His technique for making people realize his talents was simple and effortless: he opened his mouth to lecture, or answer a question.

And so, although he was no impressive figure, sitting behind the scarred old desk, round steel-rimmed spectacles framing roundish eyes, his reputation went before him, and there was no one, including Theodore Behr, who was not in awe of him.

Professor Pablo Padeyevsky's connection with Theodore Behr began in a most tenuous fashion. In the first place, he deserved the title of professor by virtue of only one course. He taught a graduate course in the history and philosophy of science each semester, spending one morning each week at the university. The course was done mainly as a favor to the dean of the graduate school of the university: he had convinced Padeyevsky that the school's reputation-and it was already considerable-depended to an extent on continuing to include Padeyevsky's name in its list of faculty. Pablo Padeyevsky had therefore continued teaching the one course, the fee for which was small change to him, compared to his consulting fees and other income. He ran the course, as might be expected, along iconoclastic lines, speaking from the standpoint of the administration. He required no readings, no homework: he assigned one paper or two, depending upon the interest of the student, and graded not by the footnote or the page but by the idea. In the eleven years that Pablo Padeyevsky had been teaching this course, over four hundred people had gotten Bs; seven had gotten an A.

That Theodore Behr came into contact with the good Dr. Padeyevsky was sheerest coincidence. Theodore had almost never come to college at all. His childhood had been a quiet nightmare of being slow and awkward. He had only by miracles managed to achieve the tenth grade in high school, the miracles being allowed because teachers had nothing against the boy: he was not a fomenter of classroom trouble. They usually couldn't even remember who he was. And so they passed him barely, to his sophomore year in high school.

This was all the boy needed to work from. In this year, he was given his first pure science courses, and he took off from his zero status like a rocket from the launching pad. Before his junior year, he had been given IQ tests, and other tests: he was acclaimed a genius; he was accelerated; he was forgiven the foreign languages and athletics credits he would not pay attention to; he was graduated from high school with a near-perfect grade record at the tender age of sixteen, and enrolled post-haste in pure sciences at the local university, where Pablo Padeyevsky taught his single course.

Theodore Behr's own attitude towards his environment had not changed just because it had begun looking at him as a genius instead of a dodo. His eye had always been a cold eye, an outsider's eye; he hadn't meant it to be, but there was only one way his mind worked. And that was, apparently, one hundred and eighty degrees from the way everyone else's minds worked. When other people thought he was a dodo, he agreed with them. It was self-evident. He could not understand what made his classmates' jokes funny, what made their lives interesting enough to continue with. He had never met anyone he considered worth talking to. Therefore, he was most likely a dodo, a real out-of-step person. And when the people around him decided he was a genius, Theodore could again see what they meant. He knew the answer to most scientific questions because they seemed self-evident. Obviously, this self-evidence was unusual. Other people didn't see it. So, all right, they could call him a genius. To himself, it simply felt normal to know what he knew, to think what he thought, to speculate as he did speculate.

But both the genius and the dodo are lonely types, and Theodore was very lonely. He had had a brief hope that in college he would meet someone worthwhile, someone with whom to share his ideas, his developing philosophies. The hope did not last. He was accelerated again; he approached the age of nineteen and the status of second semester college senior without meeting a soul to talk to.

Just on a whim, he decided to sit in on the graduate course on the philosophy of science taught by Dr. Pablo Padeyevsky. He was not eligible to enroll in the course, for he was not in graduate school, but it was quite common for the brighter undergraduates voluntarily to fill up the back seats in his lectures, simply to listen. Because, when Padeyevsky was on, when he was letting his mind run, when he was talking about hermetic philosophy or theosophy or alchemy or the relativistic implications suggesting the worlds of anti-matter, he could hold a group of coupon-minded, professional-student-geared grade getters in complete thrall. He could work miracles of spellbinding. It worked on the students who had come to learn; it worked on the ones who had come to get a degree; it worked very strongly on Theodore Behr. He was, in fact, inspired to write and hand in a paper to Dr. Padeyevsky, even though he was not officially a member of the class. The chance to share his thoughts with the first man he had ever met that might appreciate them was irresistible.

Pablo Padeyevsky was reading that paper through for the fourth time, now, in the light of early morning. He was refreshing his mind on each inflection of thought. He had found this paper remarkable, exciting, surprising. He had summoned Theodore Behr when he had read it, because he wanted to see the boy who had done this work, and because he couldn't imagine an undergraduate, or even a graduate student, having the background necessary to write this paper. The technical competence was outstanding, but the insight linking physical science with metaphysics, the maturity of mind that could produce such exploration, was a puzzle and a joy to him.

The young man had begun by listing quite a few basic equations in the fields of electricity, quantum mechanics, relativity, and atomic physics. In each equation was found the value "c," which was the symbol for the velocity of light. The fifteen pages of the paper answered the simple question: "why were so many basic equations dependent on a property of light; namely, its speed?" The paper was replete with many mathematical analogies to metaphysical concepts, and was sophisticated and incredibly accurate in detail, but the basic postulations were even more incredible, and were much simpler. The young man had said that there were two basic substances in' the universe: light and consciousness. From these two substances, one physical, one non-physical, were formed all the various physical materials that we know of, collectively, as matter, in each of its various and infinite configurations. He postulated that consciousness acted upon light in order to form these varieties of matter, and further postulated that all changes, all of what we call evolution, came about as a function of changing and evolving consciousness. He went on to state that consciousness was a field of energy that gained its power from duality, or polarity. Just as there were positive and negative poles in the material or physical universe, so were there positive and negative poles which affected consciousness. These poles were known, he postulated, as good and evil. He set forth the theory, in conclusion, that the physical phenomena which body themselves forth as the physical universe, were reflections of corresponding phenomena within the realm of consciousness; that duality of good and evil in consciousness was responsible for the physical interactions and changes that made up the material world. All energies in the physical creation were aberrations from total perfection. These aberrations resulted from a corresponding energy bias in the good/evil potential difference which moved consciousness away from its total perfection.

So had spoken Theodore Behr, and Dr. Pablo Padeyevsky was very, very eager to meet him. His office hours were, admittedly, a bit odd, seven to eight in the morning, but that was the time of day that suited him best; he liked sunrises and sunsets, and went to bed as early as he could, whenever he could. He sat, cheerful and sturdy in his big chair, almost elf-like, and very expectant.

Theodore was expectant too, but the feeling partook much more of nervousness. He had told the truth about what he thought in the paper, and had gone out on a limb emotionally by showing it to another human being. Theodore was no fonder of ridicule than anyone else. And he expected that, having exposed himself to the outside world, he would get ridiculed. His relations with that world had been so uniformly unhappy that he waited in apprehension for the emotional blows to fall. What a fool he had been, to think that anyone would ever be in sympathy with him. He threaded his way through the morass of short hallways and cul-de-sacs and finally discovered where the capricious numbering system had deposited Pablo Padeyevsky's office. He knocked tentatively on the frosted glass door.

"Come in."

He opened the door to the ocean of books, and his eyes rebelled for just a minute; then he found the moving entity in their midst. Padeyevsky was bouncing towards him, beaming at him, one plump hand stuck out for a warm handshake. Holding on to Theodore's arm, he steered him through a two-foot avenue in the stacks of books, and sat him down on the chair beside the desk.

"Have you eaten breakfast?"

Theodore stared. He kept on staring. This was the ridicule he had been afraid of? This was the biting and satirical barrage of gibes about his paper? "Ah, no, Professor Padeyevsky, I, ah, no, I haven't."

"Very good. Sweet rolls, lemonade ... do you like cheese? Here's some milk, just got it today, and instant coffee, if the water's hot." Padeyevsky opened a gap in the wall of books that turned out to be a refrigerator, and removed things. He checked an aluminum break in more book stacks that turned out to be an electric heating plate. "And call me Pablo. You'll sprain your tongue with Professor Padeyevsky." He spooned coffee powder into two dubiously clean cups. Behr took things into limp hands, ate first bites, and stared, until he discovered he was being stared back at. Then he found that it wasn't such a bad idea to return the warm, friendly appraisal which Pablo's bright, black-button eyes were giving him. He didn't mind being a specimen under this particular microscope.

Pablo Padeyevsky was staring, staring with rising elation. It was too good to be true. This boy was the one he had been looking for, he and his two fellow experimenters, for years. He examined Theodore's features. The slender, pale face, with its high cheekbones, its wide-spaced, rather deep-set eyes, the high forehead, the carefully modeled, almost arrogant discipline of the nose and mouth, all bore an uncanny resemblance to his niece, Esmerelda Sweetwater. The same features that made for startling beauty in a girl added up to totally unremarkable, quiet good looks in a boy. He judged Theodore's height to be about six feet; that was right, Esmerelda was exactly six feet tall. And Theodore was of the same blonde coloring that his niece enjoyed. There really didn't seem to be any doubt.

Padeyevsky held up the paper he had just been rereading. "I was wondering what the source of these thoughts might be." Theodore considered. "Really, there isn't any source. I've been doing my own research in the natural sciences for quite a while now, since I was about fifteen. And philosophy has always interested me; I've read a lot of it. But these particular ideas are just my own, I guess. I've never read them anywhere. It just seems to me to be the way that things work."

Dr. Padeyevsky's face was incandescent with his smile. "Perfect, perfect. I'll tell you what, Theodore. I'd like for you to work with me on a special project."

Theodore was having intense difficulty believing what he had heard. The man hadn't even begun to discuss the paper. Now he wanted the help of an undergraduate. "Uh," he said.

It is a very unusual experimental project. Are you interested?"

"Uh," repeated Theodore.

Pablo Padeyevsky waited.

Theodore got part of himself under control. "Why me?"

"Because I believe that you are an alien. In fact, I believe that you are the one alien that we have been looking for for years."

"Oh, no, sir. I was born right here in this county, lived here all my life. I've never even been out of the United States."

"Not that kind of alien. I think that your spirit has dwelled other places than this planet."

Theodore sat in stunned silence.

"Do you know what I mean by 'spirit'?" Padeyevsky spoke gently, taming his exuberance. "Have you run across the words 'mental body' or 'astral body' or 'soul' in your reading in philosophy? Meaning the true body, the one that does not die when the physical body dies?"

Theodore had indeed run across each of these words.

"Then that is what I mean. I believe that your mental body, your soul, is not native to this planet. It is an alien to Earth." Theodore's mind was beginning to function. If Dr. Padeyevsky hadn't held such a very high place in his estimation prior to this meeting, Theodore would probably have left. As it was, he sat and munched absentmindedly on cheese and Danish, and tried to follow the peculiar conversation. "You mean you think I lived other places than here, before I was born?"

"Exactly." Dr. Padeyevsky's beam extended still further towards each ear. "Every particle of consciousness, Theodore, has to come from someplace. You have explained how consciousness acts and how it changes in your paper, and you are to be given full credit for that. Now, it should make sense to you that each particle of consciousness continues, through these changes, and grows with each new experience, whether it is the consciousness of a rock, a tree, an animal, or a person. This individualized consciousness continues with the evolution, grows with it. Do you not agree?"

Of course Theodore agreed. It was, more or less, in his paper. "Very well then. In the case of some human entities such as you, Theodore, the consciousness that assimilated the chemicals that formed a physical body for you to use here, upon the surface of this planet, was a consciousness alien to this Earth. Totally alien, in nature, in knowledge, in understanding. Haven't you ever felt like an alien here?"

The question was easy, Theodore had answered it, to himself, many times. "Yes, I've always been different from everybody else. In fact, I always noticed one simple rule. If society believes something is right and correct and proper, then it must be wrong. Because society always seems to look at things just the opposite of the way I do."

Pablo reached over the desk's heaps of books and pounded Theodore heartily on the shoulder. "That's wonderful. Just wonderful. Now, I repeat. I have reason to believe that you are an alien. And, because of your thinking, and the fact that you and my niece have a great similarity of physical appearance, I believe that you are the alien, the one that we have been waiting for, for several years. Will you join me in working on this experiment?"

Theodore had never been an unkind or surly person; he had just been alone. Now, for the first time in his life, he was being offered a part in something by someone he could respect and admire, even if he sounded strange at the moment. "Yes, sir, ah, Pablo. There's nothing I'd rather do."

"Excellent. I'm almost sure that you're the right one, but of course the acid test will come when you meet my niece, Esmerelda Sweetwater."

Theodore nodded, uncomprehendingly. "I'll give you a map. Do you have a car?" Theodore nodded affirmatively again. "That's fine. Can you visit us this weekend?"

A third nod from the very happy and very confused Theodore. He accepted the accurate pencil map of the way to the Padeyevsky farm, and thought of very little else for the rest of the week. The October days seemed as crisp as his anticipation; he wondered about the experiment, about the person known as Esmerelda-an odd name, an interesting one- and, most of all, about being an alien.

Finally Friday's classes came to an end, and he was soon moving down the highway out of town, as per Padeyevsky's instructions. The map he had drawn had detailed the twenty or so miles of winding road which led off the main highway to his farm with clarity, but had said nothing about the great beauty of these roads, the October radiance of the trees shielding the blacktop like a tawny arch in the late afternoon sun. The autumn glow of the maples lent a russet sweetness to the fields and woods Theodore passed, and he felt like the solitary viewer of a perfect and fleeting work of art. He mused on the conversation that had so interested him in Pablo Padeyevsky's office. He must practice saying Pablo, instead of Professor Padeyevsky. What had he meant by it all? Well, he thought, if the map was correct, he would soon find out; the map stated that there was a gravel road marked with his name just beyond this single-lane bridge. The map did not lie, and Theodore's middle-aged Ford passed under an even more richly furnished. canopy as it began to follow the winding, hilly private road. The driveway extended nearly two miles; there was an abandoned farmhouse, nearly leveled by years of weather, at the head of the drive;

there was a side road and a mailbox marked "Mathpart Fendler" off to the right; these were the only dwellings close to the Padeyevsky house. The good doctor certainly had privacy.

Then the "farm" itself opened up in front of Theodore. FARM, he thought, as he slowed the car to an idle in the broad, circular driveway which spread generously from the gravel road. This was no farm: it was an estate, a domain, a plantation. The circle of drive was bordered with peonies; there was thick forest on each side of the house. The house itself was three stories tall, and had the look of a grand ship that had come to rest on high ground. It was brick, with a veranda across the columned front and going around on the left side to form a covered, open-sided porch; the right side of the house was indented for half a room, then it elled asymmetrically into an enclosed screen porch. Through the long windows across the front of the house, Theodore could see the elegance of draped velvet curtains. He began to feel obscurely apologetic for everything: his casual clothes, his venerable and never dignified automobile, his unprepossessing face, his unassuming personality. He awaited the liveried footman.

None appeared. As he parked in the shade of a huge, low-branched walnut tree, a collie bounded up to him, tail wagging happily, no sign of the watchdog personality about him. Theodore took an instant liking to the friendly animal, and got out of the car to pat him. The beast put his head down to enjoy the greeting and was standing, leaning against Theodore's caresses, when the boy looked up to see a girl walking towards him.

The dog nearly fell over as Theodore abruptly took his hand away and straightened up, staring. Now he understood the mansion: no other background would have been suitable as a frame to her beauty. She came walking across the drive, the gentle bloom of autumn trees against her face, and Theodore hoped with all his heart that this was Esmerelda Sweetwater. Because if it was, he was the most fortunate of men. He remembered to breathe just as she neared, and held out her hand.

"Hello." Her voice was as light and strong as her smile. "You must be Theodore Behr. I'm Esmerelda Sweetwater."

He shook her hand, looking at her hard, attempting to speak. The first try was a solid failure; he had temporarily forgotten how to breathe and talk all at the same time. He managed finally to acknowledge that he was Theodore Behr. He let her hand go.

There was a period of silence, while he looked at the girl in front of him, and tried to think of something witty to say. She was as tall as he, and as blonde. Her hair grew to below her waist, and she wore it unbound, the bangs across her high forehead wisping past straight eyebrows, the sides and back falling free down her shoulders. Her height was in such proportion that, away from reference points with which to judge her size, she would have appeared light, delicate. She was the most beautiful woman Theodore had ever seen. He could think of absolutely nothing to say. For what seemed to be about five years, he worked on the difficulty. Finally, he remembered his first impression of the house. "Say, this place looks just like the setting for a Civil War movie."

"It was the setting for a Civil War movie," said Esmerelda, putting her head to one side and grinning at him. "A movie company bought it and remodeled it for a film about fifteen years ago, and Pablo bought it from them."

"Oh," said Theodore. He breathed again, with an effort of will. Esmerelda held out her slender hand. "Come up to the house," she said, smoothing his intense shyness with her gesture. "I'll give you a tour of the rest of the movie set. It's really a very pleasant place to live." She kept Theodore walking, to relieve his tension, and chatted about the history of various pieces of furniture. He began to feel more at ease in her presence, as her good humor and simple friendliness began to ease him away from the worst of his awkwardness. She stopped looking so unbelievable to him and began looking right, just perfectly right. Her face began to seem very dear, very familiar; her slender body seemed to float in front of him; he began to have the vague feeling that he could remember how she felt. He watched the golden hair move as her head moved, and listened to her talk, and all his senses seemed to come alive to her. Though he was still tense, in a way he began to feel comfortable for the first time in his life. As though he had come home.

" ... and Uncle Pablo told me that he thought you might be the one," she was saying, "and he wanted me to help him find out for sure."

He came out of the reverie, no longer shy, no longer uncomfortable, but peaceful, fulfilled. Nothing seemed to matter right now. He looked at the girl he had come home to. "Hmm?" he said.

She was smiling warmly, her blue eyes sparkling with their moving flecks of gold. "Let's wait for Uncle Pablo to talk about it," she said, moving to a small couch and pulling him gently down beside her. They looked at each other and Theodore felt somehow as though they shared some knowledge, some understanding. "Hello, Ted," said his mind. He started slightly, and looked closer at Esmerelda. She regarded him with the same warm expression. "Is it all right if I call you Ted?" she said aloud.

He thought, "Yes, it is," and before he had had a chance to verbalize it, she had stood up and walked the few steps to the front windows. "Very good," she said, pulling the windows down halfway. It was beginning to be chilly outside, with the swift chill of October evenings after sundown.

Theodore sat watching her. He thought of saying something about the fact that they seemed to have communicated with each other without speaking, but his mind felt warmed again, and reassured, and he knew that he had indeed discovered telepathy with Esmerelda, and that communication between them was going to be effortless. And so, instead of speaking, he simply projected his realization of the situation, and his enjoyment of it, and immediately he felt the pressure of her agreement and understanding.

"It really doesn't need saying," she said, turning back to him and reseating herself beside him on the loveseat. "But I shall say it anyway, just to make it official. I completely agree with Pablo. You're the one, all right."

He nodded. He still had no idea of what he was the one for, but that he belonged here, with Esmerelda, was unquestionably so. The rest would come in its own good time. Theodore sat back comfortably, his arm across the back of the small couch, his fingers playing with strands of Esmerelda's hair that had fallen across his arm when she sat down.

"This house is fantastic. I can't imagine how Pablo was able to buy it, on a professor's salary, but it's the greatest place I ever saw."

"Oh, Uncle Pablo does a little bit of a lot of things. He doesn't just teach and do research for the university. Mostly, he consults, with corporations all over the United States. He's even done work with the army. He flies all over the country, and has a long waiting list of clients."

"How did he learn all those different fields?"

"He has a rather unusual ability," she said, "to assimilate knowledge more quickly than most people. He's been developing these techniques for years with a friend of ours, who is a magician. When he wants to get inside a new subject, he just gets the relevant literature together and absorbs it, in a few days' time. Sometimes he even manages to do better than do most of the slower readers of the books, because he has some ability towards reading between the lines." She gave Theodore a mental picture, of a book acting somehow as a link between two minds, the reader's and the author's. "He can see past a lot of awkward language, and sometimes understands what the author means better than people do who have to depend on the written word alone. So many good minds have the ability to understand, but not to express, what they discover. Probably more important, though, than his knowledge of any single subject is his ability to link supposedly unrelated fields so as to produce new methods in technology. He has a very associative mind."

Her eyes watched Theodore's carefully, and she waited in his mind for his reaction to what she had said.

He mentally grinned at her, feeling clear at last about the reason for all those books in Padeyevsky's office. "Oh," he said. It was all right with him; he welcomed the whole unique set-up-a house with lovely trees, refreshing breezes, and a totally successful collie dog, and most of all a girl who was, improbably but certainly, his girl, his companion, his mate. It sounded strange, but it felt fine. It felt like home.

He felt her understand all these thoughts as he thought them, and the mental grin spread to his normally sober face, as he reflected on how much an "oh" could convey, if it didn't have to be dissected by language.

"Meow," said the next room.

"Here comes Uncle Pablo now. Has he told you about his research with animals?"

"No, he hasn't. Greetings, uh, Pablo," said Theodore, as the rotund little man entered the room, with a tiger-striped cat walking sedately beside him. She flopped slab-sided down on the rug and he was down on all fours beside her instantly. "Meow," he said, in a different tone than the first offering. The cat said nothing in return, but seemed to smile, slightly; then, abruptly, she bent double and licked her tail, one front paw waving casually in the air just above her middle.

Pablo hitched himself up to a sitting position, and then got completely vertical. He went over to Theodore with the same beaming greeting with which he had welcomed him to his office. "So you got here, Theodore. What do you think of the farm?"

Theodore was over being nervous about this household. "I think I can see now why people talk about the good old days, ah, Pablo."

"And you've met my niece?"

Theodore looked in utter contentment at the girl sitting beside him. "Yes."

Esmerelda turned her golden-flecked eyes to Padeyevsky. "You were right, Uncle Pablo. He's the one."

All three smiled their gladdest smiles. "Yes," said Pablo. Theodore knew he was the one; he'd heard it several times by now. "Can you really talk to animals?" On to other matters. "Well, it's not actually talking." Pablo squirmed around in his seat until he was comfortable; Esmerelda was putting lemonade within reach. "You've met me, and Esmerelda, but there's another member of the group that you haven't met. His name is Joshua Starr. You may have heard of him; he's the celebrity in our midst. Does television work."

Theodore shook his head; he hadn't heard of anyone named Joshua Starr.

"Well, maybe you wouldn't have; he's on during the daytime. But I thought you might have noticed his name in the credits of some of the shows that are on in the evenings. He's also a writer for TV."

Theodore hadn't heard of him.

"Well, anyway." Pablo gulped like a little boy at the lemonade. "He's also a very close friend of ours. He and Esmerelda worked on this problem with me. They have some talents I don't have. More about that in a minute. Anyhow, they studied animals, and discovered that animals transmit thoughts, using a primitive form of telepathy, and modulate the thoughts with sounds so as to convey meaning. They've helped me, and now I can interpret a good many of these animal thought-sound modulations."

"Oh."

Padeyevsky finished his lemonade and took another glass. "It probably sounds a little unusual, to you."

"Well-unique, anyway." Theodore was enjoying the situation too much to call it unusual. It was all right if Pablo wanted to talk to his cat. More power to him.

"Are you interested in magic?" asked Pablo.

Theodore's eyebrows raised, in confusion. "I really don't know anything about it."

"Most people identify magic with trickery." Pablo got up and began to pace as he talked, a habit with which Theodore was familiar from watching him lecture. "True magic has very little to do with tricks, or the production of any physical phenomena. It operates within the realms of consciousness and thought, in the astral and mental planes. And all of its objectives and purposes lie there, in the world of thought. In the case of

34

white magic, anyway. Now black magic, unfortunately, does have some objectives that lie within the physical world."

Well, son of a gun, thought Theodore. Pablo could call that magic, but it sounded to him like what he'd been writing about in his paper: the power of the thought world to affect the physical world. That wasn't unique, or unusual, after all. "Sure. That makes sense.

Pablo put his head back and laughed. "Well, Theodore," he said, finally, "you're going to be all right, I do believe." He poured him more lemonade. "It's in the field of magic that this experiment that I spoke about earlier lies. Are you still interested?"

"Sure."

"There is much to do then, Ted. Although you already know more than I do, I'm afraid. You just have the talent for it. You see, I'm not an alien."

Theodore frowned, turned to Esmerelda.

"That's right, Ted. He can't use telepathy as well as you, for instance, and he's been practicing for years."

Theodore turned to Pablo. "Still, how could I possibly know more than you do, about anything?"

"Well, Ted, this experiment has to do with an area much deeper than the intellect. Of course I know more than you, in some areas, intellectually. But this magic is concentrated upon the spirit. And so you will be working with Esmerelda and my good friend, Joshua Starr, not with me. Because I'm not much good, and they both are. They are both white magicians. You'll meet Joshua as soon as Esmerelda says you're ready."

Esmerelda's golden eyes were warm. "It won't be more than a week, Uncle Pablo."

CHAPTER TWO

Joshua Starr lay flat on his back in the middle of his living room carpet. His hand spread across one side of his face, and he talked through spread fingers to Susan Quinn, his secretary, who sat at her desk, taking down each word he said. He was speaking rather loudly because she was some twenty feet away, her typist's chair backing up to the expanse of window that constituted the entire wall of that side of the living room.

Even lying flat on the floor, Joshua looked weather-beaten and tough, with the appearance of a merchant seaman, or a range rider. His face, with its strongly marked, almost exaggerated features, and its lines of weathered humor and experience, seemed to complete the picture of Joshua as an outdoor man, carefree, thoughtlessly strong, perhaps even a bit cruel; it was only the subtle details of expression and gesture that showed to the experienced eye the high intellect that was so much a part of Joshua's human personality.

He traced a pattern in the air whose meaning was known only to himself; the tracing took only a few seconds. Susan waited, her fingers poised above the typewriter keys, and looked at him as he lay there. His face was known to millions of TV viewers as the moderator of a daily morning interview that made up a fifteen minute segment of a news and weather show that came out of Washington, and was picked up by one of the networks. The distinctive baritone, not deep-toned, but with an edge of harshness and a slight drawl to its timbre that continued the visual suggestion of the outdoor man, was also familiar to many, many housewives. But, reflected Susan, she knew in some detail what the housewives would never know, for they saw him only in his role as interviewer, sitting in anonymous chairs in conservative suits while she saw him every working day in the far more private role of scriptwriter for television. He and Susan worked well together; she was an excellent typist and quite literate enough to translate Joshua's spoken word into written syntax at a speed at which Joshua found comfortable to dictate.

He had chosen her for this talent, and had been pleased enough with her intelligent, demonstrative personality to keep her. This was their fourth year together. Susan, for her part, was strongly motivated towards keeping her job, for besides the obvious advantages of a very generous salary and a four-hour working day, there were the manifold delights of knowing Joshua Starr.

He was, today as always, an easy man to look at; although some people thought of him as a homely, even an ugly man, his physical presence was very strong, and it arrested the attention even when it did not please. Most, however, joined with Susan in finding Joshua very handsome indeed. Today his lean, deep-muscled frame was covered with blue jeans and a long-sleeved sweatshirt. He looked shorter than he really was, usually; he carried himself with the unconscious grace of an athlete, and his height seemed entirely in keeping with the proportions of his body. On the carpet, however, he looked his full six feet two inches. From her position above him, Susan could see his face upside down, features calm in concentration, dictating in the direction of the ceiling through his spread fingers, the slightly graying, heavy mop of hair tangling through his fingers and onto the expanse of floor.

"Scene Two," Joshua was saying.

The telephone rang to break his concentration, and he moved to his feet to answer it, walking the six long strides of space with the ease that was his nature. His hand paused on the receiver while he took a few seconds to reorient his thinking. He had learned not to try to do business with his mind still in the creative realms. The results were always total fiascos, decorated with confused choruses of, "But you SAID ...!" His face lost its inward-looking blankness and put on the mask of the celebrity. "Starr speaking," he said to the telephone.

There was a long pause, while he listened less and less intently. The monologue seemed ultimately to bore him, for he cut in. "Listen, Herman. I said it yesterday, and I'll say it again today. Handle the money, man, just handle the money. Don't bug me about the money. Just do your thing. You've got full authority with the money bit ... No, Herman, I won't blame you if you lose the money. Just go ahead with the plan ... Whatever you think is best ... Yes, Herman, I really mean that. I really do. Go ahead with the whole plan ... You said all that yesterday, Herman ... Well, second thoughts or no second thoughts, I think you're right. Go ahead, all right? ... OK. I'll see you tomorrow. Good-bye, Herman."

Joshua shook his head as he replaced the receiver. "He's one of the best financial wizards around. If he'd just learn to trust his own judgment, he could make a bundle for himself instead of for other people." He rose from his seat by the telephone and roamed to the glass wall which extended forty feet across the back of the house, looking down, from the crest of the hill on which the house stood, onto the informal, very extensive garden which constituted Joshua's back yard. The slopes of the valley had been cleared of wild brush and groomed with flowering bushes and rock gardens, and the ground was laid with winding paths and clearings. Its centerpiece was a white building whose roof gleamed in the late afternoon sun.

His secretary's glance followed his over the lovely grounds which fell away gradually from the window. "Don't you think you ought to keep a closer watch on Herman? If he did lose your money, you wouldn't be able to enjoy all this luxury."

"Luxury?" enquired Joshua. "This bit here with the pretty trees and all the gadgets is here for one reason only. It makes it easier to work. Luxury is a state of mind, girl. Ask anybody where he'd like to be, and chances are that he'll say some island in the south seas. Well, if I lose all my money I just declare bankruptcy and hold out a ticket for the south seas. That's luxury, right?"

"Still, I think you ought to pay more attention to what Herman is doing. Wouldn't you hate to lose all your money?"

Starr turned back from the window and pulled his hands out of their roost in his back pockets to make a mock-Italian gesture towards her. "You trying to ruin me? What about that bit about the camel and the needle, and the rich man and the kingdom of heaven? You trying to keep me out of the kingdom of heaven?"

Susie waved the thought away. "No, no, I mean you've already got enough money to be rich. You're rich whether you like it or not."

"I sort of figured the parable had to do with how you think about money, not how much of it you have. Anyway, I've got things I'd rather do than think about money. Herman knows a lot more about that stuff than I do. If I wanted to go to all the trouble of figuring out what he was doing, I wouldn't need to hire him in the first place." He walked as he talked, back to the small black cube which was Susan's typewriter table. It sat facing away from the front window, and Joshua perched one hip on it. "Now, let's forget about money and get back to writing this script. After all, I have three minutes left to work."

Miss Quinn consulted her watch. "6:14, eh? My watch must be slow. It only says 6:12."

Starr looked faintly shocked. "Gadgets! Of course your watch is running slow again. Because it is precisely ..."

Susan cut in. "I know, I know. Spare me. It is precisely 6:14. How do you know what time it is, anyway? I never even see you look at a watch."

"I don't own one. I just sort of narrow things down a little closer than people who know whether it's night or day."

Susan waited in silence. "That's all?" She hesitated, looking at him from under her eyelashes, and decided not to ask further. Questions about his various skills and oddities tended to aggravate his normal good humor; it was better to let the question drop. Not that she understood how he knew about time. But she did understand that under no circumstances did Joshua Starr work after 6:17 in the evening. He had not answered her questions about why that cutoff time, either. In fact, he was not an explainable man. She had found the outer surface very attractive; he was extremely good looking, in his rangy way; his face held great strength and self-confidence, and his eyes could be very gentle. He exuded a masculine virility that men felt comfortable with and women were always drawn to; he had many acquaintances and very few enemies.

But she had never been able to see beneath the surface with Joshua. In three years, he had yet to discuss any personal problem with her, although he was always very careful to ask about her affairs, and she had confided in him on occasion. He really baffled her; and although she was fascinated by him, she wondered sometimes what she would do if he ever asked her to marry him. A lifetime of not understanding the man you loved was not a comfortable one.

But of course, she always reminded herself, he would never ask her in the first place; which relieved her as well as being a bit deflating. That would be too understandable a thing to do, too much within the social pattern. He seemed to operate totally outside, and to Susan's way of thinking above, the normal society, rambling through life without any particular goal or deep ambition, constantly finding new things to think about, never staying mentally still, although he was a fairly settled person physically, seldom leaving his home base.

And as a professional and careful secretary, she admired the use he made of himself and of her during the four-hour work sessions. He dictated to her at precisely her typing speed, and in one day, he could turn out as much as most television writers did in three. He seldom hesitated for a word and never for an idea, and what he wrote was good, very good. She suspected that he could have worked much faster if it had not been for her limitations of typing speed and the need to change the paper in the machine; he had tried dictating into a recording device, but had found that he was used to having an audience, and, besides, he liked to roam while he was creating, and without the ability to move around freely and get rid of some of the energy his body constantly put out, he found himself unable to work nearly as well. And so they had gone back to, and stayed with, the two two-hour sessions in the afternoon, with his goal being one television hour's worth of material at each two-hour session. He hadn't missed that goal in a long time; when he did, it was only because the telephone rang too often.

Now the work was over for the day. Joshua put his palms on the carpet and inverted his body, walking across from the desk to the bar, which was at one end of the room, on his hands.

Susan watched with great affection as he reached the bar and flipped himself to a sitting position on one of the low stools there; she had had no idea he could do that. "Learn something new every day," she laughed, and then said quickly, "No, no, I'll do that."

Josh dropped his hand from the gin bottle as if it carried an electric charge. "OK, OK, officer, I promise I'll never do it again." He put his hands back in his back pockets and began to roam in his habitual way across the room. He stood still when he came to the far end of the back window; the sun was in its last moments of setting, and the brassy orange half-disc poured its last thick rays over the far distance and into the valley. He spoke very quietly. "Thirty-eight trips around that star, and it's getting to me."

Susan was coping with gin and ice; the clinking of glass on silver obscured his words. "What?"

"Thirty-eight trips around their star. I shouldn't be this worn out after only thirty-eight trips. Look at me, breathing like a beached whale, and all I did was walk twenty feet on my hands."

"What are you talking about?" said Susan. "I've got no idea what you mean. Here." She handed him a shaker full of martinis. "Now thirty-eight trips around what star?"

He took the shaker and began to do the honors. "Look. Why should I be so worn out after only thirty-eight trips around this star?" He gestured towards the setting sun. "I mean, that's not any distance at all. This is really a weird place."

Susan was catching up now. "You mean you're thirty-eight years old, you've been around the sun thirty eight times?"

"Right, that's what I said."

"I never thought of it that way, but I guess that is how we tell ages. By how often the planet goes around the sun." The thought interested her;

she had an active mind, and thoroughly enjoyed playing with new thoughts. "But you don't look thirty-eight, Josh, you don't really look thirty, except for the gray in your hair."

"It doesn't matter. I shouldn't look even that old. Going this short distance shouldn't have had any effect at all."

"Distance?"

"Right. Using a heliocentric coordinate system, and assuming a circular orbit-Josh paused, mentally calculating-well, the planet travels about five hundred and eighty-five million miles a year. So I'm about twenty-two billion miles old."

"Time equals distance, eh?" Susan's mind was racing, trying to encompass the new concept. "Well, there goes philosophy. If space and time are the same thing, then the only one who had it right was old Heraclitus, who said that all things were one. And even he didn't think he could step in the same river twice."

"Don't forget the twentieth century." Josh was shaking the martini mixture gently; "Philosophy isn't the thing any more. It's all science. And most of that has gone the way of Einstein. They haven't come right out and said it yet, but if everything is relative to everything else, then it looks like the old idea that time is time and space is space and never the twain shall meet is wrong. And I am twenty-two billion miles old, and feel about a light year older than that."

"Tell you what, old man. Get on the next space flight out and go counterclockwise around the earth for about ten years. That should youthen you."

"The fountain of youth at last. That's good, Susan. We could sell tickets. Get on our spaceship and unwind!"

"Listen, if we could do that, you could forget about writing for TV. I know a terrific market. The whole country wants to be younger." She stopped, intrigued by another thought. "How far am I?"

"Oh, you're just a short distance runner; let's see, you're a mere sixteen billion." He decanted ice-cold martinis into two glasses. "Wow, does that look good," said Susan, reaching for hers. "You really wear a girl out with that machine-gun dictation." Josh grinned, the lines at the corners of his eyes crinkling into crows feet. "A toast to the fastest typewriter in the east."

The telephone interrupted their first sip.

"After business hours," said Susan, putting her hand on top of his to keep it from moving.

He patted her hand with his free one, and disengaged himself. The phone rang again, and he looked intently at it for a few seconds. "This isn't business." He picked up the receiver. "Hello, Pablo. How's the funny farm?"

Pablo Padeyevsky's voice came clearly into the quiet room, his clipped accents quite audible to Susan. "Fine. Listen, I've found just who we've been waiting for."

"What? You mean for the contact?"

"Yes. We all knew it would have to happen sooner or later, and it did. He just walked into my office at the university."

"That's what I would have expected. It never does any good to go looking for things; he was bound to show up. But it's still hard to believe it's happened. Are you sure?"

"Well, I was fairly certain, but Esmerelda says she's absolutely sure. And he's here right now, Esmerelda's been working with him for a week or so.

Josh was tangling fingers through his hair in his excitement; the fingers stopped moving. "I wondered why she didn't show up for work in the temple." Josh started pulling at his hair again. "Well! Great! Beautiful! Can we go ahead with it now? Can you get over here pretty soon? Do you think we can go ahead with the communication attempt?"

"Well, I thought we might all get together tonight and talk about it. How about our dropping by your place later?"

"Any time. Like, how about any time in the next ten minutes."

"We can't make it quite that soon. But we'll be there."

"I'll be expecting you." Josh put the receiver down and looked up at Susan. She smiled at him. "You look like a little boy who just found out there are two Christmases this year."

He reached over and took her by the two shoulders, his hands tensing with excitement. "There are for me! I've been waiting for this for years."

"Waiting for what?"

"Well, that's a little complicated. It has to do with some of my experimental work."

"Which I don't understand, nor never will. You tried once to tell me what went on in that garden of yours, and it just sounded strange to me. But I'm very happy for you. Really I am. Here, drink your martini! Celebrate!" She held his glass out for him.

"Nope. I'm on the wagon as of right now, and for a few weeks to come."

Susan put the glass down, picked hers up, and sipped it thoughtfully. For Josh to stop drinking was a great departure from his normal habits; it told her just how important this call must have been to him. Not that Josh was an alcoholic, he was able to function with or without his evening drinks. But he did have periods of fairly heavy drinking; often lately the martini hour would end after dinner and find Josh wandering out to the porch or garden chairs, carrying a bottle of Matuselum. There he would sit, sipping steadily at his drink, looking off into the deepening night sky until the stars came out. Susan stayed some evenings, at his request, and during these periods would find things to do by herself, for she sensed, and quite rightly, that these moods of his were solitary. He never seemed depressed, nor could she say that he was moody; he just became very detached, and withdrew into himself. She thought of them as times of adjustment for Josh, a sort of substitute for an analyst.

In actuality, although Joshua respected Susan's competence, and enjoyed her intelligence, he was aware that she would never come close to understanding him. She thought that he sat alone to realign his thinking, get the kinks out of his days; the purpose was quite different: he sat on a planet he had been weary of for some time, dulling a little the daily pain of living in a mental atmosphere that was completely the opposite of what he desired to find, and he looked up at the creation, the millions of stars, and thought of the greatly remote suns as one would wish for home. Susan, he knew, thought of him as an entertaining, but ultimately shallow, person, a person who did not take anything at all seriously. In fact, he was a man who had taken himself so very seriously that it had put him completely alone for a long time, for he had found no one else who paid any attention at all to what he considered utterly central. He had, long ago, found Pablo, and they were friends because Pablo did at least attempt to search for wisdom. And with Esmerelda, Joshua had found one other person who cared as much as he did for her spirit's welfare. And together they had practiced the rituals of white magic in the temple Joshua had built in his garden.

But, because Joshua had worked with Esmerelda first as a child, he had never discovered her full personality; he thought of her as part of his own consciousness, part of his spiritual strength. Her daily world and his had never meshed at all. And Joshua continued finding the people that he met to be like Susan, aiming at some goal in the temporal future, thinking about their lonelinesses and adjustments and chances for success and chances for failure, and worrying endlessly over things he could only think of as foolish games. And, more and more, he sat alone on a planet to which he was alien, sipping rum, and looking at the stars.

Susan was quite right in thinking that Joshua would never ask her to be his wife, but she had no idea why. She would never have considered herself as lacking in qualifications as a candidate for a wife. But to Josh she was hopelessly inadequate. She was pretty, intelligent, and useful, but she had no ability whatever to warm him, to make his spirit rest. She thought he had no desire to be married; on the contrary, he was already settled, and the very coziness of his home made his aloneness in it more intense; he would have been most happy to fill the place with the genuine warmth of a family. A long, long time ago, he had decided that there was no hope, on this planet, of finding any woman who could be a family to him, and he had closed a door in his mind, and stopped looking. He had grown accustomed to seeing his environment as an alien one, and not expecting anything but foolishness from his fellow humans. The one thing still worthwhile to him had been his research, by himself, and with Esmerelda, and for the past seven years increasingly with Pablo, in the realms of ritual magic. Now, at last, things wished for on spiritual planes were coming to pass in the physical. There was no loneliness in Joshua tonight. He looked at Susan's surprised and quizzical face and said, "Imagine that, Susie. Me on the wagon! What's this world coming to?"

Susan gave up again on trying to understand him. "I heard you say that they'll be over soon. Is it time for me to go?"

Josh put one hand back of her shoulder and shook it, gently. "You sure you don't mind?"

"Not at all. Are you going to be tied up more than tonight?"

"I really don't know right now. Can you call in tomorrow, or do you want me to call you?"

Susan thought. "Tell you what. I'll call tomorrow morning after you're through with your work at the studio. You tell me then when to report in. If you need some time, I'll just have the answering service switch all your calls to me. You can call me to give me instructions."

"Good," said Josh, steering her to her light coat and helping her with it. "We're ahead on the writing anyway, and this really might take some time. I've got some interviews taped, too, for that matter. You can handle

44

the routine stuff for quite a while. If I don't phone in, just do what you think best."

He kissed her lightly, and she responded, putting her hand to his cheek. "OK, Josh. I'll bankrupt you, or Herman and I'll do it between us. He'll probably have a heart attack, come to think of it, without you to talk to every day. But don't worry. I'll like you just as well after I ruin your finances."

"Good girl." He walked her out to the three car garage which tucked under the first floor at the rear of the house, using the slope of the hill for space. His Lamborghini Muira sat small and elegant next to another car he had owned in the past and never sold; the third space belonged to Susan's convertible; she was an inveterate driver-with-tops-down, thoroughly enjoying four gears, and driving quite well: she drove the way she typed, quickly and without error, her mind set far ahead of where she actually was, taking all available hints as to her whereabouts in the immediate future, and putting them to good use.

Joshua watched her taillights recede down the driveway and around the first bend in the road. He felt some relief that she was gone, which he would not have felt any other night. But, with the news of Pablo's discovery fresh in his mind, he was thinking only of the group's imminent arrival. Lean and dark in the twilight, he hurried back into the living room and cleaned up the bar and tables, removing glasses and wiping up rings of moisture. The typewriter went under its table and the piece of furniture became a simple black cube, sitting between two comfortable chairs. Then, placing himself by the back window, he took off his shoes and squatted to the floor, crossing his legs Indian-fashion, looking out at the sky and the first stars, and waiting.

CHAPTER THREE

Pablo had just finished the telephone conversation with Joshua about Theodore, and set the receiver back in its cradle, when it jangled at him. On its third ring, he picked it up. "Padeyevsky," he said into it.

"You win this time, too," said the voice on the other end of the line. The New York people have to do it your way. Unless some accident befalls you."

"I'd be very careful about threats, if I were you," said Pablo. "Of course, I'm sure you didn't mean that as a threat."

"Take it any way you want," said the voice. "We don't have room to deal in threats, do we? You win."

"Well, just look at it this way." Padeyevsky grinned into the telephone. "Money is the root of all evil. I've just cleared a broad path to your reform."

The voice at the other end shook slightly. "Look, Padeyevsky, don't give me that. Just tell me what you're going to do, that's all. What are you going to do? You know you can't let this go on."

"Yes, I can," said Pablo, cheerfully, "and I have. The whole thing is finished now. You're through. Be a good sport about it. Look at the advantages of financial disaster: no more wearing conferences, no more late nights, no more …

The voice cut in, hard and tight with rage. "I'll get you Padeyevsky. If it's the last thing I ever do, I'll personally get you for this. Do you hear me?"

Padeyevsky smiled very coldly into the receiver. "The moving finger writes," he said, "and, having writ, moves on." Very slowly, he lowered the receiver to its cradle. There he sat, his mind moving with satisfaction over the recent conversation, one small hand to his chin, his portly body relaxed. Perhaps he'd better make a trip to New York soon, just to be sure. His small black eyes wandered blankly over the familiar hall, narrowing in their creases as he saw Esmerelda for the first time, standing by the door from the back of the house, hands pressed together, body somehow huddled in on itself.

"Esmerelda! You startled me."

She said nothing, only continued looking at him.

"Is there something wrong?" he asked. "Something happen to Theodore, or …"

"Oh, Pablo," she said softly, trying not to cry. "Oh, Uncle Pablo, your aura. What is it, Pablo? While you were on the telephone, it was full of such darkness." She gave up and started to cry into her clenched hands, walking towards him. In spurts, she said, "I don't understand it. It changed, and then it changed back, so fast, when you saw me. It's all right now, the way it always is. Oh, Pablo! How could you let it get to you?"

She was close now, and Pablo stood up and held her against him awkwardly, letting her cry against his vest, eyes no longer creased but as soft as their blackness would ever get, with his love for his niece. "My dear, there is much in this world both of good and of bad, and each of us has a little of each. You have discovered this in me and I am sorry. But this is the world we live in, and you have to face both sides of it. I am very, very sorry that you saw this, for I have kept many ugly things from you for a long time, and this ugliness is the one closest to you. But your good old Pablo is still here too, still real."

Esmerelda cried on into his shoulder, and Pablo stopped speaking, aware now that there would be some waiting, while she got cried out. Women, he thought to himself with affection. He patted on in silence, while his vest got quite saturated across the front, and his arm went to sleep. Finally, Esmerelda raised her pink face from his shoulder.

"All right, so it's there, all this negativity," she said, not quite steadily, "and my own Uncle, the safest man in the world, has it too, but no matter how long I face it I won't get used to it. You can make me face the darkness, but you can't make me turn from the light just Because the darkness exists. I'm as tough as it is, Pablo. I can face it, and understand it, and see it for what it is."

"And what is that?"

"Separation," said Esmerelda. "Times when somebody has forgotten the one who is all, and has begun making up his own universe and his own reasons. Times when a person hides from Being kind, and makes up rules that hurt people. Times when people are scared, and run away from the creation. You can make me look at it, and make me see it in you, but it still looks like separation from the light to me. And I stand with the light."

Pablo's voice was gentle. "And why do you stress the separation, nay child? The light and the darkness are one thing. Two faces of the same creation, only subtly different. You think the chasm is so wide between the two, my child, and yet only your intellect can find the difference great, and your intellect is of no use. It only makes you put the bogeyman from you, so you won't have to think about it. But evil is as respectable as good, my dear. Don't be shallow. For evil is all around you, more evil by far than good, and you shouldn't discount it."

He looked at her then, and saw the expression, and stopped his lecture in the middle. "Oh, Esmerelda, please forgive me. I'm sorry. I only wanted to make you see that everything that is positive can be negative too. That there is only the smallest difference between the two. My child, can you forgive me that?"

She looked at him, confusion and repugnance melting into quieter emotion. The Santy Clause smile, as she had so often called it, was there again, and his aura was gentle and clear, as she had seen it for years. And yet, a few minutes ago he had been a rude and ugly affront to her consciousness, his aura dark and evil. It was going to take considerable meditation to compass this in understanding.

Pablo was still waiting for her to say something. She cast her mind back and found the thread of the talking. "It's all right, Uncle Pablo. I am only here to learn. I only wish that I had met this a long time ago, so I could have begun trying to become one with it. How could you let me be so sure of myself, when you knew I had so much to learn?"

She didn't sound angry, or even irritated. Pablo looked at her closely. She shook her head. "No, I'm not getting ready to cry again. That's done. But talk to me. What draws you to this negativity? That must be what really confuses me. I just don't feel any pull to it at all."

"There is much confusion to be cleared away, my child. By you, by me, by us all. What makes you think I am consciously drawn to negativity? Perhaps it simply finds a channel in me. You have named it evil, and yet is it not simply a pole, in a dually polarized universe? Why should one pole be better than the other? You have recoiled against my duality. And yet, in a dual universe, why not be dual?"

"All right, Pablo. I'll understand in time, and meanwhile you're still Uncle Pablo, and I cherish you. Nothing could change that. But this has all been very sudden. I thought you were one thing, and now you have me thinking you are two, like Dr. Jekyll and Mr. Hyde. I was sure, and now I'm not sure at all. I thought you and Joshua had taught me everything. Now I know differently."

"My child, my child," said Pablo, standing in the dim hall wishing he had never begun this lesson, and anxious to have it done, now it was begun. "I have taught you nothing. For I know nothing."

"Then, Pablo, where are we going?"

Pablo stepped the one step that separated them and took her head again to him. "Put your feet back on solid ground, my child. We aren't going anywhere. There is much for us all to learn. You will learn this, and when you know it, you will be where you were before: at one with wisdom, yet knowing nothing. For we can know nothing. This is not an environment that allows wisdom. We must simply act. Am I not right?" He smiled at her, feeling abashed at his uncharacteristic bluntness towards his niece.

"I suppose so, Uncle Pablo." Esmerelda smiled back at him, her face clear again. "And, speaking of action, we're due at Josh's, aren't we? Ted's ready. I'm ready."

"I'm ready too," said the Doctor. "Shall we?"

She took his arm, and they walked out to Theodore, waiting for them beside the Mercedes.

CHAPTER FOUR

True to Esmerelda's prediction, the meeting of Theodore with Joshua Starr had taken place only one week after Theodore came to the farm. Joshua had seen very quickly that Theodore was the missing link in their planned experiment, and the training towards the ritual went on apace.

Theodore had spent the ten days of preparation working harder than he had ever worked in his life. He had potential, of course, strong potential towards the positive, and Joshua's lessons sat well with him. He tentatively began to learn the disciplines of magic. The meditations took a great deal of emotional strength, for the physical self is not geared to the contemplative life. The concentration which these disciplines demanded made Theodore feel drained, mentally and emotionally; he often doubted that he had any aptitude for this at all.

But the days were better spent than he thought; although he did not gain the confidence in his magical personality that is so important to the success of ritual magic, he did become able to clear his mind of the daily personality of Theodore Behr, so that his very positively oriented light-body could be sent forth to the aid of Esmerelda and Joshua. He had no real idea of what he was doing; it takes years of apprenticeship for that. But what they needed was developed: Theodore could take a secondary part in the ritual. His teachers were well satisfied with him.

They had spent far more time than Theodore in preparation for this experiment; their magical personalities had been years in the making. Joshua had practiced white magic since before Esmerelda had been born. His childhood had been spent in England, and a magician there had had a leading to the boy. He had taken him into apprenticeship when he was ten years old. Joshua had worked each day within the realms of the thought universe, gaining with slow sureness the proper emotional biases for power within the mental planes, developing his will towards the good. He was an alien, as had his teacher and his teacher's teacher been; he had progressed until, in early manhood, when he had come to the United States, he had no peer in white magic in the western world.

Because he was an alien, he shared with Theodore and others of his kind the lonelinesses of his difference. The consciousness of one of the more highly evolved entities drift like pollen across the universe; most are sown close to their homeland. Only a few stray on long journeys, and come to be warmed by suns not their own. When Joshua had met Pablo Padeyevsky's little niece, ten years ago, he had recognized a fellow wanderer in her. Padeyevsky had taken the child in and grown to love her because she had lost her father and her mother. Joshua had loved her because she was orphaned on this planet.

Esmerelda had become Joshua's apprentice, at the age of nine. Through the years, she had in her gentle way assumed more and more of the true magical personality, until she had reached and passed Joshua's flexibility in the role of magus. Her discipline, for all its being hidden within the inner folds of her woman's pliant self, was very intense, and she was able to overtake her teacher's successes in the sphere of occult manipulation, just as Joshua had become more skilled than his teacher before him. Esmerelda's successes pleased Joshua greatly, for the bias towards the positive which she generated filled his consciousness with light, and he felt her strength added to the small community of white magicians on Earth, and to their aggregate polarity.

As Esmerelda had grown in years, she had gained much understanding of the more subtle emotional realities of the world she lived in, and her wisdom was far greater than her chronological age. She had kept herself apart from the contact with others of her own age that might have made her vain of her beauty, or eager to influence others by it. Her most intense physical desire was towards living quietly in the rural contentment of her uncle's farm. She spent her days supervising the care of the house and its environs with the help of a daily housekeeper and a twice-weekly outdoor man, in reading and studying on her own, and in her daily times of meditation alone and with Joshua in their temple. Although she had turned nineteen now, and was full-grown, Joshua thought of her still in terms of an apprentice. And Esmerelda, seeing the difficulties with which Joshua would have to deal, if he ever saw clearly that she was now his equal, was content to remain in the supporting or reinforcing role. She saw the doors that he had closed against his loneliness. She had watched the moment when Joshua might be able to take comfort in the warmth of her new womanhood come and go.

She was content, therefore, to let him think of her as a child still. And so she treated him also as a child, cherishing him and humoring him, happy in her ability to support him in his ritual work, happy to lend her will to his when he spoke the ceremonial words, and etched his forms of light in the air.

Not that Joshua was an incomplete magical entity. Years had taken their toll on a man ill fit to withstand easily the foolishness of the culture in which he lived. His social personality had deteriorated somewhat; he was not wont to expect sanity from people, and he had nearly lost the art of being open to the outside world. He could not see Esmerelda clearly because of the growing limitations of his daily thinking. There were other details of the physical world that were also lost to him.

But this in no way hindered his magical personality. It remained strong, as repeated summoning lent it more and more substance. Indeed, it was extremely well established now, and Joshua could slip into it with the slight amount of will it takes the normal person to decide to put on a piece of clothing.

Joshua and Esmerelda had worked for a longtime together, and as they progressed in strength, they graduated to the ranks of what Joshua called experimental magic. Because they were both aliens, they had often sent their consciousnesses past the mental planes, searching for a planet closer in positivity to their desire. They had found such a planet, and during their research on it, they had discovered a potential that transcended the illusions of space and time. There had been a partial transfer of mind from this planet to Earth. One of the two mind segments transferred was the being now known as Esmerelda Sweetwater: in her searching, Esmerelda had happened on her homeland. It had now been determined that the other mind segment was the individual called Theodore Behr.

This discovery had been the basis for all of the planning that had led up to the coming ritual. They had carefully brought the ingredients of the experiment together through the years. Finding Theodore had been the last requirement, and the time of action was now here. The ritual was about to become a reality.

Because the ceremony was so important, the purifying preparations had been more careful than usual; the occult preparation for the coming of the people from their sister planet involved the purging of all negativity from the temple to which they hoped to call their counterparts, their higher selves, that had remained behind on the planet of light.

They had done this purging ritual many times before. But it had never been so important to them before, because this time, they were not simply purging the place of their magic, they were also attempting to raise the purity of this place and its surroundings to the level of a far purer planet's. They wanted very much to succeed in this, for the actual landing of their counterparts seemed to promise in reality much that they had worked for in faith for so long. Therefore, all four had fasted for the last seven days: for Joshua and Pablo this had been hardest to accomplish; Esmerelda and Theodore were abstemious anyway. Their amorous inclinations had been left to atrophy for the same period of time. For this time, Esmerelda and Joshua worked together in their place of ritual, preparing their consciousnesses together for the ritual to come. In silence and in reflection, Joshua sent his consciousness into the light, and Esmerelda sent hers towards it, finding and becoming totally one with it with more and more ease. These were days of nearly total peace, and later Joshua looked back upon this preparation period with much happiness.

The eleventh day was the day of the ceremony. In the morning the Padeyevsky faction came to Joshua's house, and the group sat and chatted through the noon hour. In the early afternoon, they all sat in silence together for a while, for the Doctor and Behr were to be within the ritual as secondary members. As the afternoon hours passed, Esmerelda and Joshua removed themselves from the other two and went, each alone, to a final preparation.

It was dusk when Joshua and Esmerelda opened the door of the five-sided building that stood, small and quiet looking, in the middle of Joshua's European garden, lending to its casually placed lawns and plantings the centrality of the old-fashioned garden alcove. But this building was for more of a purpose than the spending of summer evenings under the stars. It had been built by Joshua. He had placed every nail, and set every stone, long ago. This was hardly in character for the man: Joshua looked as though he spent every day on the open range roping wild longhorns. In reality, his whipcord strength had always been maintained in spite of his temperament, not because of it. He never did any physical work that was not necessary.

But he had built his garden chamber because it was quite necessary that he be its builder. For it was a magical chamber, designed for his magical personality's use, and the strength of the talisman of the building's being his work was considerable. And for ten years, he and Esmerelda had studied and done their ritual work here. Here lay the forms of the eternal channels of power, strengthened to an almost independent life through the long and constant repetition of their invocation. This was, before Joshua and Esmerelda began this central ritual, already a place of light, where spirits of healing and wholeness dwelled, waiting only invocation to join with the consciousness of the two magicians in achieving the motionless and timeless praise of the dawning light of the one who is all.

Joshua walked in his golden robe into the chamber and moved towards the altar, a table in the middle of the chamber, twice as long as it was wide, and covered with a golden cloth, a candle, and an open Bible. Esmerelda also moved towards the altar, then stopped and beckoned Pablo and Theodore to come towards her.

She halted them two paces into the small chamber, four paces from the altar, and placed them on a line with the sides of the altar. Joshua stood motionless, facing the door on the eastern side of the chamber, his hands held over his breast in an attitude of prayer. Esmerelda touched Padeyevsky's hands and then Ted's to form them in the same posture. There was a pause, during which Theodore attempted to calm his mind, and Pablo, his mind already calming, reflected and then released thoughts of a church he had been taken to when he was a child. He had never thought to have clasped his hands in prayer again. Amen, he thought. So be it. Ritual is ritual, and I don't suppose they could help using some of the same symbols.

Esmerelda, robed as was Joshua in gold, and wearing a cross on her breast of a very complex and intricately carved design, walked counterclockwise with slow steps around the chamber, and stopped by Joshua. They stood, shoulders touching, their eyes opening with a vivid clarity. "We are ready," said Esmerelda.

Ringing with power and authority, Joshua's voice pronounced the word, "Shemesh." The sound vibrated through the temple and Esmerelda and Joshua seemed to see it with their eyes, watching it echo and strengthening its sound in the still air with the force of their will until there seemed to be, in front of their gazes, a bright place that shimmered with the effect of sunlight sifted through clouds; formless, but full of an untouchable life.

Esmerelda lifted her countenance towards Joshua's, and her eyes closed briefly, just skimming shut, as though in some acquiescence. He bent his head to hers slightly, and they moved closer together behind the table. There was a pause, while silence seemed to settle about their touching shoulders like a mantle. Then, out of the silence and as a continuation of its protection, Joshua uttered the word, "Tiphareth." Again, his voice seemed to vibrate with a timbre completely unlike his usual baritone speaking voice; it seemed quiet, but with the quiet that comes to the ear when it has heard a great deal of noise, and can no longer distinguish the actual volume it perceives. Again, the two pairs of magicians' eyes stared into the atmosphere in front of them, watching its emptiness as carefully as the eagle watches the ground a mile below. There was no prey awaited here of earthly nature: they waited only for the blessing of the one who protects this planet, the one whose rays are the flashing light of the sun, and whose name had here been called.

The pause was as short as any time of concentration is short, as long as any time of desire. And then the motes of shadowed sunlight that had seemed to dance in front of Esmerelda and Joshua brightened, and for a tiny second of time, there seemed to be a flame about them both, and a blazing light in the whole temple. Pablo and Theodore stood nearby terrified by the evident power in the chamber with them, but the light seemed almost to become a part of Esmerelda and Joshua, as they who invoked this blessing accepted and assimilated it.

It was time now for the ritual itself, the purification of their place, which was the necessary prelude to a successful contact with the planet of light. There was a nearly imperceptible movement of separation between the two magicians as Esmerelda became again and more obviously Joshua's assistant. He made the sign of the cross on brow, breast, and shoulders, very slowly. At each point of the cross he spoke a word: "Ateh, Malkuth, Ve Geburah, Ve Gedulah." As he crossed his hands on his breast, saying, "Le Olahm Amen," it seemed that the flame that had been about the two began to shine as the tracings of the cross. Joshua drew out more of this light as he drew in the air a five-sided figure with the top point at the top of the cross, and its five sides like a star superimposed upon it. After the star had been drawn and had begun glowing with the light of the cross, Joshua moved his hand in a swift and short stabbing motion in front of his breast and said the name, "Yod-Heh-Vau-Heh."

With Esmerelda at his side, eyes focused in total concentration upon the forms in front of them, Josh turned from east to south, then west, then north, then back to the east again, building the five-pointed star in each direction and speaking the ritual words. "Ah-Doh-Ni" he spoke at the south, at the west "Eh-He-Heh," at the north "Ah-Gla." The words bodied forth into the shining air the shapes he drew, and he and Esmerelda were surrounded, at the end of their turning, with forms of light that all but hid them from Theodore and Pablo. The fence of white right shimmered before them for several minutes, while Joshua slowly raised his arms to make one great cross of his body, and Esmerelda closed her eyes and stood, chin lifted, arms at her sides, lending all her will to his.

Then Joshua spoke once more, his voice still vibrating with that fullness which marked Joshua the magician. "Before me, Raphael. Behind me, Gabriel. On my right hand, Michael. On my left hand, Uriel," he said. And the watchers saw the light burst into colors and glints of substance: yellow, blue, red, green, and all the complements and undertones of those colors, one at each of the four directions. There was the breeze of gentle air, the soft gleam of light through water, the hard sheen of steel, the smell of ripe wheat and fragrant hay. The two that watched wanted to hide their eyes, and yet the will that would have raised their hands or shut their eyes was not theirs to command, for it was caught up in the power of the ritual, practiced many times by the two white magicians before them but never accomplished with such visible strength. For only now did the wills of the two practicing these rites come into complete union; only now was the work done completely. And as the strength of the two at last reached the perfection of its use, Joshua spoke the words that ended the ritual of preparation:

"For around me flame the pentagrams, and above me shines the six-rayed star."

The ceremony of preparation was over; it was time now for the summoning. Esmerelda stepped the four paces to Theodore, took him by the hand, and placed him with her, directly in front of Joshua, between him and the altar. They stood, hand in hand, their eyes closed in concentration, their posture straight with it, lending all their will to Joshua's. There was utter silence for a long pause; they could feel a building tightness in the air. Then the many-colored light became white again, and two centers began to appear in the whiteness, molding light to themselves until all the light was built into two forms, two people made of light, with a twin shaft of light uniting the two forms of Esmerelda and Theodore, and continuing from them both into the air above their heads, disappearing through the ceiling of the little temple.

"Will you come?" asked Joshua.

"We will come, and we will serve," they spoke in reply.

As these words faded from hearing, the forms faded from sight, taking the magically charged light with them and restoring the atmosphere inside the chamber to the normalcy of quiet, everyday air. The ritual was over, and it had succeeded.

The four members of its performance stirred, and began to walk to the door of the temple in silence. The waiting was over, and the action had begun. So thought Padeyevsky and Theodore, and so thought Esmerelda, until she took a close look at Joshua. He wasn't really sharing in the moment of triumph, she thought; he was apart, somehow. She gazed at him until he felt her eyes, and returned the glance. Over his eyes a veil had been drawn; she would have to leave him to himself for now. Following the other two, who were quite unaware of this interchange of unspoken thoughts, she hastened towards Josh's house. But, as she hurried, she felt the shadow descend into her mind: something was not as it should be. For Joshua's gaze had held an unexplained, but very real trouble. It would be necessary to wait until he was ready to talk about it. Esmerelda gave a mental shrug and left Josh to himself.

Joshua had remained inside the temple, with the trouble in his mind. His eyes lifted their veil, and he sat down on the floor of the small chamber, his back to the altar, facing the door, as he often sat during his times of quiet and study. As he sat, he looked before him, and very quickly a form of light began to solidify in front of him. Unlike the two young, slim forms that had appeared during the ritual, this form was in the image of wisdom and age: a gaunt face, bearded, with its features and bones seemingly cut from chalk stone, white as its long robe. The sage's long hair moved upon his shoulders as he looked down at the form of Joshua, which had bowed to the floor, and he spoke:

"Rise, my son, and be of calm spirit. I come, because you have called, but not to bring you the answers that you seek. For these answers are not within the realm of this planet's aura. You have this evening done a thing that few on this planet's surface have dared to do: you have summoned from the light of another planet counterparts of two of your number that are much more polarized towards the good than is thinkable on this planet. You have summoned, from the purity and the blackness in us all, the purity which does not dwell within us on this planet, but yet dwells in our total selves. You have acted as a part of the one who is all, and you have done as you think best, using your free will. This is your privilege, and I say to you that if you had not polarized very strongly towards the light, you would not have been capable of this act. It was your choice to find light, and it has been your choice to bring it here. We of the teaching realm could not instruct you towards any act; we could only make suggestions regarding your thinking and your intentions. This act cannot be either approved or disapproved by us, for such thinking is beyond our knowledge and understanding. I can speak to you only of the peace and the love of the Infinite One, which shall be with you always in your efforts to serve Him. I leave you in His love and in His light. Farewell, my brother. Farewell."

The image of the teacher faded away as Joshua stared at it, until it was completely gone. The darkness of night had come to the garden, and Joshua sat against the altar no more than a shape, still and shadowed. His eyes closed and remained so for many minutes, opening only once, as his private thoughts brought him to his teacher, and a brief expression of exasperation crossed his face; his eyes flickered open.

Then his eyes closed again, and he was still, seemingly lost within the huddled shape of his physical body from that earthly essence that was Joshua Starr, the virile, surefooted man, and equally lost from the powerful, wise magician of the ritual. The spaces within his crouched body had become vast and empty, and within them, sitting small and lonely, was a third Joshua, a Joshua without personality or pattern; a formless entity whose essence was of this Earth but which yet partook of none of its stimuli. It was simply an entity, nothing more, as a tree was an entity, and the entity roused Joshua up at last and took him outside, to stand in the darkness of his garden. He seemed to have lost his sense of time; he only stood and blended, with the trees, with the ground that nourished them, with the air that stirred them. And as he stood he spoke to the infinity of darkness that was within him and without him; his Creator was everywhere, and to himself did he speak his thoughts. For it had happened that, at the time of his greatest doubting, Joshua had no one to speak with except this audience. His friends were up a hill in a house made tiny to his eyes by the distance it stood from him; he could not join them, and the Joshua that had brought him to this time of doubting had lost the ability to ask them to join him. And yet, in the loneliness of this night, he stood as a continuation of the abundance of the creation all about him, and he could speak his thoughts. And he opened his heart and he spoke.

"Out of the shifting sands of a thousand deserts comes the changing outlines of the surface of the planet; the mountains stand for a little while, to our eyes strong and unchanging; the sands come, and the mountains slowly are no more. People are far, far less permanent: the mountain is of flesh only, and the eroding elements have no need to be as harsh as the biting pieces of sand. And the thoughts of people are even less permanent than the people. Their shape is unknown to human eyes, for the material which makes them up is stuff too delicate to see: it is the medium of dreams, and its texture is thin and loose as air.

"And I stand here, on this living planet, and it breathes in, because it is night. Tomorrow, it will turn to the attraction of the day and exhale the sun's light. Its rhythms are long, compared with the quick breaths of men, who breathe a thousand times before the planet has respired once. And the world within this pulsating mankind, the world of thought, has a respiration a thousand times quicker than even that of lungs and atmosphere: it thinks and thinks in unnumbered themes and variations, pausing long, long between each thought, pausing for the time it takes the creation to become fuller by each thought, pausing to turn to the sun or to the darkness for inspiration to think again.

"And men do not move separately, nor think separately. The atmosphere of one man's thoughts touches other atmospheres, other thoughts, and their interaction becomes part of the creation. The meeting of world on world is perceived only dimly by us, because its nature is a thousand times beyond language and intellect. And yet thoughts, and the uniting of thoughts, are powerful, and move the universe.

"And where, in this combining of thoughts, does responsibility lie?" Joshua turned his closed eyes even higher to the night sky. "Who is responsible for this thing that we have done together this day.

"In truth, am I not responsible for all that is to come, in that my will was the leading one? What changes in their lives am I not responsible for, now that I have done this thing?

"And yet, I attempted nothing but the good. But what good is an attempt? What can we know, we creatures of the intellect, who can use only tools which are worthless? What conclusions did I come to by the use of this intellect that could be of any good?

"But if I was not placed in the physical world to act, then why was I placed here at all? For without action, there is no use for the physical environment. And all action is somehow a product of our consciousness, and all we can do is direct that consciousness towards our goals as best we can. What am I but the energy and the bias that is called consciousness, which has assimilated a chemical body and learned to stand erect upon the surface of this planet?

"And this energy that is myself moves with each of my actions so as to polarize, either towards the good or towards the evil side. With each of my actions I move from the center towards the unity of light or towards the separation of darkness, and yet how can I know when or how far I move, or in what direction? For I have only this intellect to use, this idiotic game-player of a mind.

"But Esmerelda and I tried, so long and so hard, to learn anyway, even on this plane and with these tools. And in our strength we decided to act in this way so as to bring this planet towards that positive pole of light.

"And why, why did it not strike me before that to bring outsiders here is to violate that goodness which is free will? For is it a good or an evil thing to force anyone to do or think anything? And is it not by force that we shall disrupt the evil on this planet, if we confront it with the light of a truly positive being, a pure product of a planet of unity? Can any evil ignore it? Can those who do not seek avoid finding?

"Oh," said Joshua, "surely there is no doubt that what we have done, intended so for the good, may by this error be evil enough to cancel out the good, and bring confusion instead of peace?

"But perhaps my intellect is only producing these thoughts in its confusion; perhaps the fact that is important is that I have acted with all my strength on behalf of the one who is all. This is my gift to Him, my gift to the creation that is His.

"But of my wisdom I am not sure. I have lived, and I have acted, but I can never comprehend all that I have seen and done. "And yet I wish you peace, my planet, for now I am your child, and am humble before you. Peace, beloved planet; peace, peace be with you, creation of the Father."

Then the Joshua who was a stranger to the strength of his body began to take its leave. His everyday self began to fill up his earthly frame, and a Joshua capable of facing the house up the hill, with his beloved friends inside, began the walk towards the house, preparing himself to remove the robes which kept him from them, dropping from his consciousness that lack of identity, that oneness with the creation, that he had assumed. What he had puzzled out in his time alone could not be dropped from his mind, for he was a man, a creature of intellect, and doubt was not to be shrugged away. But he put it away within himself and took the burden of its presence as his own burden, as he turned from the dark paths of the garden and walked, head lowered for the climb, up the hill to the waiting house.

Joshua's bonds with the three who awaited him were both strong and subtle. There were real affinities between him and Pablo Padeyevsky. Both were ruthless men. Padeyevsky was ruthless because of a lack of subtlety, and grew slowly wise through straightforward faith and seeking, using his tremendous intellect and ability to concentrate in equal doses. Joshua had become ruthless slowly and because of an unending subtlety of nature, and because of a sense of humor that partook more and more of pain, until when he laughed, it was as if he cried, and he ceased both to laugh and to cry.

His wisdom was built on this pain and its surcease, for such is always the road to wisdom for a subtle man. He had become outwardly congenial, simple, and successful as a product of his pain, and he had studied white magic as a product of the only part of his thinking that pain could not touch: the faculty of hope. Joshua the man, having decided to enjoy the accoutrements of success, decided to work in the mass media. What better place to be successful, if you understood the folly of so many people? Joshua had the reputation, as a television writer and personality, of turning every project he touched into pure gold. His excellent, intuitive mind had no trouble manipulating the minds of his audience.

And he and Pablo shared their success and their will to succeed, their ruthlessness and their minds' abilities. The combination was a good one for friendship. Neither of them had other close friends. Pablo had no other friends at all; Joshua had many acquaintances who thought of themselves as his friends, without knowing that he did not reciprocate the feeling. No one except the small group waiting for Joshua fathomed anything of him past the first shell of personality, the good-looking, magnetic Joshua who could always be counted on to say something witty, or biting, or both, in any conversation. Pablo alone sensed the ruthless quiet beneath that congenial character, and Joshua felt correspondingly more comfortable around Pablo than around other men. Joshua understood Pablo too; he saw and forgave the coarseness of thinking that accompanies lack of humor, and saw also the seeking thirst for knowledge that actuated the man. They genuinely liked each other, and found each other's mental atmospheres very capable of combination.

But Joshua's strongest bond among the three who waited for him was not with Pablo; it was with Esmerelda. In terms of instinctive thought-by-thought matching it was not strong, for although Esmerelda was capable of closely reading Joshua's expressions and moods, his ability to understand or even fully notice her was limited severely by the fact that he still thought of her as the nine-year-old that he had begun teaching as an apprentice ten years ago. And yet, even though the time for speaking their bond into anything more than friendship had come and gone, there was still more to their relationship than the simple bond of friendship. For they were man and woman, and the feeling between them partook of that polarity. To Joshua, Esmerelda represented all that he hoped for: all good, all positivity. Esmerelda in her turn looked upon Joshua with the fuller understanding of which she was capable, and saw the great sadness of his deeper self, and took that sadness for her own, though she never spoke of it. She saw his love for her too, and cherished it as well, although this was never spoken either, and in silence she gathered him mentally to her and comforted him with the medicine of her gentleness. She did not understand the real wilderness of his lack of feeling for the world: she did not understand any part of negative thinking first-hand, and could not conceive it to be so. She missed the same ruthless lack of feeling for the rest of humanity in Pablo. They helped her miss it, and so the cold side of their natures was always turned from her. Which did not void the very real mingling that these three spirits enjoyed.

The fourth member, Theodore, had little real closeness with Padeyevsky or Josh. He was closest to Esmerelda; she had given his naive and inchoate personality a center from which to build. He had met nothing in his previous life which was capable of stirring him to real emotion; Esmerelda stirred him. The two were close as people who have been married for years are close: they had become comfortable together, and his world of intellectual seeking and ceaseless spiritual wandering had expanded to fit in the strong emotions of love for another human being, and surcease from loneliness. Each thought of his touched Esmerelda's world of thought and found a companion. There was an automatic closeness between them that came, not from meeting first on this planet, as these people, but from many times of closeness in many, many times and places far separated from this present illusion, so that their thinking had blended in a final way. All his life Theodore had been totally uninterested in strength of any kind; now he had discovered his own strength. Esmerelda did not so much love him as recognize him; he was a part of her, and she of him. She, already strong, found support for her strength, for Theodore understood and cherished it. And Esmerelda, who had understood so much, and comforted so carefully, was understood and comforted.

From the webbing of thought which these four had made came power which was far greater than the sum of the strength of thought of each added to each; the power had been sufficient to raise the hand of their will and be felt.

Josh came through the door more slowly than was his usual habit, and closed the screen against the night breeze with some thoughtful deliberation. He turned, and Esmerelda watched carefully, as she had in the temple. Something was wrong. This time Joshua was aware enough of the outside world to see her glance; he returned it for a few seconds and then nodded, wordlessly. She rose from the couch and went to the bar. "I'll fix you a drink, Josh," she said. "Sit down and tell us what you think."

"I think we've done it," said Josh, sitting and accepting his glass. Esmerelda sat too, absentmindedly, on the edge of the couch and turned a face to Josh that was a tangle of several different expressions, a smile of success vying with a puzzled frown and bits and pieces of worry for Josh. "We couldn't sit here for a whole incarnation and not even try, Josh. We've been working towards this for so long now, and when Theodore came ..." She broke off. "What is it?" she said.

Josh sat looking at his glass, turning it around in his hand. "It's all right," he said.

"Is it that you're worried they won't succeed when they get here?"

"No, no. It's not that at all."

There was silence for a minute as Joshua closed his worry around himself and decided to speak no further. Theodore sat quietly, the most contented of the group. "How did you really know about me?" he asked.

Esmerelda pulled her attention from Joshua, whose mind was still in turmoil as far as she could tell. "Well, Ted, when you and I were born, we were born for a special reason. I suppose everyone is, but our reason was more obvious than some: the focus of our existence has been this ritual, its preparation and its consequences. Joshua and I discovered this, dimly at first and then more and more clearly through the years as we became more powerful. We discovered that there was to be a man involved in the ritual, and we knew you to be the one as soon as you came to Pablo. He guessed just from your being such a genius, from that paper that you turned in, and from the way you look, but as soon as you and I had been together for a little time I could tell much more surely, because of the way our consciousnesses fitted together. And, just the way this ritual echoed through time and space to call us here, so has it called our spiritual counterparts from the planetary system which we have seen in our meditations. It must be a very long way away, for it doesn't seem to be known here in its physical configuration at all. But the important thing is that these two are our counterparts, and partake of the same consciousness. And the theory is, anyway, that through this union of ourselves here and ourselves from a planet totally in the Creator's light may come an understanding of the conditions that have brought about the negativity that now resides on this planet. And, we have hoped, then we can do something, or begin something, that may have positive effect on this planet of our choosing. For we live on a planet that is diseased. And it would be a blessed thing to make it well."

"That's right," said Pablo, "and there's not very much time left, for the negativity is gaining very fast here. And, once it is chosen by enough people, by their free will, Esmerelda and Josh say there's nothing that can be done without interference with the free will of many who live here. We'd just have to leave the planet to its negative polarity."

"But right now," said Esmerelda, "we've decided that there would be no infringement upon the collective free will of the planet if we just brought a beginning, just two people here." She paused, her eyes suddenly clearing. "Joshua, is that what's troubling you? Have you had second thoughts about free will being violated by all this?"

Joshua gave her a look that she recognized as one of reprimand. "Later." He turned to Theodore. "We were so glad that you came. Without you, I don't think there would have been any chance of this ritual succeeding. One person, no matter how powerful, simply does not have the available power of two people together, and in order to be able to summon the counterparts from our sister galaxy, we had to have the corresponding two here. With you here, it seems that we were successful. We can only hope that we have done well. Many teachers have been here in the physical before, and they have striven for good, but still the negativity has thrived. Perhaps this effort too shall fail, and those that are upon this surface will be bound closer and closer to evil, until we are all spiraled deep into the abyss of blackness that has taken a few other planets from the light of the Creator. Even now, as you have already seen in your life, and spoken of to Pablo, there is little or nothing on this planet that society does that partakes of any wisdom whatever. All we can do now is hope to begin a series of events that will give men on this planet a choice between good and evil, so that they can see both sides of consciousness, both the unity and the separation, and can choose freely between them."

CHAPTER FIVE

Mathpart Fendler sat watching the cat. The cat sat watching Mathpart Fendler.

"I wonder why the cat is watching me," thought Mathpart. The cat stared back, unblinking.

They stared at each other a long time, the cat and Mathpart. They were both do-nothings, who preferred sitting to working. They were both lazy, both well-nourished, both given to stark simplicity of thought. They had much in common.

But Mathpart sat and thought a thought that he had been thinking for years. It had to do with the cat's upcoming mealtime. Mathpart had long ago realized that the cat never had to get its own meals. The cat, in fact, simply sat all day, or did whatever it wished, and food came to it. In fact, the cat was a success, thought Mathpart. The cat did not have to desire things. Things came to it.

And why wasn't he, Mathpart, a success? He had thought about this. The fact that he had never succeeded in school had been often viewed, and the fact that he had never found any work in town, but these things didn't mean success to him anyway. He had inherited enough of a farm to keep food on the table, and his work for Dr. Padeyevsky gave him the elementary luxuries. But, thought Mathpart, he had had to work for these things, carrying and planting and tending and harvesting.

The cat looked at Mathpart. Mathpart looked at the cat. And Mathpart realized that he, Mathpart, should by rights be the more successful of the two. For, after all, wasn't he more important than a cat? He was almost sure than an evaluation in the favor of men above cats was somewhere in the Bible. And if it was in the Bible, it was true. So that was settled.

And yet, thought Mathpart, I'm feeding that cat.

The cat continued to look as the reedy figure of Mathpart got up from its chair and went into the kitchen. As the refrigerator door opened, the cat slowly put its four feet under it and stretched, mouth wide in a pink yawn, and as Mathpart set out the bowl and called "kitty-kitty," the cat trotted with neat steps from its lounging place and obediently lapped, emitting a brief purring noise between drinks.

Mathpart opened the refrigerator again and brought out an orange. He dearly loved the taste of the fresh juicy pieces; they were a crop he couldn't grow himself, and had much value to him. For a long time it had seemed clear to him that, if he were the cat's God, and furnished the cat with bowls of milk, then his God should furnish him with bowls of oranges.

With this thought in mind, he went to the back door, which was the main door of the shaky-walled old house, and put his head out, craning his neck to look up in the sky for orange bowls, a ritual that he had performed every evening for a long time.

He looked fairly carefully at the colors of sunset. The sky had not yielded up any oranges this time, either. Mathpart shook his head as he sat down at the big round table, beginning to peel his orange. It did seem unfair that there should never be any oranges for him. Maybe, just maybe, Mathpart's God had retired. Or was dead. Mathpart squirmed with discomfort at the very thought. That was blasphemy! That was lack of faith!

He walked back to the refrigerator and stared at the oranges within the wooden bowl. In sudden resolve, he turned again to the kitchen door. He would look harder, much harder, this time. With the feeling of a successfully concluded resolve making his actions precise, Mathpart went through the door to his back stoop, and began to sweep the evening sky from side to side, holding his hands around his eyes like binoculars. On the second sweep, he located a bowl, at a very high altitude. No hand, somewhat to his disappointment. But at least he had found the bowl of oranges that his intellect had told him would be there some day. The great bowl seemed to him to be coming directly towards him, which was perfectly proper; still, the excitement of being visited by the hand of God began to seep into his mind, and he took the three back steps at one stride as he began to run to meet the orange supply. Ten paces later, he abruptly about-faced and raced back to the house, tripped over the doorsill, and fell into the kitchen, spooking the cat; he picked himself up and closed the refrigerator door. Turning again, he rushed in earnest out the door and across his garden, being careful not to ruin any of his plantings. The barbed-wire fence that kept the livestock out of the garden came at him in the deep-evening light; he caught an overall leg in it and detached himself. He ran on, until he'd come to the edge of his property and could see, across a small stream that marked the boundary of the Padeyevsky estate, a large pasture that the great bowl of fruit seemed about to land in. The bowl was still descending, and Mathpart could see its light. It seemed to have some religious significance; he began thinking about a religion where he was the spokesman for the Giver of Fruit from the Sky. His heart beat high as he watched the glowing bowl, and there developed within his consciousness the first expression of a religious fanaticism that had lain latent in him for many years. "The great golden fruit in the sky," he thought. He had always wanted to be a religious fanatic, but he had never before had the inspiration. Now he would certainly be able to indulge his starved appetite for ritual and drama. Perhaps he should wear a white robe on Sundays. Or, no, maybe an orange robe would be better, he thought. Hadn't he seen a newsreel or a movie about some religious men in orange robes? Were they Buddhists? Well, they were one of those heathen religions, anyway. Their orange robes wouldn't rule out his being outfitted with one.

The bowl of oranges drew closer and closer. It seemed at least a hundred feet in diameter, and he stood in awe, thinking of the terrific amount of delicious juice that could be procured from a bowl of oranges of such proportions. Spontaneously there rose in his throat and mind his first prayer, and he spoke it aloud: "Glory be to God on high, for He has certainly this day given me my daily fruit." And he knew in his soul at this instant, beyond any doubt, that there was a God. "And they thought God had died," he shouted. "Wait til they see this bowl of fruit!"

The bowl hovered swiftly closer, a symbol of the worthiness of man and the bounty of God. "Just wait til Sunday." He spoke to the bowl, giving voice to the culmination of his existence. "And they stuck up their noses at me because I wore overalls to church. Just wait until Sunday, I'll be giving testimony!"

The vision rose before him, and he was on the highest pinnacle, his dearest dream achieved. No more was he that lonesome country child, whom his parents had deposited with his grandparents and never picked up again. No longer was he the isolated occupant, now grown, and his grandparents dead, of this rickety farmhouse and two hundred acres of poor forest and pasture land. No longer would he be stupid Mathpart Fendler, following a mule and feeding his cat. Now, he would give testimony at the church and he would pray, and the people in the town would all know that he, Mathpart Fendler, was the man who deserved his own miracle. Yes, a miracle. Wasn't this beautiful, shining bowl of fruit a miracle?

His eyes closed in the inward contemplation of these delights, but he abruptly shook himself from reverie as a new thought struck him. He didn't have any witnesses. What was a miracle without witnesses? As he looked around desperately for a witness he saw that the bowl had come to rest on three legs which had grown out of its bottom. There was sudden confusion in his mind as he took in the fact that the bowl was not full of fruit; in fact, it was closed across its top surface, in a slightly rounded configuration.

Mathpart did not panic. He was stern with himself; this miracle wasn't going to get away because he'd lost his head. Perhaps it was a covered dish. Certainly! There would be birds to protect the oranges from, on its trip down through the heavens, and rain, and pieces of dust floating around. Of course it would be covered. He was contemplating the problem of removing such a massive lid when, quicker than the eye could follow, a sliding door opened in the side of the bowl. Two people stepped down from the bowl to the ground, a tall blonde man and a woman of the same height and fairness. He could see them clearly in the glow from the bowl. The girl looked, to Mathpart, somewhat like Esmerelda Sweetwater. But she couldn't be. She'd never wear one of those get-ups like those two had on. Some sort of coverall that shimmered silver in the light. And tight? Why, it was indecent, that's all. And, it hit him, what were people doing walking out of his bowl of oranges?

Mathpart was wild with rage at the intruders. As he watched them, the bowl balanced on its slender tripod and then retreated, going far more quickly than it had come, depositing not one orange, not even one, for Mathpart Fendler. Instead, thought Mathpart, it had probably been taken over. Yes, that was it. Taken over by some low stinking Commie agents. Those two were Communists. He glared at their backs over his concealing veil of stream-edge shrubbery. His indignant and rampantly suspicious eye picked out two others that were coming towards them. That girl looked like Esmerelda too, as well as he could see in the deepening evening light. They were probably all in disguise, thought Mathpart. Well, he wasn't going to stand for this!

The foursome met midway across the pasture's expanse and Mathpart couldn't make out what they were doing. He crossed the stream at a wet, creeping gait, and drew closer to them. They seemed to be hugging each other, all four of them. Just standing there, indecently hugging each other, not moving or speaking. Mathpart used the time' to get within hearing distance. But they weren't talking, just standing. Finally they broke away from each other and stood, all four at arm's length, still silent. Mathpart stared as hard as he could at them, all so tall and slim in the half-light. They seemed four of a kind, and very, very attractive. Probably hand-picked for some plot, he reminded himself, and figuring on winning our confidence with their good looks. His resolve to deal harshly with these dirty Commies deepened at this.

One of them spoke. It was a male voice. It said, "Welcome to Earth."

There was a short silence. Then the same voice said, "My name is Theodore Behr. This is Esmerelda Sweetwater. We are overjoyed to have you with us."

"Esmerelda Sweetwater a dirty Communist spy," marveled Mathpart. He could hardly believe it of that pretty young thing. The two that had stepped from the bowl of fruit spoke. "We greet you in the love and the light of the one who is all. We bring you our spirits and our bodies in service," they said in unison.

Mathpart was thoroughly confused by what they were saying. Was it some part of secret Commie code? He got a bit heartier inside at that thought. Maybe he was overhearing some kind of password that would break up the whole dirty Communist threat to the U. S. of A. Hey, that would be pretty good. After all, what was more important, when you came right down to it? God, or the obliteration of Communism? He felt definitely cheered.

What were they saying now? They seemed to be doing more standing and looking and holding hands. They were all smiling. The man who had spoken first kept starting to speak and then stopping. Finally he said, "I had a little fifteen minute welcome speech for you, but it seems pointless now. But we are at your service. Shall we go?"

There was another stationary silence. Then Esmerelda spoke. "If you care to, we can go directly to the house where you'll meet another friend. Is there anything you care to do before leaving?"

"No," said the pair, smiling still and remaining where they were. There was a further pause, while the four stood and beamed and Mathpart crouched at the edge of the thin woods by the stream, muttering their words over to himself so he wouldn't forget them. Then the boy with Esmerelda Sweetwater turned and walked towards the far end of the pasture, from where they had first emerged. Esmerelda and the pair from the bowl followed him. When they were far enough away so that Mathpart could follow without being overheard or spotted, he hurried in clumsy furtiveness after them, in time to see them get into an old car.

His mind worked with what was for him uncanny speed; it had been so stimulated by the thoughts of the afternoon and evening that it seemed to him to be working like a hero's brain. He felt like he was in the movies. It would work perfectly. They had to backtrack almost to the main road to get off the old wagon road that they were on, and then they had to drive past his driveway in order to reach their residence, or get to the highway, either one. Well, then!

Mathpart's legs, for years moving only as fast as a mule walked, fairly flew under him as he headed back to his farmhouse, and his L.C. Smith double-barreled shotgun. He'd fix those Commies. Yes sir, yessirree *bob*, he'd fix those dirty lowdown subversive fascist traitor Communists. He galloped into his back door, putting the cat into a tail-thickening swivet during which she ran around the circumference of the kitchen ten times and attacked the sink. Mathpart grabbed the L.C. Smith, loaded it from the box of shells he kept near the gun, headed out again, and went headlong into the tall weeds that obscured the eight-foot drop to the road. A vine took his ankle, and down went Mathpart, rolling onto the road at the same time Theodore rounded the corner from the wagon road. Theodore's reflexes were admirable, but the road put the car into a skid, and just as Mathpart began to struggle to his feet, the front bumper of the car nudged him none too gently, as it came to a halt. The blow knocked him back down and as he went, his shotgun was discharged into the air. Notwithstanding this slight miscalculation, Mathpart indomitably waved his shotgun and struggled again to rise, scrambling out from between the car's front wheels. "Don't move!" he spluttered. "I've got you covered!"

Esmerelda screamed "Mathpart, don't shoot! It's me, Esmerelda Sweetwater."

"Dirty Communist spies!" Mathpart yelled. In a blind rage, he leveled the gun at the car.

Esmerelda caught her breath. "Stop him!"

The man from space emerged from the rear door on the near side of the car, stepped between Mathpart and Esmerelda, and looked directly into Mathpart's eyes.

Mathpart had started to turn the gun on the intruder, but found himself instead putting the gun butt on the road. His expression turned from one of frantic anger, first to confusion, and then remorse. He looked at the man for about thirty seconds. Then he backed away. "You ain't no Commie." He looked down at the road, then at Esmerelda. "He ain't no Commie, Miss Sweetwater."

"Of course not," said Esmerelda. "Whatever made you think he was?"

"Well," faltered Mathpart. "Well-he looked like a Commie from a distance, but ... well, he ain't no Commie."

Behr, out of the car already, moved towards Mathpart. "How can you tell," he asked him.

Mathpart scratched his head. "Well, he's just good. He's just good, that's all. And Commies ain't good."

Esmerelda said, "Was that why you were shooting at us, Mathpart?"

He nodded. She got out of the car too, and went over to put an arm around him. "Well, we're not Commies. Come on back to the house with me. Let's see if you're hurt." She led a thoroughly chastened and humbled man away to his kitchen, still shaking his head and looking back over his shoulder at the two beings who had emerged from his bowl of fruit.

CHAPTER SIX

Esmerelda had walked Mathpart back to the kitchen table, had given him hot coffee, had soothed him. She had also spoken soothing words, in gentle tones, to the cat, who had been behind the stove awaiting the end of the world when they came in the door. By the time she left Mathpart's farmhouse, she had been able to help him to the conclusion that it was no use whatever to tell anything of what had happened to the authorities, who would only laugh at him. He had also talked himself into believing that Esmerelda and her three cohorts were helping the government in some secret way. Esmerelda had not denied this. She had simply told him that she couldn't talk about it. Mathpart had been satisfied. Happy to do his part to help his country by keeping silent. They parted on good terms. The cat had even let his tail unfluff and was sitting at Mathpart's feet, as was his usual habit when they were both in the kitchen.

They were waiting for her in Theodore's car, the two visitors sitting serenely in the back seat. They had really come. She had had no real doubt that they would; no one had after the affirmation of the ritual. But the telepathic message which both Theodore and Esmerelda had received while they saw the two bodies of light in the temple was a mental picture of a craft coming to rest in what was recognizable as part of Pablo's three hundred acres, in half-light. Neither of them had been able to discern whether that light was the illumination of dawn or dusk, and so they had watched both times of day. Since Joshua always got up early during the week, to visit his television studio in Washington for the daily interviews that were taped for New York, and since Pablo got up early out of real preference, those two had covered the sunrises, and Theodore and Esmerelda the sunsets. The craft had landed on the seventh day after the ritual.

They had expected the ritual to culminate in the space people's arrival; they had prepared for it; they had awaited it eagerly. But the actuality of their visit was still a shock. Esmerelda smiled at the two in the back seat. It was so uncanny to see them, almost like looking in a mirror. Esmerelda, with her tawny coloring, her six feet of height, her slender, smooth-muscled figure, was not at all accustomed to looking at someone who so closely resembled her. It was an unnerving thing at first.

Theodore was driving to Joshua's house rather than the farm, because Pablo had gone to New York early that morning on business, and had told them not to expect him back until midnight or a little before. It was barely seven o'clock now. They found Josh lounging by the front window, watching the lit screen of his big television set. They met at the front door, and after he had taken each of the visitors by the hand and greeted them, he walked them back into the room, turning off the TV. "One of my scripts. Had it on to see how badly they'd butchered it."

Esmerelda walked over to his bar, taking out glasses and fruit juice. Joshua sat the people from space down on a long sofa that went across the end of the large, windowed room, and stood looking at them. Their beauty was very bright. "Well. I've worked out what I think will be the most efficient way of orienting you to this planet, my friends. It will take some time, perhaps a week or ten days for each of you. But I think it will be the quickest way. Let me ask you right now never to leave your physical bodies under any circumstances while you are on this planet, unless I am with you to be sure you're safe. I know that this is far different from your normal habit on your home planet. But you will find that this planet is different. Will you do as I suggest?"

Both the space visitors nodded. "Yes."

"Good. I cannot quickly explain to you the dangers which could befall you here, but as you learn about us, I think you will come to understand. Now, what I had in mind was for one of you at a time to leave your physical body, and spend some time in a complete tour of the mental planes of this planet, watching our planet's history, which we call the Akashic Record. I have a trusted and competent guide for you. He has been my own teacher for many years. He can well protect you, for he is very familiar with this planet's mental planes; he has been discarnate and functioning within the teaching realm for several thousands of years. My brother, I thought that perhaps you could be the first to travel through the astral realms, and view our Akashic Records. Would this be agreeable to you?"

"Yes."

"Good. It will be a simple matter for Esmerelda and me to summon our teacher, and prepare a resting place for your physical body while you are not using it. We shall go to my temple." He turned to Theodore, all business. "Ted, can you drive our sister to Pablo's?" A room had been prepared for each of the visitors at the farm. "I'll bring Esmerelda home later, probably around one or two; late, anyway."

Theodore was distinctly taken aback by Joshua's brisk approach to conversation with the aliens. He had given them no chance to speak, beyond a few monosyllables; he had indulged in no small talk, no getting to know each other. It struck him as a little unfriendly.

"I know what you're thinking," said Joshua. Theodore looked at him in surprise.

"Look, Ted. This is a very peculiar place, this planet. Nothing we say to them will have much meaning until they've assimilated a great deal more about our history."

Theodore recovered. "OK, Josh, sure. I'll take her home, and we'll see you tomorrow."

"Right. Thanks, Ted."

Theodore rose from his seat, went over to the space girl's side of the couch, and took her hand. "Let's go." He both said the words and tried projecting them mentally, and was rewarded by a telepathic agreement which matched the girl's smile. He could do it with her, as well as with Esmerelda. Very good.

The matronly, ungainly Ford began to rock gently around the curves of country road between Joshua's place and the farm. It was the largest road in this part of the county, four-lane, though not new or smooth-surfaced. It was a pretty road to drive down, with windows down and the sound of crickets chirping past them, the scent of the dew and the dusty road on the quiet breeze. They passed a roadhouse, the sort of place that springs up wherever there are a number of fairly well-to-do people residing in a rural area. It looked like a dump from the outside, with its neon lights and pockmarked gravel parking lot; inside, it was too dark to see whether the place was dumpy or not. There was a small dance combo, a small menu.

The girl from space stirred for the first time. "A ceremony is in progress."

Theodore took a quick glance at her face, then another, longer one. "What?"

"The ceremony was there." the girl pointed.

"Oh, that? That's just a honky-tonk. A place where they dance."

"We shall see it."

We would? Theodore puzzled over the positivity of the girl's statement. Why would she want to go there? He looked at her clothing. Both she and the man with whom she had come wore two-piece outfits that looked to him like ski suits, except that they were of very thin material, like jersey. They were silver in color, and clung faithfully to the lines of their bodies. Very faithfully. As Theodore considered her appearance, it became obvious to him that she wore nothing under the long-sleeved, high-necked top of the suit; the effect was aesthetically pleasing, but in the context of

74

the American culture, unfortunately startling. He couldn't take her in anywhere. Could he?

She was looking at him, apparently sure that he was about to escort her to her "ceremony."

Well, why not? Her costume wasn't any more daring than a lot of others that he'd seen. It could do no harm for her to see the strange gyrations of his fellow humans. He backed into a side road and turned towards the roadhouse, pulled into the hillocked parking area, and found a place for the venerable Ford.

They went through the double doors of the tiny vestibule and stopped dead, trying to see into the fitful darkness. A light show was in progress, and the wall of sound was pulsating past their ears. The music was visible; it was tangible; it could be tasted. The electrically amplified guitar, bass, and organ were not in the hands of virtuosos; however, the amplification system didn't know and didn't care, and the harmonies, shaky or not, came pushing against the dancers and onlookers around the edges of the room in an innocent violence of noise. The drummer was valiantly keeping up with his amplified string-playing brethren; the beat had glorious existence here.

Theodore stood next to his new friend, watching the proceedings with the bemused eye of the outsider: he had never been able to dance or to want to dance. The panoply hurt his ears and eyes and moved no muscles to life. It was just loud and tiring. He turned to see how the girl from space was taking the spectacle; she was not there. He could see the shimmer of her clothing as she walked away from him. Her hand had been taken by a kid in a flowing shirt and modishly cut trousers; they were going to dance. Theodore groaned out loud, and pushed his way towards her through the line of tables.

But it was too late. The lights flashed on, off, on, off, on. Movements seemed jerky, exaggerated, suspended, strangely beautiful as the electronic pickup of the amplifier activated the color and frequency switches of the lighting system. They seemed to be activating the girl in her silver clothes as well. With a further, inward groan, Theodore noted that he was no longer the only onlooker who was watching the girl from space. Her lovely, taut body, outlined carefully by the clothing she wore and shimmering against the flashing lights, moved as though she were part of the music. Which got louder; the band had noticed her. She got more and more frenetic: how could she do that, wondered Theodore. She was easily the best dancer he had ever seen. Her supple body moved with the sexual, primitive beat of the music, her yard-long hair drifted and whipped with it. The go-go girl who had been matter-of-factly holding forth on the small apron of the stage jumped down, and good-naturedly motioned to the space girl to take her place. "Oh NO," thought Theodore, as the girl bounded the four feet up without missing a beat in the heaving line of music.

Now the place really began to notice her. People who had been sitting at tables at the edges of the room began moving in on the room's center, which had been already more than full of dancers, People who had been dancing stopped, and began shoving for a place. Everyone was clapping, shaking back and forth with the pulse of the music; the musicians were going mad trying to pull extra decibels from their equipment. The place was too crowded for the excited citizenry, suddenly. There weren't enough places close enough for a clear view. Someone got the bright idea of climbing up on someone else's table and the man whose table had been chosen objected violently. A chair broke under someone's weight; there was a faint moaning sound audible through the tiny cracks in the noise's surface. One man apparently felt that his lady of the evening had been rudely used by the feet of a neighboring male; there were sudden shouts, and the ominous crack of another chair; the first fist met the first face. The music went on; the girl kept moving like the wind. Theodore could see only half of the room; he counted three separate altercations. It should take no more than ten minutes for the police, no doubt now being summoned, to arrive here.

No way to get to the space girl presented itself to him until a hazy idea of finding the fuse box for the place dawned. Theodore went down the dirty little hallway that opened into the restrooms. No visible fuse box. There was a utility closet; he opened it, and found a black metal box in the wall. This looked like just what he had in mind. He pulled the lever at its side, and a gratifying blackness dropped over the little hall. The strobe light stopped, and the instruments went dead, leaving the drummer starkly alone for a measure, until he lagged-and stopped playing too.

There were several varieties of screams, and an awesome crunching sound as tables and chairs began being moved wholesale. The riot was on. Now, the object was to retrieve the girl from space, and get out the back way before the police came and tried to identify a girl who had no past. And who would probably be dragged into the station for indecent dress. Oh boy.

He checked the small rear exit. The Yale lock yielded, and outside was the parking lot. Theodore put his back to the concrete wall of the hallway and attempted to clear his mind of the confusion. Could he call her here?

Mentally, he sought the linkage between his mind and hers that he had tentatively tested once before. He summoned her; with relief strong in him, he felt her acknowledgment and, in a few seconds, her hand in his. She had had a simple time coming off the stage and through the door to the restrooms which was right by its side, out of the way of the mobbed dance floor, and the front entrance towards which everyone was shoving.

Theodore took her by the hand again and ran with her to his car. He had managed to pull out on the highway before his ears caught the sound of police sirens. They had made it. A quarter of a mile down the road they met the two police cars, their blue lights blinking, screaming down the road too intent on their destination to notice one old Ford. The danger was past.

Theodore began to be very stern with himself, inwardly, for taking his charge anywhere but home to bed. And, how had she managed to learn the dances that quickly?

The girl from space turned and beamed at him, eyes dancing with the same golden flecks Esmerelda's held. "The people of this planet are very wise."

Theodore was too numbed by relief to say more than, "What?"

"There is much growth of spirit in their temples."

Lines appeared between Theodore's eyes; his nose wrinkled. "Temples? That wasn't a temple. That was a roadhouse. A place where people go to have fun."

The girl continued to regard him with her serene, dancing smile. Her voice was calm, a little husky from dancing so long without refreshing herself. "Many of those who were there wished to mate with me. I should return."

Theodore's eyes closed briefly. Oh boy. "Hold it. You can't go around on this planet mating with everyone that wants you to." He thought to himself for a minute: just why couldn't she. "It's governed by the law on this planet."

"I know the law of mating."

Theodore knew that she and he weren't communicating. "No, no, I mean man-made law. It is not lawful to, ah, mate on this planet unless you're legally married."

"I am not aware that man can make laws. I am aware only of the Creator's law."

Theodore knew what she meant; he had thought often about the Creator's law of mating, since he had met Esmerelda, had been drawn so simply to her. It had seemed to him that the physical attraction between them was an expression of polarity made possible for them by their affinity for each other; they seemed, somehow, very much in the same key.

But the girl from space shouldn't trust to that law; there were too many people around who couldn't care less about affinities or polarity. He tried again. "No, it doesn't work like that here. People have written things like marriage down on pieces of paper, and called them laws. These laws are accepted by all the people as correct. Then, anyone who does not follow these laws is punished by the rest of the people. They put restrictions on them, and call them criminals."

The girl's eyes wondered at him. "But that is a violation of the Creator's law of freedom of choice."

It was coming clear to Theodore why Josh had been so businesslike and brusque with the people from space earlier. Until the girl got more acclimated to this planet, it was going to be impossible to communicate with her about the environment to which she had come. He smiled at her open, questioning face. "I think it will all be made clear when you have seen the Akashic Record, and partaken of the knowledge of the planet."

This was feeble, but it seemed to satisfy the girl; she accepted it happily and readily, and spoke no more during the brief remainder of their journey. The rest of Theodore's task was short and easy: he offered her food, which she declined, and showed her the room which Esmerelda had prepared for her stay. There were some clothes from Esmerelda's closet for her to put on in the morning; the covers of the bed were folded down. He left her and went across the hall and away from the head of the stairs one door, to his own room. It was almost eleven. Time for bed.

The house darkened, and then slept.

CHAPTER SEVEN

The shuttle from New York City touched down at Washington National at 10:37. Pablo got his 6.3 Mercedes out of the parking area. The driving was fairly easy that late at night; he turned into his two miles of driveway a few minutes before eleven. It was very late for Padeyevsky to be up; he ran down like a clock during the day, and was ill fit for these late hours. But the job had had to be done. He had wanted to set things up so they were unstoppable. He had succeeded.

He passed the road that turned off his driveway, the mailbox at its head marked "Mathpart Fendler." There was a Cadillac limousine parked almost out of sight down Mathpart's drive. Pablo's warning system began to twitch a little. Mathpart wouldn't know anyone with a limousine. If he was getting a visit, and at this hour of the night ... He thought back to his visit to New York. He had done his business there openly, for his adversaries to see. Could they be responding? He hadn't expected them to do anything; had expected them simply to concede defeat. It was obvious that he had moved them irretrievably into a corner.

He drove the rest of the way to the farm, his mind puzzling over it. It was thirty years too late for the sort of violent business doings that had characterized them at a more primitive time in their organization's history. They didn't take revenge any more. Did they?

He didn't like it. After he had seen that all was well at home, perhaps he would go back to Fendler's place and look around. Without being seen.

The dark house looked quiet and comfortable. It creaked occasionally, in the chill of the October night, its bones settling. It creaked, in small noises, more rapidly as Pablo's weight was set down on each of the steps that rounded gracefully up and past the second floor. The hall light had been left off. Pablo stopped by the first door on his left at the top of the stairs: that was the room designated for the space girl's use when she came. The door was half-open and Pablo listened at it. He thought he could hear breathing, slow and quiet. He looked in at the sleeping form, but he did not enter the room.

The room across from hers was Esmerelda's. The door was wide open and the bed was still made up. Hmmm.

He went into the room, verified the fact that she was not home, glanced at the door that connected Theodore's and Esmerelda's dressing rooms, then went back out into the hall. Theodore's door was open, and he was there. He was also alone. Pablo determined that to his own satisfaction, and then

79

went over to Theodore's bed and woke him, very gently. Theodore's eyes opened immediately. "Hi, Pablo. How was your trip?" Then sleep left him entirely. He sat up. "Hey, we got the two space people! Joshua and Esmerelda kept the man at the temple, and I brought the girl here. She's asleep."

Pablo's black eyes softened in the dim moonlight coming in the windows. "That's just great! Tell me about it!"

Theodore recapitulated the events of the evening, Pablo nodding and grinning from ear to ear with the satisfaction and excitement. After he had heard it all, and pounded Theodore's sleepy shoulders a few times, he rose to take his leave. "Well, Ted, I'll see you in the morning. See you both in the morning. Will Esmerelda come home tonight? What about the man who came?"

"Well, Josh said he was going to send the man on a tour of the planet's mental planes, with his guide. And he said he'd bring Esmerelda home himself around one or two, after they see the man from space off, so to speak."

Pablo nodded. He considered telling Theodore that he was going out again, then decided against it. Better to let the boy sleep. It was too difficult to explain why he was going out, anyway. "See you in the morning, Ted," he repeated.

Theodore, eyes already closing, nodded into his pillow and Pablo went out, shutting his door behind him. He pulled the girl's door shut too, as he passed it, and then went down the front staircase. Through the front windows he could see the lawn. It lay empty of human habitants. He listened. All was quiet.

He went back into his den, and shut the door. There was a massive mahogany desk that dominated the room; he went to it and unlocked one of its drawers. Inside was a long-barreled Smith and Wesson revolver. At first glance, the purpose of the weapon seemed to be target shooting, but a careful look found this to be a far more specialized weapon: a Smith and Wesson.357 magnum with an inlaid ramp-type Baughman front sight, and a micrometer rear sight. The barrel was six inches long. It was a very modern, exquisitely crafted combination of gunman's companion and target piece.

It was loaded with target wadcutters, which Pablo removed and replaced with 158 grain ammunition. The rotund, cheerful-faced man snapped the cylinder shut and looked at his weapon with the eye of one glancing at a valued friend; it would seem that he had spent much time with it, for his handling of it was easy, flawless, and affectionate.

He inhaled, pulled his trousers away from his portly middle, and stuck the long-barreled weapon in to his waistband. There was a moment of reflection; then he closed the drawer which he had relieved of its singular contents, opened the study door, and walked very quietly from the sleeping house to his Mercedes. The slight downhill grade of the circular driveway and the access road allowed him to roll out of earshot of the house's inhabitants before he shifted out of neutral and engaged the clutch. The winding road led in hesitant fashion through the creek that marked the boundary between his place and Mathpart's; briefly past the creek bed he swung the car up the embankment to a hiding place that was totally out of the way to any stranger and quite inaccessible to anyone who didn't know the land as Pablo did.

He got out of the car. He was approaching Mathpart's property from the rear fence row; ahead were the windows across the back of the farmhouse. Light showed in a vertical splinter on either side of two of the drawn shades; someone was in the kitchen. The rest of the house was dark. Pablo approached the side of the house very stealthily, and put his eye to one of the splinters of light. Mathpart Fendler was sitting at the kitchen table engaged in conversation with a man whose face could not be made out, being partially hidden from view by his position, and thrown into shadow by the lighting. Mathpart's face, however, was clear to Pablo, and on it he read a mixture of agitation and fear. Pablo could hear Mathpart's words: he was refusing to talk about the arrangement of bedrooms in Padeyevsky's house. His access to that knowledge came legitimately enough: he was employed by Esmerelda twice a week to do the outdoor work, and to help indoors with any heavy work that needed to be done. Fendler had obviously been refusing this information for some time before Pablo's arrival, for blood was dripping slowly onto his shirt from the side of his mouth. There was a cut on his cheek too; it was badly swollen. Mathpart stopped speaking, and when the other man prompted him, he shook his head. The man got up and came around to Mathpart's side, raising his hand slowly, threatening him with both the gesture and the words. Pablo could easily make them out; "Listen, friend, we're gonna pull this off about an hour from now-with you, or without you. You get what I mean?"

Mathpart cowered, but shook his head again, and the hand started down.

Padeyevsky had planned to discover what the mission of the strangers was and then leave anonymously, but he couldn't stand by and let Mathpart be killed. There was the sound of a blow, and Mathpart had another cut on his cheek. The man must have a ring on. Padeyevsky removed the magnum from his waistband, putting pressure on the trigger and the hammer spur at the same time and bringing the revolver to the full cock position, making only the slightest clicking noise. He moved as quietly as he could to the porch and stepped up on it, moving over to the door by taking small steps along the house wall, where the boards didn't squeak under his weight.

The doorknob rotated very slowly, very carefully, so that the man inside would not see the knob turning; then Pablo pushed the door open and lowered his revolver until it aimed steadily at the middle of the man with the ring. The stranger's face was as surprised as Mathpart's. He started to move his ringed hand, but he was looking directly into the barrel of the .357. He changed his mind. The motion of the hand stopped; the mouth moved instead. "Who are you?"

Fendler answered, in a blurting, out-of-control voice. "Dr. Padeyevsky!"

The cunning in the man's face softened a little; surprise was edging more into its lines. He stayed quite still, looking into the barrel of Padeyevsky's gun. He knew that gun very well; he admired it. He was all too aware of the sort of punch it had. He was also aware of the steadiness of the gun's aim.

Dr. Padeyevsky was standing on his dignity. "Now, sir. Please be aware that I am a nervous person. You could humor me by moving very slowly. Because I have a nervous condition, and my fingers are so likely to twitch at any sudden movement. Very slowly, with your left hand, remove your weapon."

"But I'm not armed."

Pablo's gun hand twitched slightly.

The man's ringed hand moved again, very slowly, towards his waist.

"I said the left hand." Pablo's voice was very quiet. The left hand did as it had been told.

"Now. Put it on the floor, and kick it over this way with your foot."

The man did so.

Padeyevsky's aim did not waver, nor did his eye leave the stranger, as he stooped over slowly and retrieved the short-barreled revolver. He put it in his sports coat pocket and looked at Mathpart briefly; he had managed to save him from too much damage, apparently; his face seemed swollen but relatively intact. However, his eyes were fixed, and his mouth was hanging open. He was breathing with difficulty, taking very short breaths.

Pablo gestured with his gun. "Now look what you've done to my friend. You shouldn't have done that. You go back to Russo and tell him to pull off his dogs, do you hear me? He's not dealing with an idiot. And I'll tell you personally, if you show up here again, I shall not be so courteous. I have a very short temper."

The tight threat was broken by the sound of a horn; car headlights flashed on and off again seventy or so yards down the hill, from the approximate location of the Cadillac Pablo had seen earlier. He glanced through the open door, and the man surprised him. He buckled and rolled like a hedgehog, and by the time Padeyevsky had seen him go down, he had almost reached Mathpart's double-barreled shotgun, propped in the corner.

Padeyevsky snapped a shot at the moving figure; he put a small hole in Mathpart's wall, but missed the man entirely. Before he could realign his weapon, the professional gunman had swung the L.C. Smith, aimed it squarely at Pablo's belt, and pressed the trigger. His firing pin snapped on an empty chamber: Mathpart never kept his shotgun loaded around the house.

Pablo had his .357 leveled again at the man sprawled so clumsily against the wall, holding the empty shotgun. "I wouldn't try the other barrel, if I were you."

The man put the shotgun down.

Pablo glanced at Mathpart again; he was in a bad way, his face gray, his position frozen on his chair. A bullet splintered the door frame two inches from Pablo's ear, and the report of the weapon that had fired it sounded down the driveway. Pablo stayed vertical long enough to pump two shots back in the direction of the headlights that he had seen a minute before, then he dropped to the floor behind the door. His .357 was stubbornly pointing at the man in the corner.

He sat there, he heard the engine of the car down the driveway start. It retreated. He knew the access road like the back of his hand, and he listened to the limousine as it reached the head of Mathpart's driveway and slowed for the turn onto the road that led to the highway.

Then he stood up, really shaken. The car had not turned left; it had turned right. The only possible objective was the farm. The Cadillac was heading towards the girl from space and Theodore.

Pablo had no more business here; he had to get back to the farm. He found a heavy door with his eye; it turned out to be a utility room. The gunman in the corner went into it, motioned on by Pablo's persuasively eloquent revolver. Pablo turned to communicate with Mathpart. "You come with me. I can't leave you here with him." Mathpart nodded in dazed agreement.

Padeyevsky shot the heavy bolt on the utility room, standing aside in case the man had another weapon. A half-used box of shotgun shells lay on a shelf above the empty shotgun; Pablo dumped its contents into his other coat pocket, grabbed the L.C. Smith, and they ran for his car.

The engine started, and he pulled it back along the road to his house faster than he had ever driven on this road. The careening Mercedes went directly across the carefully planted lawn, into the peony border which Esmerelda had nurtured for years. The Cadillac was not in sight. Pablo jumped over the low bushes, moving into the ominously open front door of his house. It was still completely dark; no one had turned on a light. He listened briefly: No footfalls at all, no movement on the first floor. He ran up the steps two at a time, his short legs stretched hard. The door to the space girl's room was open.

He turned on a light: she had gone quietly. They had taken her. He heard the sudden sound of an engine starting up, a car turning around; it was coming from the rear of the house. Padeyevsky took the stairs back down, almost running over Mathpart, who had fallen in a dead faint in the front hall, just inside the door. He heard the car slow as it reached the front of the house; there was the sound of several shots. Pablo was through the front door just in time to see them drive away from their short stop in front of the peonies. He ran to his Mercedes: one flat tire greeted his gaze. Theodore's car? No, that was much worse, for the angle of the neatly parked vehicle made it even easier to attack, and two of his tires were gone, the radiator was pouring liquid onto the driveway. Pablo turned and ran back into the house again. He met Theodore on the steps, wide awake from the sound of the shots.

"What's going on?"

"The girl from space has been kidnapped. Call Joshua and tell him to bring Esmerelda and the man from space over here right away. We've got to get her back."

"What about going after …"

Pablo waved one grim hand. His voice was clipped. "They shot both our tires out. And your radiator. After you call Josh, come outside and help me change tires on the Mercedes. Oh, and see if you can get Mathpart there onto a couch, or maybe into the guest room next to the den. He's just fainted."

Pablo went back outside as Theodore sat by the downstairs extension of the telephone and called Joshua's house. He found Josh just preparing to leave with Esmerelda; they had left the space man with their teacher for his tour through the mental planes.

Joshua grasped the realities of the kidnapping quickly, told Theodore they would all be there in ten minutes, and hung up. Theodore found this estimated time of arrival unlikely; Joshua's house was fifteen miles away over country road.

He went outside after getting Mathpart comfortable, and when Joshua's Muira rolled into the farm's circular drive ten minutes later, Theodore was just tightening the lug nuts on the Mercedes' wheel; Pablo was putting his ruined tire into the trunk.

The Muira stopped, and the sardine tin opened slowly. The Lamborghini was a small two-seater, and all three of its occupants were six feet tall or more. It was painful to see, Esmerelda had borne the brunt of the bending and folding and the space man had been sat upon severely. The discomfort was about even. They extricated themselves.

"Inside," said Joshua.

All present trooped inside. They sat. Esmerelda gave a glance around, and went briefly out of the room to get coffee. Her uncle seemed much in need of coffee.

"Well, uh," said Pablo.

He sat down. Then he stood up again, pockets sagging, a dull clicking of cartridges accompanying his movements.

"Well," he said. It was most unlike him to be at a loss for words. Starr watched with compassion. His gentle voice tried to encourage. "Go ahead, Pablo. You're among friends."

The man from space sat, holding a cup of the black liquid in his hands, not drinking it; he had not liked the taste of it. His new teacher had only just begun to speak with him, to guide him through the Akashic Record. But the beginning was enough for him to have become very aware of a feeling of unease about the mission that he and his sister were to perform upon this planet. From the little that he had seen, this planet was not at all in union with the one who is all. Not at all a planet of positivity. He had not known, before he came, how far towards the negative polarization this planet was. Now his main thought was that, very possibly, there was nothing he could do here to serve these people. For, if they had chosen separation from the light, it seemed to him an obvious infringement upon the collective free will of the planet to attempt to change the polarity it enjoyed. His brothers here could serve in their wisdom; they were native here, and had proper voice in the collective polarity of the planet. But his homeland was elsewhere.

His mind moved back to the present situation.

Pablo finally found enough of a tongue to ask, a little plaintively, what they wanted to know first.

"Who kidnapped her?" asked Joshua. "Uh."

Esmerelda leaned over the man from space and patted Pablo's shoulder. "It's all right, Uncle Pablo. I know you've been mixed up in something. That was why you were on the phone that day I came in and saw your aura, wasn't it?"

Pablo looked at her. "Yes."

"And was that why you were in New York today, too?"

"All right. Yes, Esmerelda, it was." Pablo took a deep breath, and some of the petulant confusion left his expression. He was resigning himself to telling the whole story. It was a shame that the man from space had to hear it. It was a shame that Esmerelda had to hear it. But they had to find the girl from space. "I think they were working for the biggest handicapping organization in the country."

Joshua looked a little puzzled, not shocked. "What's your connection?"

"Gambling. Horses."

Both Esmerelda and Joshua looked puzzled now. Theodore's expression was inward-looking as though he were reassessing the personality of the man who had drawn him into this close companionship. He was somewhat young to be discovering how much room there is in the human personality for contradiction, a little too full yet of the tendency towards hero-worship. This would take time. "Gambling?" prompted Josh.

"That's right. Most of my money has been made at the track." Esmerelda put lips together, trying to sort it out. "Then all that consulting you did wasn't real?"

"No, that was legitimate. But that would have only made me comfortable. I am more than comfortable; I am very, very rich. It started about five years ago. You know the work I've been doing with animal language. Well, about five years ago, I found an interesting detail while I was studying the complexities of animal motivations. Joshua and I had been watching horses, among other animals."

Joshua nodded; he remembered that; he had helped Padeyevsky considerably, with several different animals, in the early days of Pablo's animal research.

"I discovered that I could trace one emotional tendency in horses that seemed always evident in the winner of a race. At first I noticed this by accident. Then I got interested, and discovered that if I observed all the animals in any race, the winning-oh, say, half of the field would have this emotional tendency. The losing half would not.

"So, I started betting, in a small way, just to test my theory. At first I did only fairly well, about six wins out of ten. Then I started refining the methods I used, and after a couple of years I found the average increasing to the point where I was winning almost every time I bet. Well, I didn't get greedy until last year. Then Padeyevsky looked sheepish-I did start betting rather large sums. Placing them with bookies, spreading them around. But someone in the organization finally deduced that they were losing too much money; they put men on it and traced the constant flow of funds to me. They threatened me. I told them that if they continued to harass me, I'd ruin them. I could do it, you know. Just by letting certain people know my methods. I went to New York to arrange that very thing today. A rather complex arrangement, and, if the man I had my little discussion with doesn't back off, quite inexorable."

"You mean you can't stop it at all? Could we get the girl back if we stopped it?" Joshua began to comb his hair with his fingers. "I don't think it can be stopped. I haven't tried, of course. But I set it up to be unstoppable. The thing now is to get the girl back ourselves. The organization has no intention of letting her go. I'm sure of that. They don't want my money. They just want me stopped."

"Well, go try and untangle it."

Pablo got up, heavily, and went into the hallway to use the telephone. He was on the phone for twenty minutes, and he came back looking grim. "No, I can't stop it. Not fast enough, anyway."

He stood, a dejected and ungainly figure in the middle of the pleasant room.

Joshua stood up. "Well then, we'll have to try and retrieve the girl ourselves. They think she's Esmerelda, of course."

Esmerelda looked up, startled. That was really obvious, but she hadn't thought of it that way.

Joshua looked at her. "Esmerelda, you're closer in thought to the girl than anyone here except our brother. Can you contact her in thought?"

Esmerelda looked at the man from space. "Can you find your sister?"

The man from space closed his eyes and almost immediately said, "Yes."

"Can you lead us to her, then?"

The man from space had no idea what that question meant, and sat confused and silent. Esmerelda herself closed her eyes and sat for several minutes, then turned to Josh. "Yes, we can do it."

It looked like they could at least find where the kidnappers had taken the girl from space. That was a beginning. Joshua went out the big front door. "Come on, let's go."

They filed out of the house together, into the darkness of the autumn night, Pablo still laden with the arsenal, and Esmerelda and the man from space hand in hand.

CHAPTER EIGHT

"Let me drive the old lady," said Josh. "You look pooped, Pablo."

The round doctor was visibly frayed, and his eyes, hooded with fatigue, got lost entirely in his grin of relief. "You do that, my good fellow. And be careful to keep her on the pavement. I believe I shall take this opportunity to rest a bit in the back seat. This is a real car, you know, not one of your toys."

Josh grinned in return, lounging into the driver's seat of the Mercedes. "I'll do what I can, if I can find roads big enough for her to fit on."

Theodore and Esmerelda Joined Pablo in the back seat, and the man from space was offered the right front seat. He had not spoken since he had been asked about his sister, and sat in a state of trance, oblivious to his physical surroundings, except for the link which he and Esmerelda had. Esmerelda was very quiet, and kept her eyes closed in concentration, but she could be spoken to, and Josh did so, as the door slammed shut and he started the engine. "We're off, Esmerelda, but where to?"

She looked at the space man and pointed roughly northeast. "That way."

The space man gave a brief nod of agreement. "OK." Joshua steered the car along the driveway.

"That means the highway will take us approximately the right way." He kept the car in the first two gears until they came off the access road and then took it through third and into fourth with the smooth actions of the car buff. The engine responded lithely, then settled and cruised, purring steadily. Joshua settled too, moving his shoulders back against the seat, straightening his arms. "Not bad for a staff car," he said, looking at Pablo in the rear view mirror and chuckling at the sleeping professor.

He glanced more carefully in the mirror, and caught Theodore's eyes. "I think we're being followed."

Theodore looked out the back window. "You may be right. That car has stayed with us for a long time. It's been sitting right there, about a half a mile back, ever since we turned on to the highway."

Joshua was still consulting his rear view mirror. "Think they're tails?"

Theodore nodded. "Well, if they're not, they're trying to look like it. Why don't you speed up a little and see if they try to keep up?"

"Might do that. See what this barge'll do, too." The speedometer needle drifted past a hundred as the car kept accelerating, sounding easy and smooth even as it crept past 120 and headed for the peg. Joshua passed a startled, sleepy Volkswagen, the first car besides their tail that they had encountered since getting on the limited access highway. Theodore had turned around in the seat and was watching the headlights of the second car. "They're right with us, Josh." The Volkswagen was so unnerved by the second car's passage that it pulled into the emergency lane and stopped; it was soon lost from sight as the two cars spent themselves like bullets down the straight gray road.

Pablo woke up, suddenly, becoming dimly conscious of the screaming speed of the vehicle in which he had been taking his ease. He looked out the window with bleary, half-open eyes. The eyes widened. He sat up very straight, very quickly, and bellowed at Joshua. "What are you doing with my car, you straight arm maniac?"

"Hang loose, Pablo." Joshua was talking out of the side of his mouth, for he didn't dare turn his head from the road, traveling on it at twice the speed limit. "I'm pushing because we're being followed. Take a look out the back."

Pablo did as he was told. "Who are they?"

Joshua grinned at that question. "Just what I was about to ask you, Watson. I'm not the one who's been doing bad things and getting shot at. Don't you have any idea of who these jokers could be?"

Pablo looked again. "No, unless they're some of the same people that kidnapped the girl. But why would they be following us? They already have what they came for. Maybe they're trying more than one way to pressure me."

"We are, undeniably, being followed," said Theodore. "Listen, does anybody have a map? If we could get on to some country road, I bet we could lose them. Their car has the speed, but I'll bet Josh could lose them on hard curves."

Pablo reached over the space man's shoulder and fished through the glove box until he found a road map. He pinpointed their location on it, and spotted a likely looking road ahead. He showed the map to Behr. "How about this one?"

"It's pretty good. Listen, Josh, it's about ten miles from where we are right now, so it's coming up in about five minutes. It goes off to the right there, almost a U-turn. It looks like the first paved road. OK?"

Joshua nodded. "Esmerelda, how about going more to the south?"

"Which way is that?" Joshua pointed.

"No, that's not the right way. It's that way." She pointed stubbornly and steadily northeast.

Joshua turned a bit to call out to Pablo, "Any way to get back on the road we're on now from that one?"

Pablo consulted. "Yes, after about thirty miles there's a cutoff that takes us back. We'd lose time though, wouldn't we?"

"Sure, but we might also lose these birds behind us. It's worth a try. They might be dangerous."

Pablo nodded. "There's a lively possibility of that." Theodore had an idea. "Esmerelda!"

She stirred. "Yes?"

"Can you tell us anything about the people that are following us?"

She obediently shut her eyes and concentrated, but opened them again within a few seconds. "No, I can't get near them. I don't know them, and the only way I can pick up other people is for them to be calling for my attention, or for them to be familiar to me. Sorry, Ted. Maybe our friend from space could tell us more." She closed her eyes again briefly, and opened them again in unison with the space man. "Please tell me anything you can about the entities that are following this car."

The man from space sat quite still, not moving at all except as the car moved him; this was his constant habit. He never made his arms and hands move as he spoke or thought; his fair face never colored, nor did his rather wide mouth move into any expression except a smile at any time. Theodore's face was in constant motion, the wide mouth mobile, the colors of pleasure, anxiety and thought moving rapidly across his pale skin and changing its tone constantly; consequently, the casual observer might not have thought the two men looked much alike at all, except for being of the same height and coloring. Right now, the difference was especially obvious, because Ted was on his knees facing the back window, eyes intent and dark, the flush of excitement across his high cheekbones, the muscles of his temple and jaw tense. The man from space, at the request of Esmerelda, closed his eyes, which he had opened at her summons for attention: that had been his only discernible movement. Now his eyelids were closed over the icy gray-blue of his eyes. His white skin lay smooth over the framework of muscle and bone it covered and protected. He spoke after a minute of concentration. "There are two groups."

The entire entourage turned to look at him. "What do you mean? asked Esmerelda. "There is a car with some men in it, who are half a mile behind us. These are the people that we meant. Are there additional people behind us that are following us?"

"Yes."

"How many cars are following us, then?"

"Two."

Esmerelda turned to look at Pablo, who sat with a baffled and almost petulant look on his face, eyes screwed up, looking at the back of Joshua's neck. "Ask him about all of them, then," he told Esmerelda.

She questioned him as directed, and they all waited for more information; none came. The man from space sat again like a statue, eyes beginning to close.

"Wait, my brother," said Esmerelda. "Can't you tell us anything more about these people?"

"No."

Joshua had found the cutoff and had angled the automobile nearly off the road on the far side in approach to it, braking sharply and shifting down to second, then accelerating out of the sharp turn to push the car back over 100 miles an hour. Padeyevsky seemed momentarily stunned. "I'm very glad you're driving this car instead of me, Josh. I don't mind facing people on firm ground, but I'm scared to death in this thing."

Theodore was still glued to the back window. "I see the second car," he announced, as Joshua's skill maneuvered them barely past the trunk of a tree on the bad side of a curve that put them on top of a fair-sized hill.

"I ... LOVE a parade," sang Josh in his clear, resonant, and distinctly inaccurate baritone. They were moving through one turn and curve after another, up and down rolling hills. This was indeed a country road.

"I think it's working, "exulted Ted. "At least, I can't see either one of them anymore."

Joshua was making the big car hum tunes, snicking into the two middle gears and back out as the choice between speed and handling was decided and redecided. "I'll have to admit, Pablo. Your car isn't too terribly bad, for a grand touring car."

The owner of the vehicle shrank into the back seat's upholstery. "Just drive, Josh. Just drive."

Esmerelda was smiling. "I think you're enjoying yourself, Joshua."

Josh was having fun. He almost never competed with anyone for anything, but the situation had come upon him here, and he relished it. The challenge of skidding close to death, with only his skill between safety and disaster, held his interest to the point that he could forget that he was on an inhospitable planet. He was enjoying himself thoroughly. The skin at the corners of his eyes crinkled a little, and he muttered to her, "Have no fear, I won't make a habit of this. It might be the death of your good uncle."

He geared deftly down and slipped the car into a sharp turn, barely avoiding a drift. A house came into view on one side of the two-lane road, a small, ranch-style house.

"How about pulling into that garage and shutting the door?" said Pablo.

Josh nodded. "Beautiful. A stroke of genius!" He downshifted again and pulled into the driveway of the place, and directly into the open garage. He killed the engine and got out to shut the garage door. He watched through the long-paned windows of the door as the pursuing cars raced past and vanished down the road. Their dust was still settling when a voice, very chilly, very rural, very firm, said, "Don't make a single move, any of you."

They all, except the man from space, who was still deep in meditation, turned in the direction of the voice. It was close to them, coming apparently from the screen door opening from the garage into the little house.

"Get out of that car, real easy now."

Doors opened and they complied, Esmerelda and the man from space last. No one wanted to chance getting the rest hurt, although thoughts of the chances of resistance crossed Joshua's and Pablo's minds, and even Theodore's. But all five ended up closing the car doors without having resisted at all, and then following instructions to open the garage door and line up in front of the garage.

OK, Lily, you hold the gun on them. I'll check them out." Time passed. Then, "This little fat one's got a revolver." Over Pablo's rising objections he removed it.

He moved around in front of them for the first time, so that they could see him; he was a stocky, ruddy-faced man of middle height, nearly bald, with small, well-shaped features built close together on a broad, fleshy face completed by a double chin and deep neck wrinkles under the ears. "Well, now. What have we got here, Lily?" Lily's answer never came, because one of the cars that had been following them came barreling back over the hill into view, trying to pick up the lost trail. The car's one occupant saw the group, and behind them, the Mercedes. He swerved the car into the driveway and up its length to the turn-around in front of the garage, and angled the car across its expanse so that the front bumper of his car pointed at the garage's far corner. He had seen that one of the men had a revolver. The opened door on his side of the car could be used for protection if the man could not be persuaded to put his weapon down.

The bald man had turned from the five he had been guarding, and now had his revolver pointed right at the intruder's head. There was no doubt in his mind but that this new arrival was in league with these other five, and had come here to threaten him. The man in the car, in a reflex action, seeing the impressive hole of the revolver's barrel leveled at him, ducked below the windshield, and opened his car door, keeping his head below window level and bringing his own pistol up towards the bald man.

He began to speak, but his sentence was never delivered, either. For, at the angle at which the car was parked, Lily could easily see what he was doing; she saw the pistol being raised against her husband. She knew he was going to be killed if she did not protect him. And as the intruder opened his mouth to communicate, Lily put her gun hand straight out, held its wrist with her other hand, and shot him. The man fell, clumsily out of the car. His pistol bounced from his hand. He did not move from where he had fallen.

The baldheaded man lowered Pablo's revolver slowly, looking incredulously across the driveway at his victim. He looked back at the group, then at the hidden Lily. "You shot him."

"Yup."

He stood immobile for a few seconds, at a loss. "Keep them covered, Lily. Not one move out of any of you. Lily's a dead squirrel shot. She wouldn't miss."

He trotted over to where the sprawled body lay, disengaged it from the car entirely, and examined it cautiously, keeping the revolver ready. He picked up the gun the man had dropped, and put it in his pocket. Then he sat down next to him, looking at Lily behind her screen door. "He's dead. You killed him, Lily."

"He would've killed you if I hadn't." The unperturbed voice held a trace of righteous indignation.

He turned back to the newly arrived dead and began to go through his pockets.

The five from Pablo's car still stood with their hands up, getting more and more restless. Pablo had stopped feeling guilty about the kidnapping; he had stopped feeling frustrated at failing to right the damage; he was on the verge of real fury. Joshua was, characteristically, having a good enough time: he was looking vaguely up at the green and golding leaves above him and mentally rewriting the entire incident for television. "If I only had a tape recorder," he was murmuring to Esmerelda, who stood, nearly undone by the sight of the carelessly executed killing. Theodore was trying to think of a plausible way out of this situation. Only the man from space continued quite unmoved; he stood with his hands up; Esmerelda had explained to him that this posture was required. His eyes were still closed and his thoughts were with his sister from space, for this was the initial request of his hosts, and he would continue, regardless of the circumstances of his physical environment. The four other sets of arms were getting exceedingly weary of being held up.

The owner of the house spoke as he went through the dead man's pockets. "I'm a deputy sheriff in this county, and I reckon I got a right to protect my property and the common peace. Ain't that right, Lily?"

"Yup."

The repeated agreements from Lily did nothing to bolster anyone's confidence in his abilities to extricate them from this. "We really had something bust in on us here, didn't we, Lily?" Theodore raised his voice, very meekly. "Could we put our hands down, if we promise not to do anything suspicious?"

"Nope."

The deputy was still going through pockets. "Here we go. Here's his wallet. Wonder what gang these hoodlums are in. And with a girl too. Must be real …" The man's healthy color left his face. He looked sick and then, abruptly, sicker. He read a piece of identification. He reread it. He looked at the man's face, lying there on the grass, lifeless.

"Lily," he intoned, with a thin, bemused dignity. "There's something funny here. Come on out."

Lily came. Lily bent and looked. She turned the card over and looked some more. "What's the Criminal Investigations Division of the U. S. Army?" she asked her husband. "Is that some kind of code?"

"Lily, we shot a government man."

The deputy sat. In unison, they turned and looked at the miserable five standing, arms dead weight against them in the air. "Now, look," said Pablo. "I'm Dr. Pablo Padeyevsky, and we're not gangsters."

"What's going on, then? This man chasing you, was he trying to catch you?"

Pablo looked a little stupid, as he always did when he was trying to think. "Well, we were ..."

Pablo was stumped.

"I'm Joshua Starr," said Joshua.

Lily looked him over carefully. "He's telling the truth, Hubert. I know him from the TV. I seen him on the TV lots of times."

"What is he, some kind of actor?"

"Well, not exactly. But I seen him on the TV."

"OK. We got one of you identified. So what's going on?"

"Can we put our hands down first?" Starr spoke to Lily. "Let 'em, Hubert."

They lowered their arms with great relief, the space man following their lead.

Pablo spoke now. "We are on a mission of some importance. We are working on the same side as the Army man. You are holding up five private and decent citizens. I tell you, we've got to get back on the road."

The deputy sat so still on the grass that Lily spoke to him. "What's the matter, Hubert?"

The white-faced man tried to speak through the pallor, and his voice came out pale as his face, and much, much thinner. "I think he's telling the truth, Lily."

Without saying another word, he heaved himself upright from his sitting position and walked into the house.

Lily started after him. "Excuse me, but something's wrong with Hubert. I got to go look after him." She turned to Starr. "I knew you couldn't be no gangster, Mr. Starr. I seen you on TV." She walked into the house after her husband, a shapeless, short, and infinitely dignified figure.

Joshua, Pablo and Theodore ran for the car. Esmerelda again contacted the man from space, and brought up the rear. They slammed the doors, and Joshua maneuvered around the CID man's sedan and let the

Mercedes start to roll back down the driveway. It had rolled about half the length of the drive when its occupants heard a command that was beginning to sound drearily familiar: "All right, stop that car and get out with your hands up."

A car had pulled into the foot of the driveway, blocking them. It was no use trying to outrun these new voices, the other car which had been following them was now in position to block the driveway completely. With the steep ditch on either side of the drive, there was simply no place to go.

Joshua bowed to the inevitable and put the car back to sleep, set the parking brake, and removed his long body from its seat behind the wheel. The others followed suit, clambering out and lifting arms still tired from the last bout of hands-up.

Two men got out of the car blocking the driveway. One of them watched Pablo with a slight smile, not friendly, but full of recognition.

"Col. Church!" Padeyevsky's by-now bloodshot eyes took in his acquaintance. "What are you doing here?"

"Always the confidence of a rhinoceros, Pablo. But we'll be asking the questions here. Where's Capt. Crouse?"

Pablo inclined his head towards the body in the grass by the garage. "That's none of our doing, Colonel."

The Colonel motioned his confederate forward and told him, "Watch them." He walked up the long driveway to the inert, prone form of Capt. Crouse, examined it thoroughly for signs of life, found none, and walked soberly and with some determination back to the little group by the Mercedes.

"Padeyevsky, I have a personal impression of you as a man of some ability, and I assure you that we will listen to whatever explanation you have." His voice was sharpening and developing in volume, though not in pitch, with each word. "But an officer of the United States Army is dead. And if you had anything to do with that, you're not going to be asking any questions for a long, long time. Understood?"

Padeyevsky nodded his head. "Oh, yes. Now. You see …"

"Wait a minute." The Colonel turned to look at the house. "Anybody in there?"

"Yes, the woman who shot your Captain Crouse, and her husband. He's a deputy sheriff."

The Colonel squinted a little in vague disbelief and said, "Wait here, Armstrong." He moved cautiously up the drive and towards the front of the house. But there was no sign of defense of property, and he disappeared in the front door, to come out again three minutes later.

"I want all of you in the house," he said from the front steps. They all filed up the drive in the front door, with Armstrong's prompting. There was a brief domestic flurry as Lily produced chairs enough for the population, then the deputy and Lily returned into the kitchen, apparently as per the Colonel's orders.

"All right, Padeyevsky. She shot the Captain, all right; I can tell that just by the way the deputy's acting, even if she hadn't already admitted it. Now, how about you explaining how it all happened."

Pablo roused himself from the torpor of utter exhaustion that kept threatening to overcome him, and did a creditable job of truthfully outlining the series of actions that had placed him here. "The five of us are involved in a personal matter that has nothing to do with the death of your man. We had an urgent reason to leave my house very early this morning, and we discovered after our departure that we were being followed. In an effort to elude our tail, which we have now discovered to be you, we took a side road, and pulled into this driveway, which was chosen randomly and on the spur of the moment as a way of avoiding the cars that had been following us. However, while we were on these premises, the deputy threatened us with his revolver, and forced us to remain here. We have been here ever since, and wish only to be on our way."

Church listened to Padeyevsky's story with apparent belief. "OK, that sounds right, as far as it goes. But you have left out one item that is of utmost importance here. Why did you leave your house in such a hurry, at that time of night?"

Pablo's lined, rather oily face took on an expression of chagrin. "Well, I'd rather not say."

Church began to look dark in the face. "Look, Padeyevsky. I'm being very patient with you. But a man has been killed, and I'd rather you did say. And right now."

Pablo shifted in his seat. "What we left the house for has nothing to do with you or the Signal Corps, Colonel. But I'm afraid that if I tell you our mission, it will endanger the life of one of my friends."

"Who is this guy, anyway?" Starr wanted to know.

"I've done some consulting work with his technical people," said Pablo. "We worked together for several months, over two years ago." He turned to the Colonel, moving slowly. "I'm very tired, Church. But I assure you these people had nothing to do with me before we turned into their driveway. We are involved in a strictly private matter, and I have already …"

"Murder is not a private matter!" The Colonel was on his feet. "Now look here, Padeyevsky, you're in hot water, whether you know it or not. I can have every one of you locked up as material witnesses to murder, and what's more, I'm sure that if we look hard enough, we're going to discover that you and your party caused the whole incident, and should be blamed for the murder of Captain Crouse as well. Now you come clean with me."

Pablo took some more meat out of his lower lip. "If I tell you what the difficulty is, will you promise not to repeat the confidence to anyone, after you see that it's really the truth I'm telling, and this is a private matter?"

"If it's not germane to the case, I think I can promise to keep it confidential."

"All right." Pablo reluctantly opened his mouth to speak and then turned to Josh, who nodded as if to say, "That's all you can do, Pablo."

Pablo began. "I am, as you know, Colonel, a rich man. I have been the victim of a successful kidnapping attempt. They thought they were getting my niece, Esmerelda, but unfortunately they mistook a guest we had staying in the house last night for her. We are trying to get to our guest and redeem her, as we believe that she may be in some danger."

"Those people that shot out your tires. Are they the kidnappers?" asked the Colonel.

Pablo nodded.

"We have been watching you, Padeyevsky, as well as everyone connected with the project you and I worked on together. We got intelligence that someone had been working on that project overtime. For the other side. And when we looked closely at you, we discovered some connection or other between you and the syndicate." The Colonel waited.

"Look, Colonel, there is a connection. But it has nothing to do with the case your people are working on. I'm not selling secrets to anybody. Besides, I don't think that there's anything to sell. Telepathy just can't be developed for military use."

"All right then, what connection did you have with the syndicate?"

"Gambling." As the Colonel's eyebrows began to raise again, Pablo added hastily, "Oh, it was just betting on horses. I just figured out a, well, a sort of system, and I won more than the syndicate thought I should. So they were out to get me."

"Oh!" said Esmerelda. She stood up, suddenly, in great agitation. "Our friend is in great danger. And I can no longer find her!"

"What?" said the Colonel.

Esmerelda quickly came to herself and looked at the floor, blushing. She sat back down. The Colonel looked at Padeyevsky. "What's she talking about?"

The group seemed to be tongue-tied, and sat looking at Esmerelda and the man from space with expressions of greatest concern on each face. The Colonel brusquely stood up again. "Sgt. Armstrong, call Headquarters and see if they can send someone to take care of this matter. I'm not going to get any more out of them here."

"Look." Pablo was on his feet now, too. "I've told you the absolute truth, Church. We have absolutely nothing to do with your Signal Corps. There is no threat to your people at all. I have divulged no secrets. And this is very, very serious. What my niece just told us is that the girl who was kidnapped is now in even greater danger than we thought she was, and that she has lost contact with her."

"Lost contact?" The Colonel stared at Esmerelda, who was clad in a dress, a light coat, and sandals. "Padeyevsky, is she using telepathy?"

Pablo hurried on. "Yes, she has the gift of telepathy. Although you couldn't use it for military purposes, I assure you. She is using it now to try and keep contact with the girl who's been kidnapped. We aren't trying to outsmart you, or keep back information. We just need, very badly, to be on our way. It's a matter of life and death. We've got to leave."

"You don't have to tell me it's a matter of life and death. You just killed a man!"

"But we didn't kill him!"

"Well, it looks to me like you're responsible for it."

"Look, if one of us stayed behind, say me, to answer your questions and cooperate with you, could the rest go on? You know you can't help us; no government or police people could. We've got to do it ourselves, as private citizens, or risk getting the girl killed. And we've got to do it now."

Everyone in the room was on his feet by this time, with the exception of the man from space; all were seconding Pablo's suggestion. The Sergeant was suspended in motion towards the telephone, and stood in the doorway looking alert and hostile. He was sure the entire room was filled with either kooks or criminals. The Colonel's eye caught the one seated figure. "Who is that guy? What's he doing with his eyes closed like that?"

Pablo hastened to speak. "He's another friend of mine, who has the gift of telepathy, and is trying to locate our friend who has been kidnapped."

"What's your name? The Colonel walked over to the man from space and addressed him. He was ignored, not on purpose, but because the man was not aware that he was being spoken to. "Ah," said Pablo.

"He's a friend of mine, an actor," said Joshua, moving beside Esmerelda and pointing her, very gently, towards the man from space.

"And who are you?"

"I am Joshua Starr."

The Colonel, not being a devotee of daytime television, was not impressed.

"I work in television."

"Well, does this man know where your friend is?" Esmerelda spoke. "No, he doesn't."

"Well, how do you know. Let him tell me. What is this? Can't he speak for himself?"

Esmerelda summoned the man from space, and his eyes opened immediately. "My brother, please tell this man here what you have found out about your sister."

The space man calmly turned his head until his level eyes met the gaze of the Colonel. "I am not in thought with my sister."

"That's an act, all right." The Sergeant was coming back into the room now, having determined to his own satisfaction that these people were lying completely, and needed a firm hand. "Colonel, I say send them all down to police headquarters and let them cool their heels for a while. That'll cure them of this stuff." Padeyevsky nearly bounced down Colonel Church's throat. "No, no, don't do that." Josh was moving forward too; Esmerelda was showing signs of being ready to cry with worry; Theodore was holding Esmerelda's shoulder and talking to the Sergeant, saying, "We're not acting; can't you see that this is really ..." The Colonel was turning pale again, except that a spot showed in each cheek which indicated that he was just as upset as before, only not quite as out of control.

The man from space cut through the confusion without raising his voice. He simply stood up and walked towards the door of the small living room.

"Where are you going?" The Colonel stood in the man's way. The space man calmly moved past the Colonel's bulk as though it were not there, and the Colonel was too dumbfounded to restrain him. The man walked out the door and down the steps.

The Colonel watched him go. In a state of almost total disbelief, he sputtered, "Halt, I mean, stop!"

The figure, unwaveringly and without hurry, walked on.

"Padeyevsky, make him stop. Tell him to stop. I'll have to shoot him.

"Ah, wait a minute," said Padeyevsky. The space man walked on.

Esmerelda stood, looking blankly at the front door. Theodore shook her by the shoulders. "Esmerelda! You've got to stop the space man!"

The Colonel turned around. "What? What do you mean, space man?"

"Uh," said Behr, realizing his slip too late.

The Colonel shrugged that minor question aside. "Halt, stop or I'll shoot."

The man walked on.

The Colonel raised his pistol and aimed it at the space man, then carefully moved it, raising it slightly so that it would send its bullet ten feet or so to the right of the man, and above his head. He fired. The man paid no more attention to the sound than to the snapping of a twig. He walked on. There was another shot, from the open window. The man from space fell forward on the ground and lay there, unmoving.

The Colonel looked to his left to see Sgt. Armstrong holding his match .45, the spent casing just rolling off the porch. "You idiot," he shouted. "I wasn't aiming to hit him. I was just warning him."

The Sergeant looked at the Colonel as though he'd lost his senses. "But, sir, you warned him ..."

The Colonel took the steps and the few yards of lawn that lay between him and the man from space and dropped to his knees beside the still form. He put his ear to the man's back, then held his wrist. There seemed to be no signs of life.

Both Padeyevsky and Joshua attempted to follow the Colonel down the steps. "Hold it." The Sergeant was motioning with his .45, which he was patently ready to use. They held it.

The Colonel came up the steps looking as weary as Padeyevsky. "It's no use. He's dead." He collapsed in his kitchen chair. So did Padeyevsky and Joshua.

"May I go to him?" Esmerelda had waved away Theodore's comforting arm; she seemed calmer than before the shooting had actually occurred.

"No," said the Sergeant.

"Of course," said the Colonel.

The Sergeant's gun lowered. Esmerelda went down the steps of the front porch and to the space man.

The Colonel turned to Theodore. "What did you mean by calling that guy a space man?"

"Oh," said Theodore. "He's just an actor who …"

The Colonel gestured him to silence with one hand and turned his eyes back to Padeyevsky. "Wait a minute, here, Pablo." He sat and contemplated him for a minute. "You know, if anyone could do it, you could."

Esmerelda opened the front screen door. "If we can purge a volume of space, we can save him."

"What?" the Colonel's voice rose incredulously. "He's dead." No, wait," said Padeyevsky. "If she says she can save him, she can." He sat, forward and low in his chair, thinking. "All right, Church," he said at last. "We've got a man from another planet, an alien, and your man has shot him. But Esmerelda says we can save him, if we let her and Mr. Starr do it. Will you allow them the freedom to save him?"

"Look, Padeyevsky, there's no way in the world to bring the dead to life again. Is there?" The Colonel sat, momentarily brought to a standstill by the dawning thought that this just might really be a man from space.

"Not for anyone on this planet, Colonel. But this man has powers of healing that I don't suppose we have. Is that right, Esmerelda?" She nodded. "Yes. All we have to do is purge a volume of space of its negativity. He hasn't severed the silver cord yet."

"Excuse me, Colonel," said the Sergeant, "but I think these people are trying to put something over on you."

"Listen," said Padeyevsky. "We've got to act fast, if this is going to work at all."

"Well." The Colonel sat immobilized by indecision. "If he really is from space, I'd hate to lose the chance to get him back."

"Please let us save him." Esmerelda leaned towards him, eyes imploring.

The Colonel moved, his mind made up. "OK. Bring him into the house."

Esmerelda moved closer to the Colonel. "No, not the house. Not here. The negative vibrations generated here within the last few minutes are enough to make the task impossible. I must find a place of reasonable vibrations."

The Colonel looked at Padeyevsky. "What's she talking about?" Joshua responded to the question. "It's complicated. It's just another kind of medicine."

"OK, then, we'll take him to a hospital."

Esmerelda reacted very strongly to that suggestion, putting her hands out in horror and saying, "Oh, no. That would be the worst place of all. All those negative astrals. They permeate the mental planes in a hospital, feeding on the suffering."

"What's she talking about?" iterated the Colonel. "What's this negativity she keeps talking about?"

"Can we carry him just a little way outdoors?" Esmerelda was pleading, "Just let us put him out of doors. You can watch us. All right? Please?"

The Colonel waved his arms. "All right, all right. But I'm going to be close behind. Don't take me for a fool."

Behr and Starr moved quickly to the fallen man and lifted him gently between them. Esmerelda ran lightly out of doors, and down into the cleared area in back of the house. There was a small, rough-cut clearing, nearly covered with goldenrod and the last of the wildflowers.

"Bring him over here."

They cradled him carefully, and laid him down in the densest profusion of flowers.

"Please get back." Esmerelda's hand swept the Colonel and Padeyevsky further up the slope. "Could you wait in the house?"

"Young lady, I do not intend to move back one step further. I told you not to take me for a fool."

Esmerelda viewed him, and then turned to Joshua. "Is he far enough back now, do you think?"

Joshua shrugged. "It might take too long to move him further. I think we can manage."

The Colonel sat down on the slope, Padeyevsky and Theodore retiring further, and sitting on the back steps of the little house. Joshua and Esmerelda walked a few feet away, and began to look up into the first dim light of the coming day.

CHAPTER NINE

The large man took the girl out of the back seat of the Cadillac and carried her into the cabin, which wasn't a cabin at all, but a plush vacation home, designed for luxury and supreme comfort, within the American tradition of pretentious rural architecture. There was a fireplace and much wood paneling and visible rafters, walls of glass giving views of the landscaped outdoors and the spring-fed lake.

The big man took her across the thickly carpeted fire-front area and into the master bedroom. He laid her on the bed and went swiftly from the room, closing the door behind him. The little man had a key; he used it to lock the bedroom door and then put the key on the coffee table nearest him. There had been no need to shut windows: they had prepared for this by nailing the bedroom windows shut and shuttering them from the outside. The bedroom doors had been covered with cardboard on the outside so that no light showed through the cracks. The room had a thoroughly adequate bathroom; there was also a small refrigerator running. It had been stocked with milk, bread, cheese, cold cuts, a few other foods, all in plastic containers. They had no intention of seeing or speaking to their hostage. Their orders had been simply to bring her here and wait for further instructions.

Which they had done, and would now do. And so they settled into the comfortable furniture of the living room. But they did not settle with much conviction. They stared at each other, one a big man, powerfully built, with a weather-beaten and experienced face; the other thin for his very small frame but very hard looking, with a face dominated by an oversized, beak-like nose which was unredeemed by any chin that admitted more than a ripple in the retreat of the face from nose to chest.

The little one spoke through his nose. "Come on, Marv, let's get out of here, right now. We could prop some furniture against the door, and unlock it, and we'd be miles away before she even wakes up, much less gets the door open. This is the only cabin on the lake that's got anybody in it, this time of the year, and the nearest town, even if she should go that way, is an hour's walk easy."

The big man sighed. "You just can't get decent help these days. You've been griping about this job ever since we took it."

"Well, I ain't never had nothing to do with no kidnapping before."

"Look. We contracted for this job. Now, if you're ever going to get ahead in this world, you've got to be smart. If we pull through with the package, it's going to be money in our pockets. We got the girl, and as long as we got her, we're going to get a nice little bundle."

"I know, I know," said the small man nasally. "But what about the police? What if Padeyevsky saw us? The police would get onto us for sure then."

"In the first place," said the big man, "Padeyevsky couldn't possibly have seen us. But even if he had-wait a minute. Let me think." He sat laboring at the mental task. "In that case," he said with flair, "we simply dump the girl and take off, because then it'd be too late anyway. Let's just sit tight here for a while. We're safe enough here."

The big man got up, went over to the light switch for the living room, and turned off all the house lights except the ones in the master bedroom. Then he rotated a picture on the wall which joined the living room with the bedroom; behind the picture was a small hole. Through it, he could see the girl they had kidnapped, sleeping peacefully, just as they had left her. He watched her for a minute or two before he gulped audibly. "We don't have the Sweetwater girl."

"Jesus," said the little man. "What do you mean, we don't have the Sweetwater girl?"

"I mean we don't have the Sweetwater girl." The big man put the picture back into place and turned on the lights. "Here," he said, finding and handing the little man a snapshot. "This is a picture of the Sweetwater girl. Look at her hair. Bangs, right. Well, the girl we got ain't got no bangs. And nobody ever grew three feet of hair in one day. Besides, look at her face. It's not the same girl. See for yourself."

They turned off lights and the little man looked through the small hole. Somberly, he looked. Slowly, they turned on lights again and sat. The similarity between the two girls was remarkable, but the differences between them were no less obvious. They did not have the Sweetwater girl.

"Jesus," offered the little man. "We are fouled up, Marv. Let's get out of here."

"Wait a minute and let me think. I'll call the boss."

He walked to the phone and dialed long distance. There was an immediate answer. He spoke into the instrument. "We picked up the package. But we goofed. We have the wrong package."

"What?" said the voice at the other end.

"That's right," said the big man. "Very similar, but the wrong package."

There was a four-minute pause. The voice then returned, speaking quickly. "You got her at Padeyevsky's house?"

"That's right."

"Then hold the package. It may be just as good." The connection closed.

"Jesus," said the little man. "We've got to get out of here, Marv." He watched as the big man put the phone back on its hook. "I don't care what the boss says. I don't like any of this." He wandered into to kitchen and came back with two glasses of tap water. "Listen. You take my part. I'm leaving. I never did no kidnapping before. I don't want no part of this kidnapping. I mean, Jesus, Marv. It's out of my line, this kidnapping. I don't want to get involved in no kidnapping."

"You're already involved. Now shut up." The big man looked at the half-empty glass of water in his hand and grimaced. "Now you've got me drinking water!"

Elmo meekly carried the glasses back to the kitchen.

"I think we're doing OK," shouted the big man after the small retreating figure. "The boss sounded excited over the phone."

"Jesus," said the little man. "All I need, is more excitement."

"Elmo," came a female voice from the other side of the door. The little man jumped, clattering the glasses on the sink's porcelain as he set them down. "Jesus," he said. "What's that?"

It was in fact the girl from space, who had awakened and remained quiet for a few minutes before deciding that it was time to communicate with her present companions. She was puzzled over her change in environment. She had gone to sleep at her new friend's house, and had no notion of how she had come here, or who these entities were. Further, she had discovered, upon brief exploration, that this new dwelling place of hers had windows which did not open, and doors which were closed to her; this she found quite impossible to understand. And the minds of the two in the next room .were totally unfamiliar to her, and she had had no luck at all in establishing any rapport in thought. She had now concluded that, although she was very poor at using verbal communication, she would have to try it.

But how was she to initiate such communication? In order to obtain their attention, she decided that it would be appropriate to use the odd planetary custom that separated entities from each other, that of greeting by names. She found that, as was the case with each inhabitant of this surface that she had met, the name was so deeply ingrained upon the individual consciousness that she was able, even from these men's garbled thoughts, to extract their names. Having come into possession of strong thought forms, which she assumed to be names from each of them, she verbalized to the shorter man first, quite loudly.

The little man tried to collect himself as the big man said, "How did she know your name?"

"I don't know. I don't understand at all. Jesus, Marv, we didn't use our real names on the job; we used aliases, and I never even said my alias, either."

"Well, there's only one thing to do," the big man said sententiously. "Let's find out what's going on. Answer her. No, wait a minute. Let me think. I've got a better idea. I'll answer her."

He turned to the bedroom door. "Yeah, what do you want?"

"Oh," said the space girl. "I spoke to Elmo, but I am pleased to speak with you."

The two men sat congealing inside their skins for a few seconds. They stared at each other through the fog of their mutual confusion. "Jesus," finally offered the smaller of the two. "What are we gonna do? We got to find out how she knows my name. Because, Jesus, Marv, we don't know what she knows, if she knows my name. I mean, she might know all about us. We got to find out where she got her information." He was running words closer and closer together in his panic. "I mean, Jesus, Marv, whatarewegonnado?"

"Simmer down," said the big man. "That's how come you never got ahead in this business. You get panicky. Wait a minute. I'll find out how much she knows." He walked over to the bedroom door. "Hey you," he shouted. "How come you know Shorty's name?"

"It is evident," she replied.

"Come on, come on. How did you know his name? What's coming off here?"

The girl stood next to her side of the bedroom door, trying to understand what the man had asked her. She had tried to answer his first question, but she had apparently failed, for he had asked it again. She could not understand the second question. After thinking carefully, she decided to verbalize her desire to join their company. "My present environment is limiting," she shouted through the door.

"Jesus," said the little man. "She talks like a book."

"Stupid. She's just one of them high class dames that uses high class language."

"Jesus," said the little man. "If she knows my name, she might know what we look like."

"Wait a minute," said Marv. "Let me think. I'll just see what she does know." He talked through the door. "What do we look like?" The space girl could not understand this question, and did not reply.

"There, see?" said the big man. "She didn't see us." He turned again to the door. "What color hair have ! got?" he yelled. "Brown," she said, picking up the man's mentally projected answer.

"How about my eyes?" he asked, after some thought. "Brown," she said.

He was extremely perplexed at two right answers. He walked over to another chair and sat down very close to the little man. "She must be working for somebody," he whispered. "I think maybe we've been set up for something."

"You know I never had nothing to do with no kidnapping," said the little man.

"Well, it ain't exactly kidnapping," said the big man. "We ain't asking no ransom."

"It carries the same penalty," said the little man.

The big man sat and thought, visibly, his face red and furrowed. After a long pause, he said to the smaller man, "No wonder you never got nowhere in this business. You ain't got no initiative." He walked over to the bedroom door, having imbued himself with a new sense of purpose and direction. "OK," he shouted through the door, "What's my name?"

"Marion Percival Bartman," said the girl.

"Jesus," said the little man with relief, "she didn't get that right." The big man spun around to face Elmo. He looked murderous. "Don't you ever tell anyone that, do you hear me?" he bellowed. "Jesus," said the little man. "You mean that's your real name?"

"YOU EVER TELL ANYBODY THAT AND YOU'RE A DEAD MAN," he shouted, apoplectic now.

The beaked nose wagged up and down hastily and fervently to show understanding.

"Well," said the big man, somewhat more dispassionately, "she's got us cold. I don't know where she got her information, but something's fishy here. We're going to have to do something. But wait. Let me think. Let me think. Don't jump the gun. That's why you never got nowhere in this business, Elmo. You always jump the gun. Wait a minute. Nobody knows my real name, not anybody. Because nobody's called me that since I got big enough to clobber anybody that tried it. Nobody's even heard that name for twenty-five years, except my mother."

"I didn't know your mother was alive," said the little man. "Shut up. Let me think. She's got to have somebody high-powered behind her. We may be in serious trouble, Shorty."

"Don't call me that," said the little man, "or I'll call you Percival." A roundhouse blow very nearly connected with the beaked nose of the small man, and he screamed, "Jesus, Marv, you almost hit me. You'd kill me if you hit me." He tripped over the couch. "Listen," said Marv, climbing over the coffee table after him. "If you ever call me that again, I'll wring your shriveled up neck until ..."

"Marion," came the girl's voice.

"Jesus," said the little man, "there she goes again. What're we gonna do? What're we gonna do?"

"Wait a minute. I'm thinking, I'm thinking." The strain lines around the big man's mouth and forehead set and reddened.

"I got it," said the little man. "Let's get out of here while the going's good. You can't tell what's up here."

"Look," said the big man. "That's why you never got no place in this business. You're a quitter. You don't know how to use your brains. Now shut up and let me think." There was a strained silence, from which the big man surfaced with the look of renewed strength that thinking always gave him. "I'm going to let her out of the room. And we're going to find out just how much she knows, and how she knows what she knows."

"Jesus, she'll see us," said the little man.

"Stupid. She already knows what we look like, and our real names. She probably even knows where I live."

"Twenty twelve South Park Drive," came the well-projected tones of the space girl from behind the door, as she picked up the automatically transmitted thought.

The big man picked up an ashtray from the coffee table and hurled it against the inner wall of the living room, where it made a very loud business of its demise. He glared at the rubble. There was a filter tip which had fallen onto his shoe. He kicked it off. The little man backed further into the cushions of the couch.

"Jesus, Marv. Let's get out of here."

There was a car coming up the driveway: they both became aware of its engine sound, of the crunch of its tires on the gravel. Marv looked double-take at the little man, but he obviously didn't know who it was; he was almost dissolving into the couch, abject and useless with apprehension at the rapidly crumbling situation. "Come on, Elmo, maybe it's someone from the organization." Marv went over to the front curtains and pulled at them just enough to make a place for his eye to see. The car was new, a light blue, four-door Ford, with a rent-a-car sticker on its bumper. The man getting out of it was no one Marv knew. He looked to be in his early forties. He came up on the porch, and his knock sounded lightly on the door.

"Jesus," said the beaknosed man. "What're we gonna do?"

"Stupid, we'll just let him in. He's probably in the organization. Who else would know about the place? Besides there's only one of him, and there's two of us, and we got guns. Tell the girl to shut up." Elmo went over to the bedroom door. "Shut up in there," he said in a half-whisper.

She did not answer. Marv opened the door to the man, who confidently strode in. Looks like he owns the place, thought the big man.

"Trostrick's my name, Marv. J.E. Trostrick. I guess you and Elmo have things pretty well under control here?"

He held out his hand for a handshake.

Marv looked at the hand. His own right hand was in the coat pocket, closed snugly around the butt of his Colt. He didn't plan on letting go of the pistol just to be pals with this one. But he might be OK. On the other hand, if he had been scheduled to meet them all along, why couldn't they have been told? Marv had been given the impression that all their instructions were going to be by phone.

The intruder's black hair was perfectly in place, lacquered smooth, gleaming subtly. Trostrick smiled easily at the two men. "Relax, boys." He paid no attention to Marv's refusal to shake hands, nor did he appear to notice the bulge in the big man's pocket. He walked easily over to the couch and sat down beside Elmo, who quivered.

"Your job is done, boys. I'll pick her up, and be on my way." Marv didn't like the sound of that. "Hold it. Where's the payoff?"

"That will be taken care of. It has to go through normal channels."

"Yeah?" The big man had never heard of such trust. He and Elmo were only doing this on contract; they didn't work out of D.C., normally. And they'd get their money in the sweet bye and bye? Not a chance.

"No dice, Trostrick. The organization doesn't work that way. Now who the hell are you?"

"You weren't told?" Trostrick's voice held polite surprise.

"No. And one, I get paid, or two, I get direct orders from the boss. Or else the girl stays with us."

"I assure you, Marv, that all this is in order. The plan simply didn't work out quite as predicted, and the boss is afraid that this location is not suitable for a longer stay." He got up and found the bar, under a counter. "Drink? Scotch?"

Marv shook his head. "No."

"You, Elmo?"

Elmo was happy to get a drink. He had overlooked the bar, earlier.

"I am to get the girl out of this area entirely. Don't worry. You'll be paid for your work. But I had to move too fast to be given your money."

"No dice." Marv began to look menacing, his free hand began clenching as though he couldn't quite control it. "We contracted for this job, and we're going to see it through. I never worked here before this week, and I ain't never seen you. Now put the money in my hand, and you get the girl. Otherwise, get the hell out of here."

Trostrick's eyes dropped, with exaggerated alarm, to the lumpy pocket of Marv's coat. He looked back up at Marv's face, eyes wide open now, surprise exaggerated in the stare. He kept on looking at Marv's eyes.

His eyes are very, very black, thought Marv.

"Jesus," said the little man. "Give him the girl, Marv, and let's get outta here. They'll pay us. I know they will. Here is the key, Mister." He flipped the key to the bedroom door to the man, who caught it in the air, hardly glancing away from Marv's eyes.

Marv broke the glance with difficulty. "All right. Both of you just hold it. Nobody goes anywhere until I get my money, or hear from the boss." His gun was out of his pocket now. "Elmo, frisk Trostrick."

Elmo did so.

"He's clean, Marv. But, Jesus, can't we ..."

"No. Sit down."

"Can I have that drink?"

"Yeah. Go ahead."

Elmo did. Then he sat, on the edge of the couch, his trembling hands lifting the glass to his lips.

Marv looked back at Trostrick. There were those black eyes again. He gazed at them in spite of himself, and began to feel stranger and stranger sensations. He couldn't look away. He couldn't think. He couldn't control his mind. Then he could think; he couldn't stop thinking. He was thinking thoughts he had thought, often before, in the night. He didn't want to think these thoughts. They were beginning to take over the room. The big man stood staring into Trostrick's eyes, and for the first time in his life, he began to explore the sensation of fear.

CHAPTER TEN

Joshua reached into a small inner pocket in his trousers waistband and brought out a ring, made very simply of gold and holding a stone that looked like a ruby. The mounting seemed to be the least simple thing about the ring; it was a series of golden threads, woven about the stone so as to make a sort of pattern, complicated and asymmetric. Esmerelda turned from the view of the Colonel and unfastened a smaller but very similar ring from her clothing. The two then turned to face the dawn again and, with the light of morning on their faces, surrounded by the small wild flowers, they raised their hands in unison and put the rings on the ring fingers of their right hands, slowly drawing the metal and stone down their fingers; even more slowly turning the stone inward so that the woven mounting was against their palms. The ceremony had begun.

Even the Colonel, who knew nothing of magic, could realize immediately that there had been a beginning. He watched the two simply-clothed people, one a man, one a woman, shake off their sexuality and assume a stature completely different. Their posture straightened but, more importantly, their entire system had become responsive to a different group of thoughts and intelligence, and the bodies that carried these entities reflected the change in numberless ways. They seemed to have suddenly put on more substance, becoming more patently who they were than they had been, and the first light seemed to concentrate, suddenly, on them.

The two held their hands up for several seconds, then placed them palm to palm, and lowered them.

"I desire to know, in order to serve." They spoke in unison, their voices nearly of the same pitch: very low, even lower than Joshua's normal speaking voice, and almost hushed, but with a quality of intensity that made each word so clear to the Colonel that he almost felt the sounds impact upon his body. His emotions stirred, and as Joshua began to go through the ritual that banished negativity, he involuntarily began to lift from his own earthly body that part of him which was mental, and move into harmony with the speakers.

"Ateh."

"Malkuth."

"Ve Geburah."

"Ve Gedulah."

Colonel Timothy Church, for fifty years an unthinking ally of his corporeal reality, began to see things he could not explain, things that seemed to him more real than all previous experience. His emotions were riveted by the magnetism generated by the magical personalities of Joshua and his apprentice, and he began to see the light not just as parts of undifferentiated sunlight around them, but as what it really was: their thought images of their magical selves, which they had, with the turning of their rings, brought forth into the physical light beside them, linking their astral and physical realities. Church could see with a totally sensitive eye that these figures were hooded and robed; in fact, were clothed as Theodore and Pablo had viewed them the day of the ritual that had brought the space visitors to this planet. The signs Joshua made with each vibrated word flamed in the air, until the Colonel could hardly see the two standing over their friend in the blaze of articulated light.

Then Joshua built the five-pointed stars, his ritual words bodying forth into the air in light forms, given power by the concentrated thinking which Joshua and Esmerelda had expended over careful years of steady application. And the Colonel saw each shade of color, each sensation that smote the air around him, for he was, more than either Theodore or Pablo had been, a completely receptive instrument and a natural student of magic, with a talent for visualization that does not normally come without much practice. He saw far beyond his capacity for understanding, and his personality came closer and closer in those minutes to a drastic change. For the key to his thinking had changed, and a new key had been minted and honed, and was waiting to turn. Just as a new entity learns to walk, and then to think clearly, so Timothy Church had taken the first step towards a totally new activity. It was never the policy of any master to allow such novices as Church to be exposed fully to the power of ritual magic without preparation, but Joshua had had no choice. And so the Colonel absorbed in a few minutes an experience that normally requires years of preparation.

The ritual of banishment was over now, and Joshua and Esmerelda lay down beside their brother, in the same posture as he: legs crossed at the ankle, hands folded across their breasts. And the Colonel saw the hooded thought images become more and more vital, until suddenly replicas of both magicians' bodies, bathed in light, loosed themselves from their prone forms and took residence in their hooded projections. The two light forms glowed, pulsing with moving life, connected by a shining cord to the now sleeping magicians. And the thought forms, in which now resided the total consciousnesses of Joshua and Esmerelda, began to move towards the man between them in the flowers. They stood at his head and laid their ringed hands in gentle pressure on the space man's head, as a bishop does in Confirmation.

"As the silver cord pulls, so we beckon you to follow, my brother."

Esmerelda's hooded face turned towards the speaking Joshua, her mental body lending his all its power, sending into the higher planes of the astral light all its love.

"Through many planes we call you here, and through many more might you have given your being its choice of sight, for there are things unseen to us that are open to you, my brother in light. But we summon you back to this plane."

And the Colonel began to see the silver cord that connected the physical body of the man from space to his mental body; then the mental body itself materialized. It was not hooded and robed, as were the two magicians' spiritual forms, but was rather swathed in a form of light, without stitch or fold of material, fitting him like a skin.

And three consciousnesses instead of two took up physical existence again. The light around them remained, losing form and gaining luminosity until its special brightness filled the meadow, and the Colonel felt himself bathed in its flow of cleansing substance. Fire and water, he thought in confusion, how could fire be so cool? Or water so bright? The two magicians woke from their sleep, and knelt over the body of the man from space, their earthly hands now on his temples as their astral hands had been before. The light ebbed and flowed about the form, which seemed at first to do no more than shimmer in its glow, but then Col. Church could see that there was some slight movement of the space man's diaphragm.

Esmerelda stood up and faced the rising sun again. Joshua stood beside her. They raised their hands, and turned their rings so that the stones faced outwards once more.

"Amen."

The ritual of healing was over.

The Colonel sat numbed by the power of the ritual, and the authority of the two magicians who had summoned that power from the astral light. His breath was ragged, and the two turned towards him, hearing the sharp intake of air. Joshua had become his ordinary self again; he grinned at the Colonel with jaunty ease, and walked over to him. "How did you like the hocus pocus, Colonel?" Esmerelda stood beside the man from space still, looking down at him. "He will be fine now, if we can just leave him here long enough to gain the strength to walk by himself. It won't take long."

She walked the few steps over to the Colonel. He was still sitting, in precisely the same posture he had been using when the ritual started. Joshua's words had caused him to look up, but he couldn't speak; in fact, his expression was on the edge of fear.

A glance passed between the two magicians, and they looked at him more carefully. "Tell me," said Josh casually. "What did you see down there?"

The Colonel swallowed, his sharp, tenor voice hoarse, his precise delivery muted to slow words. "You left your bodies behind and went off in other bodies. They looked like they were made out of light. I saw the man I thought was dead come back in the same kind of body, and then you all got back in your real bodies, I mean, the ones you're in now …" He paused and swallowed again.

"Yes," said Esmerelda, sitting beside him. "Go on."

"Well, you drew crosses and some other figures in the air, and they stayed where you drew them …"

Joshua waved him to silence. "Col. Church, I am sorry that you were introduced to ritual magic without any previous preparation. We didn't expect you to see anything at all. I hope that you understand that we use this power only for good. I must ask that you keep this utterly secret, as our rituals and keys are not things that could be used by anyone except us who have worked with them. And if someone knew about them, and wished to harm us, he might be able to hinder us from our work. For since these keys are created by thought, they can also be affected by thought. Will you promise not to tell anybody what you saw?"

Church's thin lips moved into the first genuine smile Joshua had seen. "Who would believe me if I told them?"

"By the way." Joshua stood still and lean, with a look of real interest on his face. "You seem to have an unusual amount of aptitude for magic. Would you be interested in pursuing it?"

"I certainly would."

Joshua nodded. "I'm not sure that I would be the correct person to help you, but at any rate I can give you some books to read, and start you on the first disciplines. As soon as this business is over …

The man from space sat up, slowly and without visible difficulty. After he had become totally aware of his environment, looking all about him and completing whatever preparations for action he felt necessary, he arose without a word and walked, steady-legged, to the Colonel, and past him, to stand beside Esmerelda and Joshua.

"You are again with us, my brother." Esmerelda got to her feet and reached out to clasp his hand. "How very glad I am to see you are all right again."

"From Kamaloka to Maya, I am unable to contact my sister." The man from space gazed without blinking at the two.

"He means from the astral plane to our world of illusion, Colonel. The astral light was that which you visualized earlier. It is another kind of universe than this one, much fuller and more vast."

"I can't find her either, my brother," said Esmerelda.

The man from space stood waiting further instruction; Joshua took the Colonel, who was still sitting dazedly on the ground, by the arm, and helped him to his feet, and then led him off towards the small house where Padeyevsky and Behr were waiting. Esmerelda and the man from space followed, reaching the back steps in time to see the Sergeant come barreling through the door, eyes and mouth wide open. "Christ! It's a miracle!" He turned to the Colonel. "If we could teach that to the medics, think of what we could do in combat!"

The newly aware Colonel turned and looked at Sgt. Armstrong as if he were an offending infidel, his mouth tight with scorn, but he could think of nothing to reply. He shook his head and went in through the door, followed by the trio of new-style doctors and patient. The space man was made comfortable on the sofa; he was almost immediately in a state of trance.

"Is he dead again?" the Sergeant wanted to know.

"No, he's just concentrating all his energy on completing the healing process now. He sort of closed off everything he wasn't using, so that he could mend faster. He just needs to build up his strength."

Padeyevsky's face was full of concern. "Did he find anything out about his sister?"

Esmerelda shook her head, long, light hair moving on her shoulders and back. "No, he couldn't find her. I can't either. What can we do?"

Padeyevsky faced the Colonel. "Church, you've seen that this problem is really one of people from another planet." He held up a hand. "Yes, I mean people. You've seen the man. Well, the girl that was kidnapped comes from the same place he does, and looks as much like Esmerelda as this man here looks like Mr. Behr. That was why she was mistaken for Esmerelda. And neither he nor Esmerelda can find her. They don't mean physically, of course, they mean that they can't communicate with her in thought."

The Colonel was still dazed. "What could have happened to her?"

"We have no idea. That's why it's such a life and death matter for us to get going and trace her as far as we can. I think we can at least get to where her physical body was last. Can't we?"

Esmerelda nodded, affirmatively.

Sgt. Armstrong, feeling that the Colonel had been hypnotized somehow, and had lost control of himself and the situation, pushed forward. "Don't listen to this bunch, Colonel. They've figured out some miraculous cure, and they're going to try to get away with the secret. Can't you see that they're all nuts?"

"Sergeant, please withhold your comments." The Colonel turned back to Padeyevsky as though the offending Sgt. Armstrong weren't even present. "I am convinced, Padeyevsky. I don't know how I'm going to explain this to my superiors, but I think the most important thing right now is to help your friends, and the planet they represent, on behalf of the United States government, and the world. Tell me what to do. I'll give you all the help I can."

The Sergeant found it impossible to hold his tongue at this. "Colonel, what about Capt. Crouse? He's still dead, remember, and there has to be some police action taken. You can't just let them go, can you? He had an afterthought, and turned to Esmerelda. "Hey, can you bring him back to life, too?"

Esmerelda shook her head regretfully. "No, Sgt. Armstrong, I'm afraid that in his case the silver cord was severed almost immediately after his physical body had lost its ability to remain conscious. We cannot bring him back. I'm terribly sorry. Was he a friend of yours?"

The Sergeant, who had spent his time in this house looking either scornful or angry, lost those violences from his rather indistinct, stubby features, and took on a look of earnest sadness. "Yes, he was. We worked together for almost two years. And now he's dead, and he wasn't even in uniform. He was a West Pointer, you know." His face threatened to dissolve into tears. "And, if it's your fault ..."

Esmerelda spoke as earnestly as he. "Sergeant, please believe me. We had nothing to do with this terrible accident; we were being held prisoner by the same gun that killed your friend. And we are telling the truth about the need for hurry in finding our other friend."

"Maybe he has a uniform back at headquarters. I could put it on him before we go to tell his wife." The sergeant sat heavily, stocky body somehow less firm than before. "Are you really going to let these people go, sir?"

"Yes, Sergeant, I believe I am. I wish you would think about the magnitude of this. These are representatives of another race. We should do all we can to help them. If you can't realize this yourself, please just follow my orders."

"Yes, sir." The Sergeant sat back in his chair, his mind boggling at the possibility that the Colonel might be correct. What if these were people from outer space. He'd seen lots of science fiction movies, and he knew all about extraterrestrials. Sometimes they sent a few spies down first to get everything ready, and then they always tried to take over the planet.

The havoc wrought by interplanetary war rose in his visions. He contemplated it sourly. Of course the United States would win: the United States always won. But meanwhile, men in uniform had to give their lives-for these spies.

Well, maybe he would go along with the Colonel for a little while. But after he got back to headquarters and told what he knew, there would be people who thought like he did. The spies would be caught, and their information and mission ascertained. The important thing was to make sure that they didn't lose sight of the space man while they went haring off after this alleged girl.

"Well," Padeyevsky was saying, "the most important thing is to find the girl from space as quickly as possible."

"Would a helicopter be of help to you?" asked the Colonel. "A helicopter?"

"I thought perhaps an air search might be faster. I might be able to get one."

Pablo's lip went into his mouth again. "Esmerelda, could you follow the trail in a helicopter?"

"Yes ... yes, I think so. It shouldn't be any different than in the car."

"Can the space man go with us?" asked the Colonel.

"No, I don't think so." Padeyevsky's eye sought Joshua's for advice.

"No," said Joshua. "I should think the best thing for him would be to go somewhere where he could rest. He can do it anywhere really, now that the process has been internalized into his own body. But it would be better in my temple, or at least someplace relatively peaceful and quiet."

Theodore moved forward. "I could drive him back in Pablo's car. I'd be able to give him food, or anything else he might need. I'm the most expendable of the group right now, anyway."

Sgt. Armstrong was listening narrowly, and had found his chance to obtain an amount of control over this situation. "You're not going to let him drive this man off without a guard, are you, sir? Let me go with them, as guard. Crouse's murder still isn't settled yet, sir.

The Colonel looked at Esmerelda. "Would it hurt for the Sergeant to be with your friend while he recovers?"

"No, I don't think so. Could he stay outside the temple, though? No one goes inside the temple without some preparation, usually. It's on Joshua Starr's property. It's a private place."

"That sounds quite reasonable to me. Right, Sergeant?"

"How many doors are there?"

"Just one," said Pablo. He held out the keys of the Mercedes for Theodore, but the Sergeant appropriated them. He reached into his pocket, and handed a card to Theodore, after thumbing through his wallet to produce it. "Here's the name and telephone number of my lawyer, Ted. Any trouble, just give him a call."

The Sergeant was walking jauntily out of the front door. "Let's go.

Sergeant Armstrong was smiling as he went through the door of the little house because he was pleased with himself. He had managed to achieve partial control of this so-called space man, and he was sure that the U. S. Army was, ultimately, going to be very happy with him for that. This business about the helicopter excursion was sheer madness. He saw Joshua come through the door with three sheets from Lily's linen closet. Those were markers for the coming helicopter, presumably. Really bad judgment.

Well, it didn't matter so much, as long as he had the man from space.

Theodore came out of the front door, leading the man from space by the arm. He had more bedding, and he installed it and the man in the back seat of the car.

The Sergeant bent into the car door. "Listen, I'm sorry that I hurt you, mister. Ah, I'm glad that you're feeling better." He stuck out his hand.

The man addressed looked at Armstrong gravely, feeling no instinctive urge to take him by the hand, not understanding what was expected of him. The glance was held for some little time. Then the Sergeant dropped his hand as though it had been stung, his guilt giving way to resentment of the man's snobbishness.

Esmerelda leaned through the other door and took the man from space by the hand, wishing him good-bye and good health. He turned to her, grave and calm. "There shall be no more actions on my part that are initiated by my own thinking."

She leaned over him, loosening her hand from his and touching his cheek. "All is well, my brother. You did well. Rest and regain your strength, and send your spirit to join us in our search when you can."

She backed out of the right door, the Sergeant backed out of the left, and then sat in the driver's seat, rubbing his hands together briskly, and looking out at Theodore. "Well, I imagine you want to get started. I'll drive, so that if your patient needs anything, you'll be free to help him."

Theodore chewed this over. He didn't like the idea of not being in control of the car, but he had no real reason to object, and the point about being free to help his charge was a valid one, as far as he could see. Besides, the Sergeant had appropriated the keys, and was already inserting them into their slot.

Theodore accepted the plan, and busied himself making the man from space comfortable, putting pillows and blankets where they would do the most good. The blonde heads, so much alike in outline, so far different in expression, were close together for several minutes, and the Sergeant, watching them over his right shoulder, could see how the kidnappers might have made the mistake they did. If that girl they kidnapped and that blonde they called Esmerelda looked as much alike as Theodore and this other man did, then the mistake would have been easy to make, especially at night, and in a hurry. Wait a minute, he told himself. You're getting to believe that ridiculous story.

Theodore got into the right side of the front seat, and Sergeant Armstrong started the engine of the big car. After such a hard run, it seemed remarkably healthy; its tone was quiet and even. "Listen," said Armstrong as he backed to the winding road and turned to retrace the path the car had taken so much more hastily earlier during the day. "How did those two get the bullet out, anyway? I didn't see any knives or anything."

"As far as I know, they didn't get it out. It's still in there. His body chemistry will dissolve the bullet, and carry it away in molecular form, just the way we dissolve different foods, and carry the nutrition to various parts of our body, and the waste matter out. Sort of a garbage-in, garbage-out thing."

"What? Oh, yeah. Computers say that, don't they. Well, nobody can dissolve a bullet. That's half an inch of lead and copper. You can't tell me he can get rid of that?"

"As I understand it, that's exactly what he will do with it. See, it's negative, but he is very positive, and he can use the natural healing powers of his body. We can't do that, because we're pretty negative ourselves."

"You make me sound like some kind of monster."

"No, that's not what I meant. I mean, we're all like that on this planet. It's just sort of a negative planet."

"And he's from a positive planet. Is that right?" Is that right?"

The Sergeant turned onto the limited access highway and drove back towards their supposed destination in silence. He was reflecting on the situation, sifting ways of putting these two he guarded in the hands of the proper authorities, who could be trusted to question them, control them, find out what they knew, not leave them to their own devices. It didn't really matter to the Sergeant whether the man was from space or not, whether Behr was telling the truth or not. If they were liars, they had, indirectly or directly, caused a murder, and deserved to be brought to justice. This was peacetime! You couldn't just go around shooting soldiers! And if the man sleeping in the back seat was really from another planet, then the military had far more reason to get him, to get what he knew. The Sergeant visualized the War of the Worlds again in passing, identifying completely with Victory by Earth and the U. S. Army. And, finally, if the two were not connected with the murder, and were not from outer space either, they had still been able to perform a miraculous healing, and this skill had great military use. If medics could heal, very rapidly, the dead and near-dead on the battlefield, you'd have an indestructible army! Sergeant Armstrong nearly took his hands from the steering wheel to rub them together.

It was quite clear that the Colonel's orders or no, his duty was to bring these two into the protective custody of the U. S. Army. The Colonel didn't really have the right to command him, after all. He outranked him, sure, but he wasn't connected in any way with the C.I.D.; the C.I.D. had just agreed to help the Signal Corps on this assignment. His orders actually came from the Criminal Investigations Division, and he was quite sure, although he hadn't had time to find out, that any new orders would be to do just as he was doing now. Bring 'em in.

But there were two of them, and he was only one. He would need to move carefully, and fool them, until he had been able to get word to headquarters to have the car picked up.

The Colonel. That was the trouble with the military. It had so many pseudo-civilians running around with uniforms on. The Colonel would probably have trusted Adolf Hitler if he'd talk well. And these people were actors. Hadn't one of them said that this man from space was an actor? Well, it was his duty to protect the military from civilian tampering. He was, after all, a twenty-year career man. And he knew a civilian when he saw one. That Col. Church was basically a civilian clear through. A reservist given an indefinite extension just because of some fancy degrees.

He couldn't turn directly and go to Fort Benson, that much was clear. He had to admit it: he was a little scared of these two. Normally, he would just have pulled his .45 and handled the situation. But he'd shot one of them with the .45, and it hadn't seemed to hurt him for long. Maybe the other one was the same way, on whatever dope or drugs had made him able to recover like that. The Colonel had said that that little fat man Padeyevsky was a genius and he could have invented something like this. What if he shot these two, and they just kept on coming, like zombies. He could be killed that way. They could strangle him. He'd seen gooks doped up, and he'd shot them two and three times with his carbine, and they'd kept on coming. The .45 was supposed to be a manstopper, but it sure hadn't stopped that space man. Sgt. Armstrong checked on the man in his rear view mirror. Yes, he was still asleep, or pretending to be asleep.

What should he do? Better move while the "space man" was still quiet. There was a rest stop up ahead, with a restaurant and a filling station, in a concrete island right on the super-highway. He pondered his situation, stubby hands clenched on the wheel, jaw muscles moving, and he devised a plan.

Theodore had been watching his driver as closely as he could, and the clenched fingers and jaw were not lost on him; he suspected the Sergeant of getting ready to cross the Colonel's orders. And he was determined not to let him do that. His long, rather narrow face was tense with that determination. The man from space had been put into his protection and, by heaven, he would protect him!

Sgt. Armstrong slowed and pulled into the island's vast expanse of concrete, concession buildings, and shrubs.

"Where're you going? Tank's half full."

"I know, son, but nature calls."

Armstrong carefully parked the car around the corner from the filling station, so that anyone sitting inside the Mercedes couldn't see into the office of the concrete block building. He twisted the key in the ignition and withdrew it in one quick motion, dropping it into his pocket as he headed for the station. Theodore had no choice but to stay put, for the man from space might awaken at any time. It was impossible, so Esmerelda had told him, to be sure just how long it would take the space man's body to assimilate the bullet. And when he had finished, he would simply wake up, totally well. Theodore had to stay with him.

Armstrong had strolled casually around the side of the station, and then sprinted to the pay phone and inserted his quarter to call the operator.

"Operator," announced the operator in the peculiar tones of her kind.

"I want to call collect to the Provost Marshall's office at Fort Benson. I want to talk to Major Harris. My name is Sgt. Armstrong."

There were clicks, buzzes, sounds of other operators' professional conversations, a snatch of popular music from somewhere on the line. Major Harris's voice cut through phantasmagoria to complete the connection, and the line quieted.

"Major Harris here."

"This is Sgt. Armstrong. Listen, sir. I got a real crazy story to tell you. I don't think I can tell you the whole thing over the phone, and I'm in a hurry. Listen, can you have a detail pick up this vehicle here he rattled off the car's license number and its description-at an intersection as soon as possible? The next exit from here is Redland Road. Can you make it in fifteen minutes? It'll take us at least that long to get there."

"We can probably do that ourselves, but I'll call the police in your area and have them hold the car until we catch up."

"Well, sir, if a civilian detail picks them up, have them take us to the hospital off that exit. There's a sick man in the car."

"Will they be likely to be dangerous, your passengers?"

"No, sir, I don't think so. But tell them to approach with caution."

"Will do. What have you got there, Sergeant?"

"I don't really know, but I'll tell you this. They're suspected of selling government secrets. And they might be spies."

"You'll have a detail, Sergeant."

"Thank you, sir."

Armstrong hung the phone back on its metallic cradle and wiped his short, broad hand off on his pants. He hated pay phones; they always felt grimy and polluted, as if they were sour and matted, microscopically, with unspeakable disease. He shoved that hand into his pocket and began to run back to the Mercedes, wishing that he had indeed had time for his ostensible errand. Theodore was sitting much as he had left him, looking casually and aimlessly out the front window; the "space man" was still motionless in the back seat. That was more of a relief than he had anticipated; this case really had gotten him going. He slid under the wheel and inserted key in starter, but there was no sound of life at all from the engine.

He turned to Theodore, who was looking with a vague air of puzzlement at his hand on the key. "Is the battery in bad shape on this car?"

"I don't know. First time I ever rode in it was this morning."

"Well, at least we're right in a filling station." He flipped the door handle and got out of the car again with alacrity, disappearing back around the corner of the station.

Behr moved rapidly, sliding under the wheel, reaching under the dashboard and grabbing the wire that he had disconnected. Replacing it against its terminal, and checking with sudden alarm to see that the Sergeant had indeed gone out of sight, he made sure that the car was in first gear, depressed the clutch, and started the engine. The sound brought Sgt. Armstrong tearing around the corner again, in time to see Theodore leaving the parking and rest area in a dead hurry, accelerator pedal to the floor. The tires made gratifying noises, and Theodore was on the entrance ramp, and then down the expressway and away before the Sergeant had a ghost of a chance to catch him.

The Sergeant kept running at a decreasing rate of speed until he jogged gently onto the ramp, stood in the middle of it, and gave up. He cursed himself at length for having fallen for such a simple trick. And after all his years in the military, too. He ran back to the telephone. A teenager's trick. It was something he was going to be ashamed to report. He'd be hearing about it. Well!

He reached the telephone, panting and beginning to sweat in the slight chill of the morning air, and picked up the sticky receiver again.

The same number was called, and the Major answered quickly. "Yes, Sergeant. What is it now?"

Armstrong told him of his loss of the two, and suggested a roadblock. The Major agreed at once.

"You might send somebody here to get me, too," said the Sergeant.

"Yes, I'll have to, I suppose." The Major's voice sounded halfway between amusement and anger. Armstrong winced, and hung up.

When Padeyevsky's automobile had come under Theodore's hands, it had not found itself in the hands of a master. Theodore was not particularly familiar with the ignition circuit, and he had no idea what would happen if he let the wire go and it came loose again, now that the car was started. Would it stop again? Theodore thought it might. Holding a wire with one's fingers, however, means shifting in some alternate fashion, and after the first, gloriously wound-out gear, there was a series of lurches, hurried steering movements, and perceptible mechanical grinding sounds while second gear was achieved. After this rather harrowing, and surely too eye-catching experience, Theodore determined to let go of the wire, and hang caution, and that seemed to work much better; the engine continued purring confidently.

It now came to Behr that he was going to have to get off of the superhighway before he could lose the Sergeant. He knew that the Sergeant had called ahead; most probably there would be someone waiting at the next exit. Well, he'd have to hope that he could drive by that exit and seek another one. If he stepped on it, perhaps they wouldn't have gotten there quickly enough. He couldn't turn around; the lanes going the other way were across an impossibly deep depression in the road. The Mercedes wasn't a Land Rover. The speedometer needle went up again, over the eighty mile-per-hour mark. In the back seat, the man from space slept quietly on.

Here was the intersection: Redland Road, the signs said, next exit. He turned onto the cloverleaf. There was a police car sitting at the foot of the ramp so as to control the intersection completely. Theodore slammed on his brakes to try and stop far enough in front of the barricade so that he could back up and try, somehow, to drive the wrong way, in the emergency lane perhaps, back to the expressway. But the waiting policeman had obviously had experience at this sort of thing. His engine was running, and just as Theodore came to a full stop and started to back up, he pulled to a stop right in front of him.

"Hands up and out of the car."

Behr considered putting that to music. It certainly was catchy. With an ease born of practice, he maneuvered the door open and swung his torso out onto his legs and balanced, hands up again. Again he was frisked; this time, for a pleasant change, his hands were being allowed to rest on top of the car. There really were refinements to this sort of thing. Lessons on polite detainment, by Theodore Behr. If he ever got his hands down, he could write a book.

One of the brave forgers of the bonds of justice was examining the man in the back seat.

"Is he dead, Charlie?"

"No … I can get a slow heartbeat. I think he's in a coma."

"Yeah. We're supposed to take them to the hospital right away. This all of you there are?" The policeman looked suspiciously at Behr.

That did it. Theodore was normally the mildest of people, the most shy. "No," he grated turning teeth to the sun in an authentic snarl. "There is a confederate in the glove box and an accomplice with a machine gun in the trunk. And if you touch my nose, I'll blow up. I'm mined!"

"OK, Charlie, give me some help with the sick one."

"Yeah. And watch this one. He's a punk."

"Where are you taking us?" Theodore was afraid he had heard the hospital mentioned.

"The hospital."

"No! You can't take us there! That's the worst place for my friend. He doesn't need treatment. He just needs rest."

No one paid any attention to Behr, and the police car drove off the exit ramp towards the hospital, with a frantic, volubly objecting Theodore Behr inside, and a man from a bright planet, with brightness inside him that was dissolving a dim bullet, asleep and calm beside him.

CHAPTER ELEVEN

The police rolled up to the hospital emergency door, and opened the back door of the car to two orderlies, who had come rolling a stretcher out the door to meet them. They picked up the man from space, very efficiently, and rolled him through the doorway into a hall at the near-head of which was a tall desk and an overflowingly fat, dark woman with a typewriter. She rolled forms into the typewriter and put fingers ready over keys.

"Name," she said.

The policeman looked at each other and shrugged, turning to the obviously upset Theodore Behr. "He doesn't have a name," said Theodore.

"Punk. This kid's a punk, Charlie."

"What's your friend's name, kid? Don't tell me that he never told you his name." The taller of the two policemen exaggerated his disbelief and nudged Charlie, who obviously was enjoying the gibe. "But he doesn't have a name, that I know of."

An intern came down the hall towards them, a very young, tired white coat in a white and old-paint-yellow hall.

"General condition ... breathing abnormally slow ... pulse slow ..." The intern started to wheel him past the admissions desk.

"But Doctor ..." The high-pitched, sweet voice did not sound as though it came from such a massive bulk of femininity. "I haven't even got his name yet."

"Admit him on a John Doe. I want to look at him now." The young, slight figure disappeared into one of the doors off the main hallway. The two policemen rushed after the intern, but failed to be first into the examining room after him, because of a mishap with a cart of oxygen bottles as the two tried to turn into the door at once. In the confusion of mutual recoil and recovery of balance, Theodore slipped through.

"Doctor, I have to talk with you. Please don't do anything to this patient. You might kill him!"

"Kill him? That's hardly what I'm here for."

Theodore was very frightened. He had no idea what the space man's body chemistry was like, and what might be of harm to it while it was in this state. He had no idea, really, of what jeopardy the man might be in because of the negativity of the hospital atmosphere against which

Esmerelda had warned. The one thing he was sure of was that he couldn't say, "My friend is an alien, and he's healing himself from dying of a gunshot wound."

"I don't mean that you would do it on purpose, Doctor. I happen to..."

"Look, buddy." Charlie was in the room, and threateningly close. "You let the doc look after this friend of yours. You just butt out. Sit over there," motioning to a chair by the cabinets on the outer wall of the room, "and shut up, or we move you out altogether."

"Can I talk to the Doctor just a minute first, please? This could be a matter of life and death."

Charlie looked at his taller partner. "What do you think, Al?" The senior officer scratched his ear. It certainly was serious, this guy being in a deep coma. Maybe the young punk did know something that would clarify the situation. Be nice of him to speak up for a change, instead of being such a little punk. He didn't want to have anything happen to harm anyone, didn't want the man lying so still there to die. What harm could it do? "OK, sure. Why not. But make it short."

"I happen to know," Theodore started again, "that this man has a very unusual medical history. He has been part of an experimental program at one of the universities in the area. There have been complications, and he has been under the care of a research physician and biophysicist who is the only one who knows precisely what the experiments and their complications were. His body is in very delicate balance, right now, and if you do anything to it at all, I don't know what might happen. You might kill him. Absolutely all he needs is rest. He'll be waking up, perfectly well again, as soon as he's had enough rest."

The young, almost unformed face above the white jacket had an expression of puzzlement. "Where did you pick up these men?" The senior policemen stepped forward. "We got them on the expressway, at the request of the military police. They should be here any time now, and can give you more information. The guy was just like that when we first saw him."

The young doctor ran one hand through hair that already stood away from his forehead, its short ends looking wispy, pre-bald. "Well, I'd like to talk to whomever is responsible for bringing you in in the first place, but until he gets here I don't see any reason to do anything drastic. But I will examine him. It won't hurt him to be looked at, or poked for a little blood, will it?"

Theodore's blue eyes were very dark, almost black, with worry as he made a gesture of ignorance. "I really don't know what might hurt him, and I really urge that you do nothing at all. As I said, he's not in need of anything."

"We'll examine him, nevertheless. He's in coma, and I can't stand here for the rest of the morning waiting for the medical answers to fall from the sky. Nurse!"

A nurse came in and, when told what was needed, left again and returned immediately with a metal basket of equipment. She drew some blood into a test tube, and left to make the tests the intern had requested. The ineffectual looking young doctor, meanwhile, began intoning, to himself and to a woman in nurse's uniform who had come in and sat next to Theodore. "Bradycardia and bradypnea indicated," he said conversationally. "Expect a neurologic problem here, something in the brain. Suggestive of uncal herniation, which has led to ischemia of the brain stem." He opened one of the space man's closed eyes and shined a small light into it, while Theodore squirmed with worry. "Eye is normal!" The intern's voice was surprised. "Thought it would be arreactive," he explained to the recording secretary, who nodded in competent agreement.

"That's all we do here." The intern spoke to the thoroughly unsettled Theodore. "We'll wait here until those lab reports come back, but I'll be going. I have …"

There were voices, then shouts in the hall. "In here, you say?" came the husky voice of Sgt. Armstrong.

"Yes, but …" quivered the voice of the overweight receptionist, as he burst through the door.

"And who are you?" The young doctor was not diffident. This was, after all, his office, for the moment.

"John L. Armstrong, Criminal Investigations Division, United States Army." Armstrong sounded as if he were reading it off a card. "These are my prisoners."

"You're the MP we picked these two up for?" asked the larger policeman.

"Correct. But I'm C.I.D., not MP."

The policeman reappraised the Sergeant. C.I.D. sounded impressive.

"Maybe you can tell me more about this man's condition," said the intern. "I have examined him, but I can't find any reason for the coma. And his eyes …"

"I put a .45 slug in him," spoke the Sergeant unhesitatingly. "Gunshot wound?" The intern was even more puzzled. He had seen gunshot cases, and they didn't put a man in a coma, unless they were in the vital organs, or unless the bullet had glanced off his head. This man didn't have a mark on him, as far as he could determine.

"That's right." The Sergeant stuck out his big jaw a little defensively.

"How did it happen?" asked the doctor.

"I shot him in the line of duty. Listen, these men are spies." The intern looked with considerably more respect at the utterly undone figure of Theodore. "He gave me some story about how I shouldn't touch him, that he'd get better all by himself. Gunshot wound?" The doctor was checking carefully all over the space man's body. "Where?"

"Should be right about in the middle of the back. I don't group more than three inches at that range."

The doctor called for an orderly, and they turned the man from space on the table so that he was lying on his stomach. There was an obvious hole in his shirt, right where the Sergeant had said there would be. It was stained slightly with blood. The man's back itself was without blemish. Neither the Sergeant nor the doctor could see any damage at all.

"Listen, now, that's the man I shot. I'm sure of that." Sgt. Armstrong turned narrowed eyes to Theodore. Maybe these guys were on the level after all.

The intern was carefully, slowly, going over the man's back. "I find basal rales on the left side. He could have inflammation there." He searched the back very thoroughly for evidence of any other discomfort, and could find none at all. "I don't know what to tell you, Sergeant, but this is not the man you shot. There is no evidence of gunshot wound, or any wound at all, except for slight inflammation on the left side of the diaphragm here."

The Sergeant's jaw was clenched. "I would stake my life that I shot this man."

The intern was older in his profession than he was in his emotional life, and his pride was stung. "Sergeant, there is no bullet in this man."

"I'll prove it to you," the Sergeant said in loud and ringing tones. "Just put him under the X-ray machine. That'll show bullets, won't it.

"It certainly would, if there were any bullet to show. But there isn't and I'll stake my professional reputation on that. For that matter, any fool can see that this man doesn't have a scratch on him."

"You're just afraid I'm right. Don't you care more about your patient than you do about being right?" The Sergeant was thrusting his jaw quite close to the insignificant face of the poor intern. "Listen, you give this boy an X-ray, and you'll find out what's wrong with him."

The intern looked at the red face in front of his for a few seconds, then pulled the cumbersome X-ray equipment from the ceiling and manipulated it briefly, taking the picture the Sergeant had requested, removing a hastily-labeled plate from the slot under the table, and sending it to be developed.

It came back in a few minutes and was handed to the doctor, who held it up to the light and stared, mouth gawking open.

"There it is," said Sgt. Armstrong. "Right where I said it was going to be."

Both of them looked for a minute at the X-ray. There was definitely a bullet there, in the diaphragm. It looked like it might have nicked the stomach, but it was lodged safely away from vital organs or bones. That must have been why there was so little blood, thought the intern. Missed the great vessels.

"Hey!" Sergeant Armstrong was puzzled in his turn. "Are those pictures accurate as to size? How big is that bullet?"

"These X-rays are very accurate." The doctor took an instrument from one of the drawers in the wall cabinet. "That bullet is almost exactly a quarter of an inch in diameter."

"But listen. I shot that man with this." The Sergeant produced his .45. "And the bullet is almost twice that big. Could you have gotten the thing on a slant, so it would distort the size?"

The intern looked dubiously at the sergeant's automatic. It was very obviously a .45. He pulled the equipment down again, taped another plate, and made a zzap sound; the negative came back in another five minutes. There was no bullet on it at all.

Theodore had retreated to the very edge of the room, and watched the brightly lit occupants cluster around the negatives and the examining table, talking, gesturing, looking strained and yellowed in the light, like men in a boxing ring, or people reciting in a classroom. He was the first to see the man from space open his eyes and then move to get up, and was on his feet instantly to give support. None seemed needed, however. As he had when he awakened in the country meadow earlier, the space man looked carefully all around the small room, examining its citizens.

Theodore told him, "We're not at Joshua's because the Sergeant here decided to have us picked up and sent to a hospital. Now that you're up again, though, I don't see how they can keep us here. See, Doctor?" Theodore nodded towards his friend, now calmly sitting and looking around, seemingly as healthy as anyone else in the room. "I told you he would be all right if you just let him sleep. And he is."

The intern quickly checked the vital signs: pulse, temperature, breathing rate. All were perfectly normal now, no longer slowed. The nurse who had drawn blood came in, as if on cue. And, as if expecting her to speak her lines next, the rather dazed group silently waited. The audience rather disconcerted her, but she rallied, and read from her paper. "'Crit 50%. Glucose 100. No ketone bodies. CBC is 6,000, with 68% poly's; no left shift noted. Lymphs and mono's 25%. That all, Doctor?"

The intern took the paper from her hand and looked it over again. There was no evidence in any of the tests that there had ever been anything wrong with the patient. No evidence of any gunshot wound, or loss of blood. "That's all, thank you. No, wait a minute. Could you please get me a test for lead?"

"Spectroscopy?" The nurse looked surprised. "That's right."

"Well ..." The nurse hesitated. She wasn't qualified on that equipment. "I'll have to hunt up Dr. Price."

The very large lady in white came through the door as the lab technician went out of it. "Doctor, I still haven't admitted this patient."

"Ask him whatever you want to, Maude. He's awake now."

"Thank you, Doctor." The small, rather pretty mouth gleamed teeth at the pale, handsome man from space. "Now then. Name, please."

Theodore jumped into the verbal gap. "He's a friend of mine, and ..."

"I have no name."

The doctor began raising his wispy, thin eyebrows and watching closely. He was attending a seminar on psychiatric techniques. The plump cheeks quivered into speech again. "But everybody has a name."

"I have no name."

"Well, what's your address?"

There was silence. The man from space regarded Maude's bewildered face and poised pencil with grave detachment.

Theodore cut through the daunted silence. "Please, don't question him. You'll not need that now. When this is straightened out, I can answer any questions you need ..."

The intern interrupted. "Wait. I believe we have some difficulty here. I'm going to put him in observation overnight.

The Sergeant pushed forward, getting ready to object. He was overridden.

"And we'll have a psychiatrist's report. But right now ...," the intern turned to the coquettish woman overflowing the chair next to the table, "I'll have the psychiatrist ask the questions, Maude. He's not responding to you."

Maude arranged herself with injured dignity, and left.

"Now, let's look at this." The doctor was getting more and more excited by the X-rays and by the man's recovery. "You say he was under treatment by a biophysicist?" he said to Behr. "Was the treatment, all or in part, for this gunshot wound?"

Behr considered and nodded affirmatively. "That's right. He was treated so that his own body would assimilate the bullet, and get rid of it internally. That's why he was asleep like that."

The doctor was nodding. "And that was why the bullet got smaller, and then disappeared on the X-rays."

He sat and thought, looking reflectively at the still-motionless man from space and thinking hard, trying to remember what he had learned in his courses about the body. Could the body be put into some sort of hypnotic state and, somehow suggestible, did it have the ability to remove a bullet?

"Mister Armstrong, what's in a .45 bullet?" asked the intern. "Lead, and some copper."

Hmmm. The copper was easy enough. There was a protein in the blood, ceruloplasm, which could dissolve copper and pass the ions to ... where would it go? It would be passed out through the feces. That could be checked. Now the lead. That was harder. That was a poison to the system. But-yes, the bullet had nicked the stomach, almost surely. There was plenty of acid there to reduce the lead to double-plus ions. That would get it as far as the kidney, and-yes, there was an enzyme in the kidney that recognized lead. Then the active transport system of the proximal convoluted tubule of the kidney would move it out of the basi recti to the lumen. It could pass from there as urine. That could be checked too, lead in the urine.

"Please tell the nurse on duty to come in here," said the doctor to one of the policemen. The smaller obliged.

"Nurse, could we please find a room for this gentleman? I want some additional tests too, please. Check the stool for copper traces, and run a midstream urine sample to test for lead."

These were most peculiar orders, and the Doctor was only an intern. "Yes, all right," said the nurse, looking askance at the young face.

"And, nurse, see if you can get Dr. Harvey in here as soon as possible, for a preliminary interview with the patient." Dr. Harvey was the staff psychiatrist; they shared him with another regional hospital in the next county.

"Just a minute." The Sergeant had been watching the apparently fully recovered "space man," and he had reconsidered his former silent agreement to letting the man stay overnight. "I'm ready to take him with me now. He's got no need to stay here."

The intern could see the paper he would write as a result of brilliantly diagnosing this case going out the window. "No, Sergeant, the patient will remain here overnight for further tests."

The door opened again. "Dr. Harvey!" The intern rushed into speech, quickly outlining the case to the psychiatrist.

"Where's the patient's information?" The mild, competent looking man, speaking quietly and briskly, looked around at the nurse with pad and pencil who was trailing him.

"We haven't been able to get any, Doctor. That's why you were called."

"Very well then." Dr. Harvey took the chair that Maude had vacated, closest to the examining table. "Hello there. What's your name, please?"

The calm, pleasant face, wide-set eyes gravely fixed on this new questioner, answered, "I do not have a name."

"What are you called?"

"I do not have a name."

Harvey looked closely at the man's face; it seemed perfectly congenial; no hostility. "Have you forgotten your name? I mean, there has to be something, some heading, that gets put on this paper." Harvey waved the admissions sheet. "What name do you suggest I put on it?"

The space man remembered well the difficulty he had caused others by initiating actions, and was not going to get up and leave, as he would otherwise have done, in the face of this utter confusion. He simply sat, trying very hard, and failing, to make any sense at all out of these questions.

"How about Charlie? Would you just as soon have the name, Charlie, for the time being? We're going to have to have your name for the record before long, but will Charlie do for now?"

There was a pause. The man from space attempted to find some meaning in those words. He could not. He sat quietly, smiling the universal small smile of well-meaning and slight embarrassment.

"Say," said the psychiatrist. "Do you feel OK? We can do this another day, if you'd rather." He ignored frantic signals from the intern.

Silence from the space man.

"Look, this is part of my job, that's all. I ask the questions, you answer them. If I ask the questions and you don't answer them, then I can't do my job."

He waited. No response.

"All right. We'll do it tomorrow. I'm glad to have met you." He stood up. "Good day."

"Don't quit yet, Dr. Harvey!" The intern was most unhappy over the brevity of the interview. "I had hoped for a diagnosis of condition, and a report, sir, so that I could work better with this patient from a medical point of view."

Harvey grinned; he hadn't seen any evidence of anything medically wrong. He said so. "However, I'll give you that report now. I'm just not going to push that boy. I want to be friends with him so that he'll talk to me, eventually, when he's ready to."

He sat back down, and the nurse hovered. "I was going to do this in my office, but I'll do it right here, if you're anxious to know what I think. You'll have to clear the room, though. Patient goes too."

"Could you wait in the hall, please?" The intern opened the door and shooed everyone through it. The space man followed, at Theodore's suggestion, and quietly took his place with the little group outside the door.

The psychiatrist dictated to the nurse: "Subject is an adult male. He appeared normal in every possible way. The only noted abnormality was a complete absence of responsive speech; he refused to respond when asked his name and, while remaining relatively pleasant, remained completely uncommunicative. The possibility of catatonic schizophrenia, or a form of other neurotic, or possibly psychotic, reaction, with catatonic symptomatology, remains a very strong possibility. A neurological work-up is strongly indicated here, particularly testing for brain damage. Affect appeared bland. There was no apparent hostility; however, it was impossible to achieve rapport with the subject."

Dr. Harvey rose and smiled at the young intern. "Will that do, Doctor?"

As the unfinished face collected itself to say 'thank you,' the older man turned and walked out the door, trailing his secretary. The Sergeant poked his head through to say, "We'll be going now, Doctor."

"Wait! I haven't ..."

"Nothing wrong with him any more, is there?" The Sergeant's jaw was shoving forward again.

"No, not that I can see. But ..."

"This is a matter of national security. Thank you for your help. Good-bye."

The Sergeant walked past the admissions desk, Theodore and the man from space right beside him, and the two policemen following closely. As the emergency door closed shut behind them, there was one last wail from Maude. "I never did admit that man!" The plump cheeks quivered with the anticipated trouble from her supervisor. "How'm I ever going to make that right? Huh?"

The intern came over. "Maude, tell you what. Forget about the whole episode. I'll take the record myself. OK?"

She nodded, fluttering her lashes. The ineffectual intern walked sadly down the dingy hall. Nothing like this would ever happen again. He would never be famous after all. He lay down on the examining table the space man had just left, and closed his eyes.

Sgt. Armstrong closed the emergency door, the intern, the whole episode out of his mind and herded Theodore and the man from space back into the police car that had brought them to the hospital.

"Better snap the cuffs on this one. He's a troublemaker. Last time he got in a car, he stole it."

The senior officer nodded agreement. "Yeah. I spotted him as a punk when I picked him up, didn't I, Charlie?" The cuffs went on. "What about this guy here?" asked Charlie.

Sgt. Armstrong looked at the so-called space man. He remembered the man's miraculous recovery, and wondered what other supernatural powers he had. "Yeah, better put them on him, too."

Charlie did so, and the metal was suddenly cold and hard against the space man's wrists. He tested his gleaming bracelets; there was almost no opportunity for movement with this device on, making it very difficult for him to serve himself or his fellow man. He puzzled this over in his mind, and found it surprising and incomprehensible. It would be a great pleasure to complete his tour of the mental planes of this planet, and find the explanation for the motives behind this rather peculiar action.

The whole ride was a series of inexplicable scenes and actions, especially after the police car was admitted through the main gate at Fort Benson and Sgt. Armstrong had given instructions on how to get to the Provost Marshall's office. The man from space sat enthralled by the various units they passed; many devices which he saw were large and complex, and yet seemed to have no meaning or purpose whatever; he was completely bewildered by the objects that passed his line of vision as they drove by part of an armored division's motor pool. The M-60 tanks seemed somehow attractive to him, with their long, slender 105-millimeter guns projecting so high and far above the stubby, heavy undercarriages; perhaps, he thought, these are art forms, and the long projecting tubes, lifted skyward, represent man's eternal seeking of truth.

This thought pleased him greatly, and he considered it for some few seconds, hopeful that he had penetrated one of the myriad mysteries that he was encountering on this planet.

He watched as a group of recruits in basic training marched by in almost perfect step, rifles carried at sling-arms, canteens and bayonets slapping rhythmically and tunefully against their thighs. They seemed most cheerful, and he wondered what possible objective could create such a unity of purpose in the entities involved. He envisioned some very complete gathering and uplifting of these men's spirits, and he rejoiced with them at their being linked so in brotherhood. How closely they moved, how complete a unity of mind and thought must exist, for they all knew what each of the other entities was about to do, and moved in harmony. Just as their police car passed the head of the column, at the command of the drill sergeant, the recruits broke into the chant so common to training units:

Left, right, left,

You had a good home, but you left.

This was a beauty of harmony between spirits that the man from space wished to express, and he turned to Theodore with eyes shining with happiness. "Those who dwell here are truly at one with themselves and with the creation. They enjoy great unity!"

Theodore turned slightly green. He could not speak in answer to the space man, but the big policeman responded. "Is this guy still on dope,

Meanwhile the man from space had eagerly turned his head again, drinking in the sight of brotherhood as they passed other marching units. When the car came to a stop in front of the building which housed the Provost Marshall's office, the big policeman took him by one arm and pulled him into the front office, right behind the Sergeant and Theodore.

"I've got to see Major Harris," said Sgt. Armstrong to the desk sergeant.

"He's expecting you."

Sgt. Armstrong turned to the policemen. "Thanks a lot. We really appreciate your cooperation. We can take care of these prisoners now with no trouble."

"Glad to have been of service. Any time," said the big policeman, under the permanent impression that Behr and the man from space were military personnel. "We'll take these cuffs with us, if you don't mind."

"No problem," said Armstrong. "Go right ahead. They're on a military post now."

The cuffs were retrieved and, with his head bent, the senior officer grinned somewhat indulgently at the obvious twenty-year army man. He'd been in the army himself, and recognized the philosophy common to such men as Sgt. Armstrong. He departed, the sets of handcuffs ringing together as he and his fellow officer went through the door.

"Go right on in, Sgt. Armstrong," said the desk sergeant, motioning Theodore and the space man to seats along the front wall of the waiting area.

Armstrong did so, coming through the Provost Marshall's door and stopping the correct three paces from the rather plain wooden desk, behind which sat Major Harris. He saluted sharply. "Sir. Sgt. First Class John Armstrong to see the Provost Marshall."

"Yes, Sergeant. Sit down." Harris returned the salute. "Now, suppose you tell me what this is all about. We were very sorry to hear about Capt. Crouse."

"Yes, sir. Well, I really don't know where to begin. But, listen, first I want to tell you about Capt. Crouse. I was worried …"

"We have a fairly full report on Capt. Crouse. Lt. Sheridan went down to pick up his body, and made a preliminary investigation, and the civil authorities have taken that deputy sheriff's wife who shot him into custody. Although, from what I hear, the whole thing sounds like a ridiculous mistake."

"Yes, sir. It certainly was. But I have brought in the two .. . well, the, ah—" Armstrong realized suddenly that his superior officer might think it a bit odd for him to claim the possession of two interplanetary spies, one of them from another planet.

"Yes, Sergeant?"

"Well, sir, I've got … well, I've got two men out there …" The Major waited until it was obvious the Sergeant needed more prodding. "I gathered that you had two men to bring in from your telephone call earlier. Now, what are their units?"

"Ah … well, sir, they don't have any units. In fact, they're not in the military at all."

"Not in the military?" The Major's face underwent a swift change from interest to the beginning of anger. "Then what are we doing with them? Do you realize what trouble you could get us into if these two men are civilians, and they can prove we detained them? This is serious, Sergeant."

"Yes, sir, I know," said Armstrong. "I thought it was, too, and that's why I sort of took matters into my own hands. Listen, just let me tell it from the beginning."

"You'd better," said Major Harris grimly. "And I do hope it's good."

Sgt. Armstrong twisted nervously in his chair, one hand going to pull at his collar. "Well, sir, it all began when Capt. Crouse and I were assigned to help Col. Church investigate the leakage of certain information about experimental work. This was all top secret. We were watching Padeyevsky because he had personally set up some of the experimental program." The sergeant took a breath. "So I was watching the Padeyevsky place, well, not the house, exactly, it's a long driveway, real long, and you can't see the house. But it's the only way you can get to the house."

He paused. The Major nodded his understanding.

"So, anyway, I saw this Cadillac go up the driveway. I didn't know who they were. But they didn't come back out, and then Padeyevsky's car went into the driveway. So I wondered whether the Cadillac had gone to the other house. There are two houses off that driveway, sir. But I went to this other place, and no Cadillac. So I thought I would walk back to the Padeyevsky place, to see if I could find out anything that way. Well, sir, just as I got fairly close to the house, here comes the Cadillac, and I can see that they're shooting at Padeyevsky's tires. So I ran back to my car and called Capt. Crouse to tell him that something was up. I guess he must have called Col. Church, because he showed up with the Captain. They both live on post, see, and I guess it would have been fairly easy

"Yes, Sergeant, said Major Harris. "Go on."

Yes, sir. Well, they both got into my car, and I was starting to tell them about the situation when a little sports car turned into the drive. We were off the road, hidden. Well, anyway, it was just a few minutes before Padeyevsky's car came out of the driveway. They must have changed the tire that was shot out. We decided to follow it, since it looked like everyone that had been at the house was in the car. The Colonel stayed with me, because he wanted to ask me some more questions, and Captain Crouse got back into his own car, and we started out following them. It ended up at this deputy's house. We missed them when they ducked into the garage, but Capt. Crouse backtracked and found them."

"Now you're getting to the killing of Captain Crouse," said the Major. "I want to see how your story compares with Lt. Sheridan's."

"Yes, sir. Well, as I understand it, it was one big foul-up. The deputy's wife just shot him before she knew what was going on. She thought Captain Crouse had his gun out and was going to shoot her husband. She thought he was a criminal. I guess she was just upset."

Major Harris nodded. "Yes, that matches the Lieutenant's story so far. But what in the world are you doing with two civilians?"

"Well, sir, I was just coming to that. You see, the Colonel started questioning the Padeyevsky group-there were five of them: Padeyevsky himself, an actor named Joshua Starr, a fantastic looking blonde named Esmerelda-would you believe that, a young guy named Behr, and another guy who looked a lot like Behr, maybe they were related, only he never said anything, and it seemed like he was crazy, or on some kind of trip. He just sat around with his eyes closed. Anyway the colonel started questioning this group, and I was just listening, until the space man just got up and walked out of the house. And of course ..."

"The WHAT, Sergeant?"

"The space man, sir. The man from space. That's why I brought these two in. I've got him out in the front office there ..." There was stony silence from the Major.

"Well, he just got up and walked out, and Col. Church tells him to halt or he'll shoot, you know, and he doesn't. So the Colonel shoots him, or shoots at him; he said it was a warning shot, but I didn't know that. So I backed him up. When the Colonel was starting to shoot at him, sir, that's when they let it out that he's from another planet. One of them says, 'We've got to stop the space man,' or something. That's when we found out. Anyway, the Colonel starts shooting at him;, and what am I to do but back up the Colonel, so I let him have it in the middle of the back with my .45 Gold Cup."

"Wait a minute, Sergeant. You shot the man that's sitting in the front office right now with a .45?"

"Yes, sir. Right square in the middle of the back."

The Major went to the door of his office and looked around the edge of it, trying to spot the victim. "I don't see any casualties out there, Sergeant. Just two youngsters, who look like they're brothers. Both healthy as horses, from the looks of them."

"The one on the right, sir. That's the space man."

"Then you missed him. Is that right?"

"Oh, no, sir. I got him right in the middle of the back. I never group more than three inches at that range."

"Sergeant, I have never heard of a man that was hit in the middle of the back with a .45 recovering, if he lived at all, in less than a month or six weeks. This man is in good shape."

"Well, sir, I know. It's one for the medics, sir. I told you it was going to be a funny story. That's why I began to believe that he really was a space man. Because he did recover."

The Major looked at Sgt. Armstrong. He looked at him long and hard. The harsh color in his cheeks, the shiny, over-bright look in his eyes-the

Sergeant could be having a nervous breakdown. He walked slowly back to his seat and sat behind it. "Go on, Sergeant."

"Yes, sir. Well, the gorgeous blonde came running up after the man from space hit the dirt, and the Colonel had examined him and said he was dead, and she said, no, that he wasn't dead, and could they bring him back to life. Well, they talked for a while, and the Colonel said they could, so they picked him up-and he was a dead one too, Major-and took him down behind the house into this field, and then they did a lot of mumbo-jumbo over him, and the girl and the actor ..."

"Where was the Colonel all this time?"

"Well, I was back at the house with the rest of the party, but the Colonel went down to the field with them, and watched real close."

"Go on."

"Well, they're waving their hands around in the air, and saying these foreign words, and after a while, they come back, and the space man's walking with them, under his own steam. They just brought him back to life, somehow. We could sure use that in combat. Anyhow, after they all came back to the house, I could see that they'd done something to the Colonel while he was down there, hypnotized him or something, because he was believing everything they said, and he did whatever they wanted him to. They wanted him to go off and rescue the space girl, who ..."

"The WHAT?"

"Yes, sir, you see they had been driving so early because the girl from space, the one that had come with the space man, had been kidnapped, and ..."

"KIDNAPPED?"

"That's right, sir. She had been kidnapped by these syndicate people, and the Padeyevsky group was after them to get her back. Anyway, that's what they told Col. Church, and he believed them right down the line, and said he would help them any way he could. Well, Sir, I could tell that the Colonel wasn't right any more, you know, that he wasn't in control of the situation. I mean, you had to be there to get the feel of the thing, if you see what I mean. Anyway, he told me to just let the man from space and this young fellow Behr go back to their temple ..."

"TEMPLE?" The Major's face had given up trying to reflect all that he heard, and a curious anarchy reigned, each feature twisting a little, in independence from the others. With its color, it was bearing more and more resemblance to a bowl of chili con carne "What temple?"

"The actor, Starr, he had a temple, apparently, sir. And we were supposed to go to it. It's very near here."

"Yes, I know of Mr. Starr. I've seen him on television. He has a temple? Well, never mind. Go on, Sergeant."

"Yes, Sir. Like I said, you had to be there, really, to get just how everything happened …"

"I know this is a difficult story, Sgt. Armstrong. Just go on."

"All right, sir. Anyway, normally, sir, I would have respected the Colonel's orders, of course, but the Colonel had this far-off look to him, and his eyes were real glazed, if you see what I mean. And, really he's in the Signal Corps, and I'm in the C.I.D., and I thought maybe I knew more about criminal investigations than he did, because he sure was letting this situation get out of hand. I mean, to let a spy from another planet just go off to some temple, if you see what I mean. So I thought I'd better bring them here, instead of going to the temple."

Major Harris seemed to be having difficulty breathing. Armstrong swallowed. "Don't you see, sir, I couldn't let these spies get away. It was the only thing to do, to bring them in here for questioning. I mean, I really don't know whether they had anything to do with the deputy's shooting Capt. Crouse, but I bet they have military information that we need."

"All right, Sergeant. So you phoned me?"

"Yes, sir. And they escaped right after I called you, but we got them anyway, and took them to the hospital. The space man was still recovering from being killed, see, and he was in a coma or something."

"And the space m …" The Major caught himself. "And this man recovered in the hospital, then?"

"Yes, sir, that's where he was, but they didn't do anything to cure him, give him any medicine or anything; they just let him sleep there for an hour or so, and did some tests with his blood, and examined him the way doctors do, you know, with a stethoscope and stuff, and then he just got up from where he was lying, and he was perfectly all right. Just like that Behr guy said he'd be."

"He was up and about with a .45 slug in him?"

"By that time, he didn't have a .45 in him, sir. It was a .25 on the first X-ray, and by the time he got up, it wasn't there at all."

"And then you took the two men and brought them here. Is that right? Is that the whole story?"

"Yes, sir that's it. So now we've got an interplanetary scout out there, and ..."

"Thank you, Sergeant. That will be all for now. If you could just wait outside, while I talk to these people." Major Harris got up and escorted the Sergeant to the door of his office. He was severely doubting the Sergeant's competence at this point, for the whole story was unbelievable, and that last part made absolutely no sense at all. None. "These men are civilians, Sgt. Armstrong. I wish you had thought of that earlier. Unless they are both very kind to us, we may be in very hot water."

"But, sir, one of them's an advance scout from another planet, so he must be in the military there. So that puts him under our jurisdiction, doesn't it? And Behr is his accomplice, so that makes him an accessory, doesn't it, sir?"

The Major ushered Sgt. Armstrong through the door without answering these queries. Spy from another planet! Any fool could see that these were just two normal boys, college kids, probably. He beckoned the man from space into his office, and with Theodore's prompting, the man complied cheerfully and sat down, at the Major's invitation, in the chair that Sgt. Armstrong had just vacated.

The Major cleared his throat. "Before you speak, I would like to read from the Uniform Code of Military Justice." The Major had absolutely no rights of jurisdiction over this man, and he knew it.

But he thought that perhaps, by reading this as was routine with military personnel, the boy would be soothed into compliance. He was reading Article 31, the part informing any accused of his right to counsel and his right to remain silent, since anything that he might say could be used against him in court.

The space man looked at him steadily as the words were read to him, trying to fathom their meaning. As far as he knew, words could not be used as tools on the physical plane, for the power they set in motion was mental. Perhaps the man in front of him was giving him some sort of information about artificial elementals and other summoned forces from the mental planes. This was very interesting; he had not known that the people of this planet were this much aware of any but the physical plane.

It was good news. This was truly a fine place, this Provost Marshall's place. The brotherhood of the people who walked about the grounds, and their harmonious songs, and now evidence of knowledge of the higher planes.

"Is that clear?" asked the Major.

"Yes," said the space man, smiling eagerly at this man, who might be a teacher. He hoped that he could be of service to him. Now that his metal bracelets were off, he was more than happy to help in whatever way might be necessary.

"What is your name?" asked the Major. "I have no name."

"Well, then ... how does Mr. Behr call you?"

"I am not called with words."

"What, then?"

"I am called with thought."

"Oh boy," thought Major Harris. The Sergeant was right about one thing, at least. We have a weird one here. He'd have to try a different approach.

"I understand that Sgt. Armstrong shot you with his pistol."

"Yes."

Harris stared. "You were shot, then?"

The space man stared silently at the major, not recognizing the words as a question.

"Where did the bullet hit you?"

The man from space put one hand behind his back and, as well as he could, touched the place where the bullet had entered his body. Harris walked over behind his chair, leaned over the man, and started tugging at his shirt. "Do you mind?" he asked. Although the man had no reaction to this query at all, not understanding its meaning, the Major went ahead and pulled the slightly stained shirt up anyway. There was no evidence at all of any wound; the fair skin was as smooth as a child's. It seemed obvious to Harris that the Sergeant had somehow brought in the wrong man. Maybe someone had substituted this boy for Armstrong's victim. He wondered how they managed to do it. Perhaps Armstrong had been right about the hypnosis. Perhaps these people had managed to hypnotize not only Col. Church, but Sgt. Armstrong as well. That was really weird. He shook his head, went back to his desk, and asked several more questions of the man from space, but they didn't seem to mean anything to him, for he sat silently, not answering or saying a word. Finally he gave up. Perhaps he could get more out of the other one. "That'll be all, thank you. Could you send Mr. Behr in, and stay out in the front office while I talk to him?"

The man from space did so with cheerful alacrity. Behr walked in looking sour, distinctly sour. Major Harris read the same words to him, and motioned for him to sit down. Theodore did so.

"Now, what's your name?" asked the Major.

"Sorry, Major, but I'm not saying anything. And I've seen enough television to know that I'm entitled to call my lawyer right now." He had Pablo's lawyer's phone number very handy.

Oh boy, thought Harris. First a nut, and now a guardhouse lawyer. But he was a good officer, and had had a long time to learn how to keep his temper while talking to witnesses and suspects. He would be kind to this one. Maybe that might help. It often did. Appeal to sympathy and all that. "Look, son, I don't want to hurt you or your friend. I really want to help you. This seems so mixed up; I just want to get to the bottom of it, so that we can all go home. Off the record, I'm rather confused as to what happened out there and, frankly, your version of the story would be of great help to me."

"Major, I'll be glad to give you my version of this, just as soon as my lawyer arrives."

The Major squirmed inwardly. The boy had him. He wasn't going to be bluffed. He'd better give up, and get these two off his hands before the whole business went up in smoke, which it would as soon as a lawyer found out that civilians were being detained by the army. "Just a minute," he said and went through the door of his office, found Sgt. Armstrong's eye, and beckoned. Armstrong came quickly. "Yes, sir?"

"I can't keep them any longer, Sergeant. That Behr fellow called my bluff. I'm either going to let them go or turn them over to the civilian police right now. Do you want to press charges against them?"

"Yes, sir. I certainly do."

Harris walked back behind his desk, and smiled a hearty smile at Behr. "You can call your lawyer from my phone, right here. Tell him to meet you at the police station in town. We're going there right now."

Theodore did just that, and then, for what seemed to be the seventy-fifth time that day, he was hustled into a car with the man from space: this time a military police sedan, with an MP driving. The Major and the Sergeant were both along; the Major did not really trust Armstrong to remain rational, and wanted to know first-hand anything that might have repercussions in his department. In fifteen minutes, they were standing in front of the desk sergeant at the police station.

"Names," droned the desk sergeant.

"This one's Theodore Behr, and this one doesn't have a name." The desk sergeant entered Behr's name on a piece of paper. "Alias on the other one?"

"No alias, either," said Armstrong.

"John Doe," droned the desk man. "What are the charges?" Sgt. Armstrong was ready for that one. "Interplanetary espionage," he said loudly.

The desk sergeant came to life for the first time, looking up from his papers and squinting in disbelief. "Did you say interplanetary espionage?"

"That's exactly right."

"You can't charge him with that. There's no law against interplanetary espionage. There is no such thing as interplanetary espionage. Give me something there's a law against!"

"But there's got to be a law against it. These men are spies!"

"Look, I don't care what there's got to be. There's no law on the books anywhere about interplanetary espionage, for Christ's sake. Make some charge we got a law for."

"But I'm telling you, these men are spies," said Armstrong. "It's treason. I had to shoot one of them for it."

"Oh, yeah? Where's he shot? Which one? Do we need a doctor?"

"No, he's OK now."

"Just nicked him, eh? Bounce off his head, or some freak thing?"

"No, I shot him right square in the middle of the back. I group about three inches at …"

The Major cut in. "Sergeant, this is a very unusual case," he said to the desk sergeant. "It's pretty obvious that we can't charge these men with interplanetary espionage, and-he twinkled professionally I'm not very sure they're guilty of that. But they were present at a very nasty little incident earlier today, the shooting of Capt. Crouse."

"A shooting? Where'd it happen?"

"Out in Spencer County," volunteered Armstrong. "Oh, that's out of our jurisdiction."

Major Harris turned to Sgt. Armstrong. "Is there anything else that you can possibly charge them with?"

The Sergeant thought as fast as he could, trying to come up with a charge, any charge at all, to hold them with while he somehow convinced someone that they were passing up the chance to get information about an interplanetary war. "Vagrancy?" he said, a little wildly. "How about vagrancy? I bet neither one of them has a dime on him."

"We are the guests of Pablo Padeyevsky," said Theodore, "and I should imagine that he is one of the richest men in this county." The desk sergeant recognized that name. The man was indeed an important resident, and the source of a great deal of tax income. He had no desire to mix with him. "If he and his friends are with Padeyevsky, they're not vagrants," he told Major Harris.

"Well, wait a minute. I know. Resisting arrest. They resisted arrest."

"What arrest, Sergeant?" asked the man behind the desk. "We haven't arrested anyone, and you can't arrest non-military personnel."

"Well, they stole the car that I was driving."

"That was Professor Padeyevsky's car," said Behr, "and we were simply driving it home."

"Is that right? Did he drive away in his own car?"

"Ah ... yes, I guess so ..."

Padeyevsky's lawyer came through the door of the police station at this point, and it was all over in a few minutes. After a very short battle, marked by several outbursts of "But these men are interplanetary SPIES." from Sgt. Armstrong, and several placating speeches by Major Harris, Theodore and the man from space walked out the door of the station, got in the lawyer's car, and drove off towards Pablo Padeyevsky's house. Theodore was very tired and very hungry, but they were free. Scot free.

CHAPTER TWELVE

Esmerelda had very little trouble following the akashic trail of the girl from space, and after almost an hour in the helicopter, they had found the cabin where she had been taken by the burly Marv and the beak-nosed little Elmo. The terrain was wooded and very rough, and there was the added difficulty of the lake and its shore; no landings could be made there. They decided to put down about half a mile from the cabin, setting down over the rise of the nearest hill from the cabin, far enough away so that they could escape detection by its inhabitants and making their approach on foot down an old dirt trail which looked as if it might have been a logging road at one time.

They had made their reconnaissance at a high enough altitude that no one should have spotted them from the ground unless he were sitting right in the clearing in front of the cabin looking straight up; the forest which covered the side of the small hill was very dense, part maple and oak, part pine, and no one could have seen them without really trying. Padeyevsky didn't think that anyone would really be trying; it couldn't be suspected that he could track the kidnappers, and even if he could, that he would have access to a helicopter this quickly.

The landing was uneventful, and Col. Church climbed down from the UH1-B first, feeling rather like the leader of an infantry platoon. He instructed the pilot to stay with his machine and wait for their return. Then he led the small group of Pablo, Esmerelda and Joshua down the road. He walked slowly, carefully down the dry dirt trail, taking in the lovely reddish glow of the turning maple leaves, the variegated yellows and oranges of the oak; this was a lovely autumn. The country was quite deserted; only a few robins and grackle that left here to sing, this late. The squirrels were making the most noise, methodically cutting on their harvest of nuts, dropping the cuttings through the branches at the edge of the forest, lying flat and still at the approaching footsteps. Shadows filtered down on the group, through the lace of the leaves, and the Colonel picked his way past a fallen limb that blocked the trail. It must have been torn down in a late summer storm; it was already quite dead. He was beginning to feel more and more uncomfortable with his decision to help these people; the momentum which had propelled him from doubt to complete belief, provided by his complete immersion in the ritual of healing, had begun to wear off, and he was beginning to feel foolish.

Col. Church was not at any time accustomed to feeling foolish; his military career had been a series of steps towards more and more dignity of being, more and more solidity of personality. He had accustomed himself for many years to evaluating situations, analyzing situations, making rational decisions about situations. This habit of mind had served him well. But now, he had failed to report the situation, feeling that if he did so, it would take hours, even days, to untangle the mess and get on with helping these people. He was right about that; it would have been one big snafu if he'd gone through channels.

But now, as he moved through the peaceful near-wilderness of this lake country, he wondered if his original reaction to the ritual had been sensible. Had he been duped, after all? Was he in the company of, not magicians and good people, but charlatans and confidence men, who had been involved in a murder?

He was, on the other hand, committed to this course, and he may as well follow through with it now to the best of his ability. He cleared his mind of doubt, and began to think about the problem ahead. After all, even if he had made an error in analysis of the situation, there was one "man from space" safely guarded by Sgt. Armstrong, a man in whom the Colonel had considerable trust. Sgt. Armstrong had twenty years' service. And, in the last analysis, he had a great deal more to lose by not helping these people, if they were who they said they were, than by helping them, and being fooled. For if these were indeed aliens, how terrible it would be for the government of the United States to rebuff them. The political consequences of that would be enormous.

Now: the problem. They had walked to the place where the old road opened into the cabin's clearing. Someone was going to have to function as scout; they couldn't simply walk up to the front door en masse, especially not with Esmerelda along. He motioned them all to halt, and went ahead until he had come to the very edge of the trees and could see the outside of the cabin quite well.

There didn't seem to be a soul around; the yard was deserted. There was, however, a car in the driveway; no way to tell how long it had been there, or if it signaled the presence of anyone in the cabin. The clearing extended at least fifty yards, and there was no real cover at all for the entire distance between the forest and the dwelling.

Col. Church went back to the group and told them of the situation; it was Joshua who came up with a plan. He was dressed in blue jeans and an old sweatshirt, and his beard was a day old; he looked a fairly bohemian type. Since it would be impossible to sneak up on the house anyway, why shouldn't he simply walk up to the door and ring the bell. He could be asking directions. Or begging for food, for that matter. And he could probably get some sort of an idea of who was in the home. With his scruffy appearance, he shouldn't be suspected at all, and should be able to return with his information. If the house was locked, he would pretend he was a burglar, and get in by a window, and when the place had been checked and declared safe, he would wave them on.

The Colonel could see nothing wrong with this plan; he said so. "Naturally," grinned Joshua. "I write for television, remember?" It was hard to believe that the man was respectable, thought the Colonel. Appearance meant a great deal to him, and the appearance of two-thirds of this small band was one of the chief reasons his confidence in them had started to flag. They just didn't look dignified. Starr looked terrible, sloppy and long-haired; the girl could have been a lovely woman if she'd just put her hair up and wear stockings. Padeyevsky looked fairly well. But right now, both he and Pablo looked too dressed up and citified to be asking for directions, on foot, in the country. And neither one of them could function very well in the role of a common burglar either; both were too prosperous looking. His confidence in the integrity of the group grew slightly. "Fine," he said. "Go ahead with the plan, and we'll watch for your signal from here."

Joshua strode out into the clearing, composing his mind for his newest role; he had a great deal of practice at grooming his personality to fit various situations, and he slipped easily into the role of a carefree wanderer, perhaps in need of company, perhaps just curious about his neighbors. His walk was that of the confirmed outdoorsman; he swung along, legs moving smoothly from supple and understated hips, back straight and relaxed, arms swinging. It was almost a caricature of the normal Joshua walk but it was done well, and looked indigenous, believable, and very healthy. He breezed up the rustic, self-consciously woodsy porch steps and rang the doorbell. It echoed harshly through the interior of the cabin; Josh could hear it go. He waited. He rang again. There was no response whatever.

He walked around the back; there was no bell, but he knocked several times, loudly. Nothing. Time for the burglar routine. Either the cabin was empty, or there were people inside in hiding, waiting for him to go away. Joshua had thought of the burglar ruse for two reasons: first, it got him inside the house; second, if the kidnappers were indeed inside, they might have enough sympathy for a criminal that they wouldn't immediately kill him. Josh had no desire whatever to be killed immediately.

He hefted a rock that was lying near the end of the driveway, by the car. It broke the window in the back door, just above its Yale lock; within seconds, Joshua was inside the cabin's utility porch. It was very dark. All the shades were drawn. There didn't seem to be anything in the room except a large pile of awnings or some sort of heavy canvas fittings. Josh left the room and went into the kitchen, which was more revealing of recent inhabitants: there were two glasses in the drain board with droplets of water still clinging to their sides. Someone, or several ones, had recently been here, anyway. He examined a bedroom, which had not been touched, and went into the master bedroom, which had been used, but not to sleep in; the bed was slightly rumpled, as though it had been sat on. Another interesting fact: the room was in total blackness; someone had covered the windows from the outside, and had nailed the windows shut. Josh tested the door: yes, it was also completely light-proof when closed. The plot thickened.

He walked through the bedroom door and into the living room; it was dark and still, like all the rooms in the house; he thought it was empty until he stepped on something next to a long sofa which backed up to the window running across the front of the house. The object turned out to be a human foot, in a shoe. It was attached, Joshua discovered after he had gotten his brief startlement under control, to a dead body, the body of a small man, short and fine-boned in life, even shorter and more wasted in death. The death seemed to be recent: the body still contained warmth. There was no visible sign of injury; however, there were drops of blood on the floor just under one of the body's clenched fists; Joshua pried the fist open and discovered that the palm was quite bloody. The cuts were obviously from glass; several long splinters were still imbedded in the palm. The other fist was clenched, but not wounded. Then Josh saw several drops of blood on the man's lips, just under the beaklike nose. He pulled the flesh back from the tightly closed lips and found more glass, a ground-edged piece of what looked to be a drinking glass like the two that were in the kitchen. Part of the lower lip had been cut through, and the glass was still tight against clenched teeth. Apparently the man had bitten the glass, and crushed it in his hand.

There were no other signs of any reason for death or even violence; the face was darkly flushed with blood, but was unmarred except for the injury to the mouth.

Joshua straightened up, his face no longer at all insouciant. He had feared something like this, but he had not spoken of it; it is no use speaking of misfortune as yet unencountered. But so much had pointed to this: the fact that neither he, Esmerelda, nor the man from space had been able to pick up the girl's thoughts, and could not find her in the Akashic Record. It took a great deal of magical skill to be able to put up that sort of barricade; only a few people could have done it. And the trail of violence of the past twenty-four hours: the deputy sheriff's wife who had without any need shot and killed a man. And the presumably trustworthy Sgt. Armstrong, whose judgment had been terribly bad; who had shot to kill a man, when there were a dozen other completely non-lethal ways of stopping him. None of it had made any sense, unless these acts of negativity and violence were being-say, encouraged, or prompted, by the magic of one as practiced in black rituals as he himself was in white magic. And, whoever this man was, he had the girl from space. And she, who did not know negativity at all, would not recognize it until it was very much too late. Not if he were very, very good at his art.

As apparently he was. Because here was a man who had, fairly obviously, been frightened to death.

Joshua started back over the house, much more thoroughly this time, working backwards until he came to the little utility room, with its pile of awnings. He found the other body jammed headfirst into the corner, behind the massive pile of heavy cloth. It was no surprise; he steeled himself to uncover the thing, and look more closely at it. As he heaved at the canvas, the corpse came briefly to life, shoving itself spasmodically into the darkness of the corner of the room, burrowing deeper and deeper into the canvas until it had covered its eyes again. This was not a dead man, just a crazed one. The large body quivered and then stayed immobile once it had achieved darkness, its 250 pounds or so curled into a fetal position, spittle drooling slowly out of his mouth and onto the heavy cloth. Joshua reached out and touched the man's sleeve, tentatively; the only response was a terrified whimpering, and a brief spasm of further burrowing.

That was all there seemed to be in the house. It was enough. Joshua went back through the front of the small, plush cabin, stood on the porch, and beckoned to his confederates, who broke into a run across the clearing and steamed up on the porch beside him. They had to wait while Pablo caught up; he was haggard with fatigue, and was too winded to run all the way. Josh told them all what he had found, cautioned them against touching anything, and led them into the house. They each examined the two men; Esmerelda was concerned about the corpse, but only because she felt that its departed spirit was not in a state of well-being; physical trauma meant much less to her than to most women, as she had been so often out of her own physical body that she did not identify its life with life itself, but only with existence in this particular time and place. The man who still lived concerned her much more, and she asked what she could do for him.

The Colonel answered first. "I've seen this sort of reaction after heavy enemy shelling. It's a shock reaction."

Padeyevsky concurred, although he had reservations about the kind of shock it really was. "Speaking as a psychiatrist, I would say you're right, Colonel. It looks like a shock reaction, or it could be a catatonic schizoid reaction, although they don't usually burrow like that. But, knowing what I know now, I would have to term it an extreme phobic reaction. He was simply terrified of something." His hooded, reddened eyes met Joshua's; both men nodded slightly.

"What scared them?" asked the Colonel. The two looked somberly at him.

He looked back at them, his skin prickling slightly; it was uncomfortable in here; the very air was dark, somehow.

"Let me try to explain, Col. Church; as long as you're helping us, you should know all that we do." Joshua took him by one arm. "Let's get away from all this first." He lightly steered the man towards the back door; they went through it, and sat on the steps. Esmerelda was wandering around by the side of the house by which Joshua had not been, and her voice came around the side of the cabin. "Pablo! Josh! Come here!"

There was fear in her voice, much more fear than there had been in her manner when she had examined the two men inside. The Colonel followed Josh and Pablo around the corner, and saw them all looking at some wooden object stuck into the rather soft ground at the side of the foundation of the house. It looked like a garden tool of some kind. But as the Colonel kept gazing at it, it seemed to him that he could see a darkness around it, and an unaccountable feeling of fear, even terror, stirred to life within him. The hair on the back of his neck rose up.

"What do you see, Col. Church?" asked Joshua.

"I couldn't say-except, ridiculous as it sounds, the thing just looks evil. It scares me," said the Colonel, his emotions jolted for the second time in one day by something which was not, but yet which was.

Joshua nodded. "Yes, Colonel, you are definitely a very sensitive man. What you see is a symbol of goodness, which is used in white rituals; it is a crucifix. The man who scared those men inside must have found this on one of the walls inside. If this house is owned by a member of the organization, it's quite likely that his family is Catholic. Black magic makes use of the degradation of the symbols of white magic. You see the way this cross is turned upside down? And shoved into the dirt, right next to shrubbery which has been cultivated recently? There's probably a considerable amount of fertilizer here, probably natural fertilizer, which would make this the most unclean earth around. Now do you see why it seems so evil?"

The Colonel was, dimly, seeing, but he wanted more information about the evil which he saw, and about why he was seeing it. "No one else at the deputy's house saw what I saw, did they?" he asked.

"No," replied Joshua. "It's really very rare for anyone to have the ability to see astral forms without a great deal of preliminary study and training. It would indicate to me that you have, in at least one previous incarnation, done a great deal of work, made great progress, in spiritual matters. Have you ever wondered why you are named Church?"

The Colonel nodded. "Yes, as a matter of fact, when I was in college I planned to go into the church as a career, and I used to think how my name fit right in with that ambition. But the year that I got my B.S. in physics the Korean War came along, and by the end of the war, I was pretty well advanced, and I enjoyed the orderly ways of the military; it seemed dignified, somehow, and I felt like I was in a position of service to my country …" He paused. It struck him, suddenly, that he had been happy in the military for pretty much the same reasons that he would have been happy working within the church: it was dignified, people accorded respect to the position, it was apart from the rank and file of civilian humanity, it had its special and protective mission to perform, it even had its own special robes, or uniform.

"Your parents were probably chosen by your higher self before you incarnated this time," said Joshua, "to help remind yourself that you wanted to resume your metaphysical studies. I'm afraid that you just got lost on the way to your first ambitions, Colonel.

The world often does that to people."

The Colonel was tentatively feeling his way through the ideas that Joshua had given him to ponder and, somewhat to his surprise, he discovered no resistance in his mind to the seemingly outlandish notion that he had been born before. His intensely logical mind, which was so good at analyzing situations, was not failing him now. Everything this rather disreputable man showed him seemed to make the simplest kind of sense, more simple and logical than all the reality that had gone before. All right, he thought, if I really believe this to be true, then I must act on it. So much for my career, maybe so much for my family. He thought briefly of his wife; she would be all right. She would be able to adjust to this shift in his thinking. She had never had any difficulty that he could find adjusting to new places, new people, new languages, new food, new ideas … she would follow. Things would be all right. "And this man, whoever he is. What exactly did he do, to frighten these men?"

Joshua paused, trying to think of a way to explain. "I'm not sure that this is just how it happened, but it's probably something like it, anyway. The two men are both criminal types, probably pretty negative. It's easy for a black magician to work with this type of personality: not too much intellect, but lots of negativity. He probably summoned from the astral plane-you are familiar with the creatures of light which were the thought-forms of Esmerelda and myself, as magicians-well, the astral plane has many, many inhabitants, some beautiful and full of this light, and others from lower in the plane which partake of very heavy astral material and which are dark and prone to evil vibrations of thought. These two men probably both had habitual thoughts of an evil nature, some obsession about some evil excess, lust or cruelty towards someone whom they hated, and these thoughts caused the heavy etheric material of the lowest astral plane to form into shapes, just like our shapes of light, except these would be horrifying shapes, monstrous forms, as evil as the thoughts were, and if the thoughts were thought often enough, the monsters would become permanently alive on the astral plane, have an independent life of their own. Do you see, so far, what I mean?"

Col. Church vaguely did, and was-as seemed normal for the things Joshua had to tell him-not surprised. He had often felt the power of thoughts; often felt, for instance, that his wife's even-tempered kindness, her perennial affection and cheerfulness had been a shield to him that had protected him, somehow, wherever he went. Yes, he could see easily enough that thought could raise forms of its own. He nodded to Joshua.

"All right," said Joshua. "What this magician did, and he could do it very easily, if he's as good as I think he is, was to make these forms materialize briefly in the physical plane. So that the two men could see them. They would be especially terrified of them, for these monsters would have been personifications of thoughts of a very personal nature."

Now the death and lapse into mindlessness was easy enough for the Colonel to understand. "But what about the girl from space? Could she have been killed too?"

Joshua seemed unsure of his answer. "I really don't know, but I suspect that she will have been protected by the fact that, on her planet, there is no part of development that is as low as this is, and she will not have been able to see these forms. Although I should imagine that the very atmosphere would have made her afraid, even though she did not know what she was afraid of. That would explain the sensation of fear-which is unknown on her planet and then immediately the blackout of her aura. The magician would have been able, once he got here and was actually in her presence, to block her out, put some sort of a mental fence around her that she would not be guarding against, since she was never in a position to know of its existence before."

"Then why was she afraid at all?"

"The higher self always recognizes danger to the spirit."

Col. Church nodded again. "Well, then," he said, his habit of military analysis and action functioning automatically, "you're a magician; what can you do to counteract his magic?"

"Our magic may not be strong enough to counteract his, Colonel."

"Blast it, man, you're on the side of good, aren't you?" The Colonel was sure that good inevitably triumphed over evil. He had seen battles won, and known that right was on his side.

"Colonel, I'm afraid that on this planet, it isn't as simple as that."

"You mean your white magic is weaker than his black magic?"

"There's more to it than just us, Colonel. I can't tell you directly why it's so complicated, but ... well, think this over. One of the basic truths of magic is that the entire creation is formed by thought, or consciousness. This consciousness has two poles, and we on this planet call the poles good and evil. The duality is what makes action in the physical plane possible, just as there is no electrical current if there is no potential difference. Since the physical plane is almost completely a plane of action, this duality is very strong here, and magicians draw their power by polarizing, or concentrating, on one of these two poles. We concentrate by using symbols that other people dedicated to good have concentrated on in the past: it's not the crucifix itself, for instance, that is important, but all the positive thinking that has been concentrated upon that symbol for so long that makes it powerful. Black magic utilizes these same symbols, and twists or inverts them so as to degrade them, and that's how it gets its power. Everyone on this plane, whether he knows it or not, thinks either positively or negatively all the time. Now, tell me, Colonel. On this planet, which do you think has more concentration: the good or the evil pole?"

The answer was obvious. "The negative."

Josh's eyes flashed, dark in his clear face, and his body moved in on itself, tightening as if for movement as he sat on the step. "That's exactly right, Col. Church. And that is why, on this planet, black magic can be more powerful than white magic. In the rest of the creation there are millions of galaxies, and in our galaxy we are a small planet, turning around a small star near its outer rim. And this, Col. Church, is Earth." He paused, lean frame hunched on the steps. "And I am responsible for bringing these innocent children here."

He got up. "Come on," he said, as if throwing off the seriousness of that last remark. "We've got to get out of here and find the girl. Can't hang around all day, man." He walked back into the utility room, where the good doctor was observing his patient. Pablo stuck his hands into his pockets and jingled keys.

"You know, Josh, it took quite a bit of skill to have this much effect on these men. I don't have any knowledge of the, ah, personnel in the field. How many black magicians are there who could have done this?"

"In this country?"

"Well … does it make much difference?"

"Yes. But still, it is likely to be an American. A very short list, Pablo: two. Marcall in New Orleans could have done it. Or Trostrick in Ft. Lauderdale."

Pablo cut in. "Trostrick? Oh my God." As Joshua looked questioningly at him, he went on. "Here it all is, Josh. In a nutshell. And all my fault. You remember when we were talking about my betting?"

A nod from Joshua.

"I wouldn't have been able to do that on my own. After you stopped working with me, I went on alone for a while, but I hadn't gotten anywhere. But about five years ago I received a visitor. Said I'd met him somewhere, some university thing I'd gone to. And I did remember him. One thing led to another, and we started talking about the research I was doing on the horses. He had a few suggestions. Said he was really very interested in this sort of project. Well, to make a long story short, he helped me quite a bit. I knew that it was magical, what I was doing. And wanted to tell you about it, about the results I was getting using these techniques he showed me. But Trostrick asked that I keep his name and activities totally secret. Just an interested observer, he said. And I was making money off the deal. So I didn't want to …" Pablo trailed off, sounding as miserable as he felt.

"All right," said Joshua. "Now we know where we are. Trostrick was behind the kidnapping, and he's got the girl. And we still can't hang around here all day."

"No," Pablo looked again at the man lost in the awning material. "I don't know how we can do this, but we shouldn't go without getting someone out here for this man. He needs help."

"I can do that," said Josh. "Anybody touch anything?" Nobody had.

"Then we'll just call the local constabulary from here, and leave right now. You all go on. I have a phone call to make myself. I know how to go through a network switchboard so the called number won't mean anything to the police. We don't want to have any connection with this mess here. Then I'll join you."

The sense of this was easily seen, and they filed out, leaving Josh to make his calls. As soon as he was connected with a close business acquaintance, he told him to contact a detective agency in Miami, in Padeyevsky's name, and have all the airports in the Miami and Ft. Lauderdale area watched for the possible arrival of two persons of the descriptions of Trostrick and the space girl. He then made a call to the police and, as the number began ringing, placed the receiver on the table. The officer on duty came on the line. "Help," screamed Joshua in falsetto.

He left the line open for the authorities to trace, and caught up with the rest of the group as they crossed to the edge of the clearing. The birds' songs had all but stopped. The sun was high, and it was time for the quiet that the heat of the day produces; the sun was warm as summer on their backs as they walked back along the wooded trail to the helicopter.

CHAPTER THIRTEEN

The girl from space sat down next to the window and looked out. She could see very little of the jet airliner that had seemed so large from the outside; men in white clothing were moving about under her window, carrying boxes and baggage, and apparently ministering to the vehicle in which she sat. It was a fulfilling and exciting experience for her, although she could not quite rid her mind of a faint feeling of doubt about the man Pablo had sent to guide her.

He sat down beside her, a man of average height, with hair so black that the highlights reflecting the light from the cabin's illumination were a glinting, steely blue. His eyes were very deep-set, very bright, with the intensity of gaze that Joshua had, although this glance was, for some reason, difficult to meet for any length of time. The space girl had found it to be of increasing pleasure to look into the steady gaze that Joshua could turn on her. The black-haired man instructed her to put around her hips the cloth and metal belt that each seat had by its sides; she did so, at a loss to explain to herself why one should desire to restrict one's movement in this way. She had much to learn about this strange planet called Earth.

The events of the last few hours were most befuddling. She tried to sort out her confusion. This man had come into the cabin in which Marion and Elmo and she had been enjoying each others' company. She had been in the bedroom, and had never seen either of the two men. The man had led her out of the rear door of the bedroom into the hall to the kitchen and back door, and they had left immediately. The most puzzling thing was that, at the instant of her meeting with this man, she had ceased to be able to see the mental planes; she could not discover the man's aura, or any of his thoughts; indeed, she discovered that she could no longer converse with her companions, the one known as Esmerelda, and her brother. They were gone. And, in the instant before they had disappeared, she had felt a vivid flash of some force that she had no way to describe, except that she had, while studying this planet's languages, repeatedly come upon words which had no referent in her own language. She had discussed these words with her brother, but had been unable to define them, or even guess what they meant. And she found it possible to believe that she had now become somewhat acquainted with the meaning of one of these words. For she could remember no specific thing, but there was a fading memory of a pain that affected both her body and her spirit, that for a second she had been unable to dispel. And always before, she had been in complete control over the stimulus which was fed to her being, on both the physical and the mental planes.

And she felt, because of these puzzling events, a little dubious about her new guide, whose aura she could not see. But he had told her that he came from Pablo and Joshua, and that he was to be her teacher. And that, for a time, she would experience different conditions than she was used to, as a means of learning about conditions on this planet.

That was precisely what she had come here to learn. She attempted to compose her mind, to relax it into the smooth and uncluttered surface with which she was used to greeting her environment.

A stewardess, coming slowly down the aisle, writing down the names of the passengers and their drink selections, came abreast of the girl from space and stopped, her mouth slightly open, her eyes widening. She simply stared at the girl, pencil poised above the pad, for several seconds; this did not at all disconcert the girl from space, but the man who was her guide cut her period of intense gazing short. "My name is James E. Trostrick, and this is Miss Mercer."

"Yes," said the stewardess, turning her eyes to her pad and writing. "Would you or Miss Mercer care for a beverage?"

"We would, my dear," said the man. "I'll have black coffee. And Miss Mercer will have scotch and soda."

The stewardess nodded and wrote, and held her composure through one more long stare before she turned and hurried back to the front of the airplane. The two had been sitting in the last seat of the section, and their order completed the first class roster. She opened the door to the pilot's compartment, and leaned close to the flight engineer. "Harry, you've got to take a look at 6-D. Most beautiful girl I ever saw in my life."

"Oh, yeah?" The engineer glanced up front. There was a minute or two before he would be involved with the checklist. He walked into the first class compartment and strode back towards the galley, looking purposeful, but his step faltered as he passed the girl and her black-haired companion. He stared, recovered, and went into the galley, fiddling with the emergency chute on the door, and staring blankly at the pressure gauge. When he had regained the expression of nonchalance, he walked back into the pilots' compartment and exploded. "You won't believe it," he told the pilot and copilot. "You just won't believe it!"

"What's that?" The captain was only half-listening.

"The girl sitting in 6-D. Before she gets off, you've both got to go take a look at her. She must be a fashion model or a movie star or something. Anyway, she's the most fantastic broad I ever saw."

"OK, OK," said the Captain. "We'll see her." He looked at the copilot. "Let's read the before-starting checklist."

The copilot read from a folded card. "Circuit breakers and radio bus switches."

The engineer shrugged. "Checked and on," he said.

The girl from space sat in her seat quietly as the big jet started to roll, absolutely delighted with the heady feeling of acceleration as the craft took to the air. It was an unaccustomed sensation; the craft that brought her here, and the smaller ones in use on her planet, did not make use of such phenomena. Its difference from all that she had known made it the more enjoyable to her, and she was very happy as she looked out the window, seeing the changing configurations of clouds and terrain below her. The only event which at all disconcerted her during her trip was the beverage which her companion had offered her. Eager to experience the environment of this new planet, she had drunk it, despite its unpleasant taste, and she had been slightly startled to note that it caused her body to suffer a mild trauma. Her thinking produced the notion, finally, that it must be some sort of tranquilizer, given to combat the tension that she had noted beginning to rise in some of her fellow passengers as the jet left the ground. Except for this, the flight was all too short, and without remarkable event, and she was sorry to feel the slight brush of the tires as they made contact with one of the parallel east-west runways at the Miami International Airport.

The passengers were herded off the craft very quickly, and into a corridor that had been placed right against its side, so that she was never exposed to the outside air at all, but walked through a large hallway into the terminal building itself. Trostrick hurried her into part of the main lobby; she would have much preferred staying an indefinite amount of time there, for she saw many different types of human entities and felt she could, as the vast crowds of people ebbed and flowed in the great concourse, have added much to her knowledge of this planet's inhabitants.

But Trostrick was hurrying down an escalator, and into a space guarded by men in uniforms. There seemed to be a great deal of attempted control of people by other people on this planet. But perhaps she was interpreting data wrongly. She would wait, and ask thus man who was her teacher at some later time.

They walked through electric doors, which opened hospitably for them and let them into the lower level of the airport's roads. Many more people were present here, and there were so many cars that the girl from space could not see the end to them, or find where they all came from, or where they could go. It was crowded here, and shady. Here too she would have liked to have stayed, and watched, and discovered what all these people, and all these cars, were doing. But again, Trostrick hurried her along the gray walkway, straining his head upwards to see over the cars parked under the overhanging rampway. It took little time for him to find a uniformed chauffeur who opened the rear door of a black Lincoln, and took the bags from his employer. Trostrick helped the girl from space into the rear seat, and then spoke to the chauffeur. "I'll be back in a minute. Please make Miss Mercer comfortable."

The chauffeur's dark face creased into a small grin, a secretive expression; then the smile was gone, as he bent into the car door to look after the passenger Trostrick had given him.

Trostrick quickly disappeared into the colorful masses of people that threatened to overflow the dingy, columned sidewalk; almost immediately, he had a collision with a man going the other way. There wasn't really enough crowding for the jostling to occur, but it did occur, the men meeting heavily, shoulder to shoulder. Trostrick paused in the second of contact and prolonged it slightly, looking intently into the man's eyes. He did not speak. The man he had bumped into walked on, but there was a blankness in his eyes that had certainly not been there before; before his face had been sharp and alert. Now, dull of expression and with expressionless eyes, he slowly but steadily walked between two parked rental cars, and directly into the path of a moving limousine. The big car wasn't traveling fast; 15 miles an hour is almost the top speed in the lower level, but it was quite impossible for its driver to begin braking before the front bumper of his heavy vehicle had pulled the man's body beneath it, and its wheel had crushed his head.

Trostrick had continued into the door of the lower level terminal, and had gone to the nearest rent-a-car desk, but he had left soon thereafter, for the clerk with whom he had had a short conversation stopped paying any attention to him, as her attention was pulled to the growing crowd of people that were clustering around the accident. Trostrick walked back to the waiting limousine and slid into its back seat with the girl from space. The chauffeur closed the door for him, the wisp of a smile moving briefly across his flattened features once more. He walked around the car, giving no impression of speed, but wasting no time; he had the Lincoln threaded around the piling congestion in a very short time, and had pulled successfully into the outer lane, past the police office, and towards LeJeune Road. A right turn from LeJeune put him on the expressway to the beaches. He drove with authority past all the exits and bewilderment of signs, and did not leave the expressway until he had passed through the toll gates. A left turn took the car northward to Ft. Lauderdale, and he cut across the north end of that city and found highway A 1 A.

The girl from space had gradually become aware that the city scenery was being left behind, and it was a very great pleasure to her to be able to look out her window at the beauty that surrounded her now. Her teacher had brought her to a place that was lovely to see, and far different from the way the green trees and shrubs had looked before she took the airplane ride. Here the trees seemed quite different; they had leaves which were as long as branches, and grew at the tops of the trees, instead of from their sides; these leaves made a sound in the constant wind that was restful, soothing, altogether comfortable. Her spirit grew close to the sound of the trees, and she celebrated with them the clean, sweet smell of life; somehow, it held sea within it. The space girl was, more than anything, held in thrall by the motion of the water in the distance; she could see white flecks move across its face and she could hear the sound it made. Upon her planet, the waters did not move so restlessly, but stirred only gently with the air which fed the life therein. Here the ocean was powerful and full of the motion that she had felt when the jet had flown. The sense of ceaselessness seemed to her to express the eternity of the spirit in an opposite, but equally eloquent way from the quiet and hush that characterized her peacefully stirring planet's life forces. They passed forests and forests of these palm trees, and she caught glimpses of secluded houses. Many people seemed to live here, in far greater privacy than could be found in the crowded city she had just left.

To her delight, the limousine pulled into a driveway that was shaded by these palms, and reddish, smaller bushes. Her teacher was out the door, and holding his hand to her in greeting; she took it. He helped her out of the car, and they walked around the patio and towards the sliding glass doors that stopped the sweet air from moving too destructively into the peaceful house. It was the most modern of houses, all glass and wood, all gleaming and smooth-surfaced. Even the wall-to-wall carpet was of an unusually smooth consistency. He took her to a hallway that led off the spacious living room and opened a door: it was a bedroom much like the one she had been in earlier this day. The differences were not striking; however, they did exist: here everything was much more impressive; here there were no carved or broken surfaces. The large bed was without posts or endboards and the other furniture was absolutely plain. The colors of the room were as muted as its furnishings, and as flat; there was nothing but restfulness here.

Trostrick walked over to the window and pulled the heavy curtain back, revealing a glass wall of the same kind that the patio had; he opened it, and the ocean air moved in through the screen and touched her nostrils again.

"I believe there is everything you need, here and in here," he said, indicating a small, complete bathroom. "I am sure that you would like to refresh yourself, my dear, before we dine. When you are ready, join me on the patio, and we will have supper."

The girl did not feel tired; it was not her habit to tire at all, until her body was in physical need of rest. It was not now in such need, so she contented herself with washing her body, and making her hair neat and clean again, and shaking out the clothing that she had on, so that it would be smoother against her. It was only minutes until she walked back through the thickly carpeted living room and onto the patio. The sun was just setting, and they watched the rays of the last rosy light drift over the moving sea, and deliver themselves up to the shores that lay very close to them. Trostrick's private beach stretched along the patio and around the gentle curve of the shoreline, its arc broken only by the shapes of palm trees that bowed under the wind's weight.

Her teacher was seated at a table made of very dark wood, and set with very heavy eating appliances; the glasses were carved of this wood; the handles of the silverware were fashioned of it too. Silver gleamed from the table, and shielded candles were lit, their illumination flickering across the gleaming wood, their smoke moving on the sea breeze.

"I have attempted to provide enjoyable physical surroundings for you, my dear," said Trostrick. He took a bottle from an ice bucket, and expertly maneuvered the cork out of its neck. She drank the liquid which he poured for her. It was much like the liquid which she had tasted on the airplane; it had the same effect, and its taste differed only minimally. It would be good to understand whether this liquid were again being given her as a tranquilizer, but she felt it would be better for her not to ask questions of her teacher yet; for he had much to tell her, and she was sure he would go about it in his own way.

"This is a very good year, my dear," said her guide, patting the dark bottle.

She did not comprehend what he meant; he seemed amused by this.

"But of course, my dear, you would not be familiar with these mundane matters. However, I shall try to provide you with some interesting sensations, here. I thought perhaps you might not have tasted an antipasto before, or a lobster tail?"

The girl simply looked at him, a little quizzically; her study of the language had not been encyclopedic, and she had learned the names of only those foods with which she had already been familiar, as she had no way of remembering the names of alien substances. Neither antipasto nor lobster meant anything to her.

"Never mind, my dear. We shall enjoy the food as it comes. It is a lovely evening to be sitting looking out to sea, is it not? The stars show clearer and clearer, don't they? This excellent evening, with its darkening sky, does it not make you homesick?"

Her teacher was very easy to talk to; he led her right to her answers. "No," she said, and felt quite at home in his presence. "I imagine that you are eager to know just what part I am to play in teaching you of your new environment."

Again, he had led her to her answer. "Yes," she said.

"I am to be your teacher, my dear, and lead you in your education concerning certain metaphysical principles that we enjoy here on this planet that you might not have been aware of on your home planet. In many cases, it will not be possible to teach you directly with words. For instance, in order to teach you of some of the limitations of awareness under which people on this planet labor, I have assisted you in temporarily restricting your mental vision. It puts you off your normal balance, does it not, my dear?"

"Yes," said the attentive girl.

"You do not mind my teaching you in this way, do you?" asked her guide.

"No."

"I was certain that you would not, my dear. As you are aware, it is often impossible on this planet to teach by using words, for the people who dwell on the surface of this planet have evolved a language with words which pertain almost totally to the physical illusion. Even words that intend to pertain to metaphysical matters are quite inadequate to those who wish to seek truth. But, you know all of this, do you not, my dear? I do not wish to bore you, but to point out a few concepts that we feel are germane with respect to seeking spiritual awareness."

An enormously bodied, heavily muscled man came through the patio door. His clothes were scrupulously tailored to his seven feet of bulk; in his darkly tanned hand was a heavy wooden tray. He took from it two plates, upon which were a variety of green vegetables.

"It would not show respect to the food," said Trostrick as the waiter retreated into the darkened house, "for us to speak, even of spiritual things, while we revitalize our bodies with its nourishment."

They ate the salad in silence. The girl was thoroughly enjoying all the variously shaped green substances, and the red ones as well. When she began to eat a bit of peculiar material on the plate, however, she found it distasteful, and would have put it aside, except that she saw that Trostrick was eating a similar substance. And so she ate the oily, salty scraps of fish too.

The waiter reappeared before they had had time to grow restless in their silence; this time the tray contained two lobster tails, with the proper instruments for removing the soft, white meat, and cups of drawn butter for garnish. There was a lesson in how to use the implements, and then the space girl was able to taste the meat. She found this distasteful too, and unlike anything she had ever eaten before. Not exhilaratingly different, but different in a way she somehow mistrusted. However, again the man who was her teacher was eating his food with gusto, and she did as he did.

Trostrick was finished, after a time, and touched his mouth with the heavy linen napkin. "Did you enjoy your meal, my dear?" She did not answer.

"I do not believe that you enjoyed the lobster as you did the green food in the salad, did you?"

It was unbelievably easy to speak her thoughts to this man. "No," she said.

"Were you concerned about the levels of consciousness of the foods you ate, my dear?"

That was precisely what had troubled her. "Yes," she said happily. She would not have known how to use the language well enough to have expressed that.

"This is one of the principles that we must speak of this evening. It has to do with our consciousness, and the consciousnesses of the others that surround us. We have just eaten two forms of life: mixed plant life, which has minimal consciousness, and lobster, which enjoys a very limited form of animal consciousness. I sense that it troubled you to assimilate this consciousness."

"Yes."

"My dear, our planet is not like yours. On your planet, this would have been a slight infringement upon the free will of the animal that you ingested. However, this planet, as I told you, enjoys certain differences in condition. Central among these differences is that on this planet all consciousness does not seek the light, as it does on yours. Many, many of the entities that enjoy the gift of physical incarnation here have become lost from pursuit of the truth, and seek in other directions, pitifully lost. This lobster was a fragment of life that had not begun seeking the light; by being assimilated into your being, it has been aided in its search, and perhaps, as its consciousness continues to evolve, it will be helped by your contact with it."

The girl was disturbed and confused by this powerful chain of reasoning. She could not fault it intellectually. But ...

"My dear," said her teacher, very gently, "I sense that you are still worried about the free will of this life form. You feel that it should be free to choose and act as it pleases, as a function of its will. Am I not correct?"

"Yes," said the girl, nodding vigorously.

"My dear, I must iterate to you that this planet differs from yours. On your planet, each particle of consciousness will seek the light without guidance, and form its own destiny, because your planet is a planet of light. However on this planet, the darkness is as strong as the light, and without the guidance of ones such as we, they would be lost and separated from the truth. It is our duty, once we have learned, to guide. Can you understand, my dear?"

She could understand the words quite easily; her teacher had a great ability to speak clearly. And yet, despite her intellectual understanding, the idea of this sort of guiding sounded to her like a violent misuse of power. She could not see how it could ever become permissible to make choices for other entities, or even to block out some choices for them. And it seemed to her, in her puzzlement, that that was what she had done to the lobster. Even if she had said, "Lobster, you may either be assimilated by me, or you may live on in darkness," was she not by her words hiding from this particle of the Creator's universe the truth of his freedom to do, not either the one thing or the other, but anything he decided? She could not make her mind settle on what her teacher had said, for it seemed foreign and wrong.

Her difficulties did not seem to be as apparent to her teacher as her previous ones had been; or perhaps he noticed them, but wished to help her out of them by other examples.

"My dear," he said quietly, "I cannot explain to you in enough ways that this planet called Earth is far different from the one you know. I can only attempt to explain to you, basically, how a certain problem exists, and how it is handled, upon this planet. Upon your planet, of course, there is a unity of purpose. Here, there are many who are confused, and have lost their sense of purpose. They do not realize that seeking is the ultimate objective of all those who dwell in the whole creation, and fill their physical lives with vain amusements."

"Now, my dear, since I am sure that you are aware of this condition on Earth, you are aware that there must be some way to reawaken the spirit of seeking within these lost wanderers. I have seen in your eyes that you are disturbed about this concept. Is it that you feel that we would be infringing upon the free will of those we helped, to help them in the way in which I am describing?"

The girl from space was most grateful that her teacher had found her area of confusion, for she sorely wished to become clear, and learn all she could of this planet. "Yes," she said.

"It is self-evident, my dear, that there is only one thing which is truly wrong, although many things are called sin on this planet, and that it is simply the infringement of one consciousness upon the free will of another. And it is equally clear that we who guide must in some way circumnavigate this sin, using our intelligence. So that, free from sin, we may lead the lost into light, and show truth to those who will ultimately seek it."

Somehow, even restated, the concept of which he spoke retained its alien and distasteful flavor; it was like the taste of the antipasto: not obviously unpleasant, but nonetheless, without virtue to her. She did not think that she had ever before considered that there might be a way to limit choices as this man was apparently telling her they did upon this planet, without infringing upon free will.

"You do not understand the techniques for circumventing this sin, do you, my dear?" asked Trostrick, watching her steadily, his dark eyes shining into hers across the flickering candlelight that was now their only illumination, except for the night glow of the moon and the stars off the ocean's surface.

"No," she said.

"It will be necessary for me to demonstrate to you, my dear, techniques for guiding and leading those who are lost. One must always be careful, as I have said, to avoid sinning, and to provide only choices which the individual, if left to himself, could eventually freely make. You are not aware that such free choice can be deliberately provided, are you, my dear?"

"No," she said.

The man rose in the soft light and took her arm. He was as tall as she, but thicker built, and very much darker. "Come with me, my dear, and we shall walk, and you will understand."

They walked across the sand to the water's edge. The sand was slightly wet from the receding dark waves. "It is a beautiful creation, is it not, my dear?" said the black magician softly. "The sky so black and studded with stars, the sea breeze so refreshing. Let us stand here, and consider freedom of choice, the freedom of choice provided by a teacher. We will consider physical bodies, which both of us now use to experience our physical environment. They are quite useful to us here, for they are acted upon by the catalyst of the physical world. This is in turn quite useful for the evolution of our spiritual selves. But let us examine the limitations of the body more closely." Trostrick had carried his linen serviette with him from the table and now, folding it diagonally, he placed it over her eyes and tied it around the back of her head. "You do not mind this little experiment, do you, my dear? I wish only to limit your physical sight."

"No," said the girl, eagerly awaiting further instruction.

The magician spoke again. "Your physical body has now been deprived of its physical sight. Now you, my dear, are able to use your mental body, and see all and more than the physical eyes can see. Therefore the physical eyes are redundant. But on this planet, very few can project their spiritual selves from their physical bodies, and the loss of eyesight is a hardship indeed. Can you see how severely this loss of stimulus would restrict learning and thus hinder the spirit's progress?"

"Yes." It seemed most pitiable to the girl that anyone should be without sense, unable to gather information about his environment. "However, my dear," said Trostrick, "a man who is blind can still experience whatever he wishes with the rest of his senses, for he has freedom of movement, and can go where he pleases. There are those whose experience is even more limited. Allow me to demonstrate."

She stood straight and still at the water's edge as he took a stout cord from his jacket pocket. Placing her hands behind her back, he bound them tightly with the cord. "Your body is now even more limited, is it not, my dear?"

"Yes." She found this a strange sensation.

"Some of this planet's inhabitants have been further restricted, and they still do not understand how to remove their mental body from this hindered vehicle. Is that not sad?"

"Yes.

"And yet, this limitation may be carried still further. But here. I shall show you." Trostrick removed another length of cord from his pocket, and placed the girl's ankles together so that he could tie them as tightly and securely together as he had tied her wrists. The girl began to anticipate the end of the lesson, for she saw that her physical body was now almost completely limited.

The magician stood up, his manipulation complete. "You may learn much from this, my dear. For consider that many of this planet's inhabitants are imprisoned in various ways. They are not usually tied, but they are kept in dark buildings, where they may not speak with anyone, or see anything of the outside world. And they are unable to leave their imprisoned bodies. Your physical body is severely limited now, my dear, with respect to gaining further experience, is it not?"

"Yes."

"It would be necessary for you, in order to gain more experience at this time, to use your mental body, leaving your physical body behind. Is this not so?"

"Yes," she replied once more.

"Now, consider this," said the quiet voice. "It is an interesting characteristic of this planet that there are some inhabitants who are as confined in their mental bodies, in what we call the lower of the astral planes, as you are now in the physical plane. They are so restricted in their spiritual bodies that they cannot experience or evolve any further than you can now, in your physical imprisonment. That is most unfortunate, is it not?"

"Yes." It was more than unfortunate; it affected her in a way that this physical restriction could not. She had never been aware that it was even possible to accomplish such gross infringement upon free will.

"Many have been so confined, my dear, and instead of being able to seek, they will be forced to live in their present state of awareness for all eternity. The only escape, it seems, is through a retreat into darkness, until the level of subjugation which the creatures of the lower astral planes enjoy is reached. The personality must totally be given up here, and each shred of light must be left behind, for the creatures that inhabit this plane are very, very negative, or, as we call it on this planet, evil. Isn't it unfortunate that they must travel so very far back along the path away from the light, in order that they may once more have their freedom, and be able to enjoy their Creator's universe?"

"Yes." The space girl was deeply shocked. This planet was a very different one from hers. She tested her bonds. They were very tight. And her mental body could be as tightly bound here. It was a thought which shook her as no other knowledge could have, and she realized that it was the one her teacher had left with her, for she could hear his footsteps shifting the firm sand as he walked away from her; hear his shoes speak against the stone of the patio and lose themselves into the carpeting of the living room. The glass door slid behind him. She was alone.

For a long time she stood, motionless, in meditation, at the shore of the ocean. It was an ebbing tide, and the water moved slowly away from her. In an hour, it had become less easy to stand comfortably. She was not sure that she had completely understood all that had been told her, for she did not feel as though she had gained a great deal of awareness; she only knew that she was most disturbed in spirit by what he had told her.

She considered her present limitations. What purpose had he had in limiting her thusly? He had talked about providing choices for the growth of the spirit, and she had not understood. Or had she? Was this perhaps an example of what he had meant? Had he provided her with the free choice between standing, helpless and alone at the sea's edge, and moving towards her teacher in her mind-body for further education? Was this the point of being so bound?

She considered leaving the physical, to find her teacher. Joshua had allowed her brother to travel in the mental planes of this planet, but he had provided him with a guide, one who had long worked within these planes. Joshua had told her not to leave her physical body under any circumstances, as she did not have a guide. She had so far obeyed him implicitly.

But did she not have a guide now, in her teacher? She wished she had command of her spirit self, so that she might speak with Joshua in thought, and ascertain more surely what he would have her do. She did not want to make an error. But her teacher had limited her thusly as part of her learning. It did seem to be showing her as no words could the terrible limitations that were in force in this planet's physical plane.

Her teacher did not return. Her bonds remained unyielding. The only thing that seemed evident to her was that she would not learn any more, standing here where she was. She remembered Joshua's warning about the dangers of this planet's astral planes, and her present teacher had described in even greater detail what these dangers were. But could she not put herself under the protection of her new guide? Together, they could gather more understanding, and she would continue to evolve. It had been so long since he left her. This must, without question, be what he intended her to do: to come seek him in her mental body of light.

She visualized her mental body, sheathed in light, made of light, pure as light is pure and was delighted to discover that, once again, she could leave her physical body although all but her immediate surroundings was still blank to her. The image began to glow in front of her on the sand until she could see it in great detail, the clothing, the features. She charged the image with the etheric energy of her physical body, making it briefly of the physical world, making it externalized. Her mind moved the form's hands, turned its head. It was now ready to receive her waking consciousness, and without a break of any sort in her awareness, she was away from her physical body and into the body of light, looking about with its eyes. As she looked back at her bound physical body, it fell heavily backward onto the sand, almost pulling her body of light back into it, and she regretted not having put it to rest before leaving it. She could see the faint glow of the silver cord. Some of the etheric material of her physical body had been used to charge this one with vitality; consciously, she returned the etheric substance to the body as it lay on the sand in a state of trance. Her being lifted in joy, exhilarated as it always was after she had shed the heavy chemical projection that was necessary for physical experience. Filled with an intense feeling of vigor and well-being, she turned and walked to the patio, and into the living room.

She passed the enormous servant that she had seen on the patio during her meal; he did not see her body of light, of course. Trostrick was not there. She walked towards the hallway and started down it, drawn with a stronger and stronger sense of certainty towards its end. The hall ended, not in a door, but in a very heavy, wine-red velvet curtain, ponderous, smooth, and utterly luxurious, as all the furnishings of this house were. There was a command now, within her; she opened the drapes with one hand and entered the large room to which her teacher had called her, certain now that she had done the correct thing in coming here. For she was expected; she had been summoned.

She waited at the door a moment, looking about the dim room. There were candles along all the walls, flickering in their thick sconces. The room was bare, except for a black marble table in the center of the room, upon which lay the naked body of her teacher. She walked over to it, compelled to do so; she watched it until she became aware that, although the body was still and apparently lifeless, there was awareness in the eyes, which were looking straight at her. She looked back. In her body of light, it was no longer difficult to return the look steadily. And the eyes caught her up, and pulled her to them, so that she leaned over him and kissed his lips, feeling within herself a trembling rise of urgency that she had never experienced outside of her physical body. His eyes were still looking into hers, and now, as a curious desire grew and dominated her spiritual body, the one known as Trostrick moved, in his mental body, up from the table on which his physical body lay, and took her mental body close to his, holding her, still looking deep into her spirit's eyes. The desire which had no place on the mental plane beat into her, and, rejoicing that her teacher could perform such wonders as this, and that he wished her to share this experience with him, she closed her eyes in complete and exultant surrender to him, that their spirits could become one. As she did so, she felt the waves of vibrant attraction pass between herself and her teacher until there was no break in their excitement, and her spirit was lost in the sea of sensation. Everything went very dark, and she felt her teacher pulling her through dimensionless space.

CHAPTER FOURTEEN

The ride back to Pablo Padeyevsky's house was broken only by snores from the rotund doctor, who had finally succumbed temporarily to exhaustion. The Colonel parted company with them as they set down in the natural landing spot of Pablo's front lawn, extracting a promise to be kept up to date in the search for the girl from space.

The small group ducked away from the bunches of debris the chopper's blades threw up as it took to the air again, and opened the front door of the peaceful house with a feeling of relief. It was good to be home again. Pablo sat down on the longest couch in the room that would have been called the front parlor if the time had been before the Civil War; he was stirred up by the intensely alive Joshua. "Come on, Pablo!"

Pablo's eyes struggled open. It was a long struggle. "Josh, now I know why you stay so thin. You never sleep."

"Oh, come on, Pablo," said Josh. "Get up."

Pablo was still having a mammoth and seesaw battle with his eyelids. Josh smiled down at his old friend sitting so wrinkled and full of sleep. He had seldom felt better.

Esmerelda walked into the living room with sandwiches, and there was a sudden pause while all three discovered that they were starving. The conversation proceeded, a bit thick with sounds of ingestion.

"Well, Pablo," said Joshua, "I've already arranged for a detective agency to watch the airports in the Miami and Ft. Lauderdale area. That's what I did over the phone at the cabin. If they spot the space girl, they'll call here. I used your name and telephone number, since we were coming here. Now, Trostrick and the girl must have left the cabin just shortly before we arrived; the small man's body was still warm. So, say they've been away from there no less than two hours. It would take about an hour to drive to the nearest airport, and much longer before they could make connections to Miami. Even if they got a flight out immediately, it would be a good two hours before they landed." Joshua was retousling already unruly hair. "And probably there wouldn't be a flight right away."

He pulled his six feet into vertical activity. "Meanwhile," he said to the somnolent doctor, "I'm going to the airport and charter a plane. If I can locate a jet, I can be at Trostrick's with no more than a two or three hour lag. Maybe four. But I know where his house is. And he took her there, if he intends to do any ritual work."

"Wait," said Pablo. "He might have gone to New York, as well. He has a place there, too. That's where I was yesterday, as a matter of fact. Is there any magical technique you could use to trace them?"

Esmerelda shook her head. "I don't think so, Uncle Pablo. We've both tried searching the Akashic Record, which is the most foolproof way we know of for finding someone. She vanished from it while she was in the cabin. It's just what a black magician would try to do: put a mental fence around her so that she would begin to lose contact with the rest of her environment. It is highly technical work; it takes an Ipsissimus to accomplish it. Which Trostrick is."

Joshua ambled into the hall and used the telephone. He announced, after hanging up, "I've found a good charter jet. It can be ready to go as soon as I get there. The pilots were there already, as it happened. No problem. I'm off."

"But, Josh," said Pablo, "how do you know it's Ft. Lauderdale you're headed for?"

"Just playing the odds. Trostrick may do some ritual work in New York, but his magical personality will have much more power if it works in the place it has used the longest. If I were he, I would go to Ft. Lauderdale."

Joshua was on his way out the door, oblivious to Pablo's objections. He paused at the sound of an engine, and all three came to the door to welcome Theodore and the space man, back from their long journey via the Army Way.

Theodore was first through the door, and he went to Esmerelda. She took his hand, and held her other one out to reach for the space man's. "Back all safe," she said.

"You wouldn't believe it," said Theodore. "But yes."

"Great," said Joshua. "Good-bye."

He was out the door.

"Where's he going?" Theodore asked.

"He found out that the space girl is probably in Ft. Lauderdale. He's going after her."

Theodore looked swiftly at Esmerelda, and as swiftly she nodded in response. "I'm going too," he said. He was out the door after Joshua.

Josh started the Lamborghini. "Too dangerous," he said with some finality, putting the car into gear.

Theodore wasted no more words, but simply opened the right door of the car and, as Joshua accelerated along the driveway, folded himself into the passenger seat and got the door closed as Joshua made the turn onto the access road. The twelve cylinders screamed away down the road, audible to the ones left behind long after the car was out of sight.

"They'll be all right, Uncle Pablo," Esmerelda soothed, leading the exhausted professor back to the sofa.

"Maniac," he grumbled, settling into the cushions again. Esmerelda took in the room: her uncle was ready to sleep, and he would want to answer the phone whenever it rang. She turned to the man from space. "Do you wish to rest your physical body, my brother?"

"Yes," he said.

"Will you send your spirit in search of your sister?"

"Yes."

"And may I accompany you in spirit for your search, my brother?"

"Yes."

Esmerelda took his hand, and together they walked into the shady, breezy screened porch, made themselves comfortable, and prepared for meditation.

Esmerelda's teacher was meditating too; not as deeply, but his concentration was so intense, as he pushed the little Italian car to its limits, that there was a calm, peaceful confidence that is discovered in the meditative state. Theodore beside him in the two-seater, had intended to explain some of his reasons for coming along, but after the car took the driveway corner, his mind was able to hold nothing except acute fright. Josh slid around corner after corner, missing trees and ditches by inches as he drifted past them at 120 miles per hour. The gear box sang as Joshua manipulated it, and the machine settled to a smoothly howling whine as Josh flattened out at 150 on the four-lane. It would be only minutes before they reached the airport.

"They ought to put a grand prix course along that road back there, and name it after you," Theodore managed, as the relatively straight road numbed his sense of fear somewhat.

"Relax, Ted." Starr was settled deep into his seat, his arms straight. "Magicians don't have accidents."

This comforted Theodore very little. The ribbon of blacktop was untangling behind them at an impossible speed. Theodore's pale skin was even paler, from the emotions he felt; his whole expression had lost its gentle sweetness, and taken on a tone of dogged determination.

The ordeal was over quickly, as Joshua rapidly downshifted, and moved more and more slowly into a left turn around and under the viaduct as they entered the Washington National Airport area. One stop sign, and they were parking at the executive terminal. Starr was still wasting no time; he slammed the car door and sprinted for the office. Theodore was out of his side of the car and running fast but lagging behind, and feeling like thunder trying to keep up with lightning.

Joshua was flagged down by a young, thin office clerk as he passed the main desk. "Mr. Starr? Joshua Starr?"

The clerk held out a telephone. "Call for you, sir."

The magician broke his run to take the receiver. "Yes?" he said, his voice impatient.

"Josh? Thought I'd be able to catch you. Told the boy there just to stop any maniac who …"

"What is it, Pablo?"

"Joshua, I just had a call from the detective agency you employed for us in Miami. The Acme Detective Agency. They reported no sighting of Trostrick, but he said that one of the men he had working on our case was accidentally killed in a traffic mishap right outside the terminal doors. Does that suggest anything to you?"

"Yeah. We're on our way."

Joshua handed the receiver back to the clerk and began to run again, past several desks and some seated customers; he was stopped again by his name, spoken by a pudgy, blonde man who was extending his hand to him. "Mr. Starr?" asked the man pleasantly.

"Let's go," said Joshua, passing him at a dead run.

The pilot joined the retinue, and fitted neatly between Starr and Theodore as they raced for the small jet. They climbed the air stairs at the front of the aircraft, and thoroughly startled a short man with a bright red handlebar moustache who was comfortably reclining in one of the executive chairs of the cabin's rich interior. The bright blue eyes looked out between the moustache and a thatch of similarly red hair. "Mr. Starr?" he said, in unconscious repetition of his copilot's greeting.

Joshua had a similar lack of tact with him. "Can we take off immediately?"

"That's what we're here for," said the pilot, good-naturedly enough to take Starr at his word, regardless of the way he seemed to disdain the amenities. He sat down in the left seat. His hand moved swiftly over the fuel boost pump switches and the ignition. He depressed the number two starter solenoid switch and spun the compressor of the right engine. The copilot raised the air-stair and put his shoulder against the plug-type door, turning the handle to lock position as the jet engine started its whine outside.

The copilot slid into the right seat and took the radio microphone off its hook under the window on his side of the cockpit and turned the volume up. "Clearance delivery, Lear four seven two eight alpha, to Ft. Lauderdale."

The loudspeaker above the copilot's head came back immediately: "Four seven two eight alpha is cleared to the Ft. Lauderdale Airport. Depart south, over the river. Noise abatement. Vectors Casanova, Gordonsville, J 37. Flight plan route: maintain four thousand. Expect flight level two three zero after Gordonsville."

The copilot read back the clearance, was acknowledged, and switched over to ground control. "Two eight alpha at Page. Taxi," he said into the microphone, his voice barely audible to Josh, but perfectly clear to the controller in the tower. His thumb flipped the mike switch, and ground control was answering efficiently: "Two eight alpha is cleared to runway one eight. Or you can use one five, if you want."

"We'll use one five," said the copilot, glancing at four air carriers in line for one eight.

The small man whose face was so totally dominated by the elegant red moustache moved his hands with professional speed over the necessary switches to complete the checklist. He applied power with the thrust levers, and they were moving at last, the wheels rolling forward across the executive ramp.

The copilot moved the control yoke through full travel, checking for freeness, and switched the radio to tower frequency. "Two eight alpha is ready when we get there," he said into the mike.

The answer boomed back, holding a tinny chuckle. "Two eight alpha is cleared for immediate take off when you get there. Traffic's three miles, final for one eight."

The pilot had the thrust levers slightly forward as they rounded the corner of the runway and straightened out on the 150 degree heading. He moved the levers up to the 2.28 limit, and the jet accelerated rapidly. It was running almost empty, no luggage, only two passengers and the crew, and the full fuel tanks.

As the nose lifted away from the ground and pushed sharply upward, the copilot contacted departure control and was cleared to flight level four one zero. Josh and Theodore sank down into two overstuffed couches in the deluxe cabin and, as the small jet moved south at mach .78, composed themselves for a brief nap. "Don't know what you were so excited about back there on the way to the airport," said the magician. "We weren't going one third this fast, then."

They slept lightly, dozing into their cushions with the slight consciousness of exhaustion at a time of continuing stress, neither fully asleep nor completely awake, until the small pilot put his fiery head into the cabin to say, "Ft. Lauderdale, coming up."

"Thanks," said Joshua, sitting up. "Could you call ahead for a rental car?"

"Sure could." The pilot had been watching Josh and Theodore with some interest. He had extreme disrespect for the usual corporate types that rented this expensive an airplane usually, going off somewhere to close one of their endless deals. He had watched so many of them climb aboard and drink until their destination was reached, without ever looking or sounding even vaguely intelligent. This Mr. Starr looked quite a different article. And his obvious exhaustion bespoke a possibly interesting recent past. He also seemed very anxious, now that he was up, to get where he was going. "What's up?" he asked Joshua.

Josh grinned. "The good guys is chasing the bad guys. Speed is essential, man."

"You're in the right place for that," said the pilot. "Listen, if there's anything I can do to help out when we land, count me in. Always glad to help out one of the good guys."

"That goes for me too," said the copilot.

"Thanks," said Joshua. "Just get me on the ground."

"Roger wilco," said the red-haired pilot. "I think we can work that out."

Theodore had come up to the door of the cockpit, and they all looked through the windscreen as they began descending. Lights spread out below them in the gathering dusk as far as their eyes could see: Highway A ı A shone all the way from West Palm Beach to Homestead Air Force Base south of Miami like a gaudy necklace. Miami was solid with light in the dimness below them, and they could hear loud speakers identifying Miami Approach Control. They were cleared down to two thousand feet for an approach to runway nine left at the Ft. Lauderdale Airport. The gear and flaps were down; the copilot had completed the before-landing checklist. The pilot pushed the thrust levers forward and the plane stabilized at a 600 foot-per-minute rate of descent, on final approach to the runway below.

"Down and three green," sang the copilot. "Full flaps, and clear to land."

The pilot made the touch-down while the copilot was in touch with ground control, and they taxied to a hangar complex at the extreme south end of the field, where a tired-looking line boy dressed in white wandered out and directed them to a parking area. The air stairs went out and down, and the copilot opened the door. "You going to a motel?" asked Josh.

"No, there's a condominium apartment that the company keeps here," said the pilot. "We'll check in there, and you can call us any time." He gave Josh a card. "One of us will make a point of being by the phone. We can be ready to go anywhere you want in ten minutes."

As the pilot started down the air stairs and signaled the line boy to top off the tanks, Josh was off and running again, Theodore close behind. He almost ran up against a rather heavy-set man, who was coming through the office door of the flying service with a coffee cup in one hand, the other hand outstretched, and a big grin on his face. "Hello," he greeted in a gravelly voice. "My name ..."

Joshua barreled past him; the man ducked quickly and then looked ruefully at his coffee-stained shirt front.

"Is that the rent-a-car?" asked Josh.

"Yes, it is. The keys are on the counter there." The paunchy man moved back behind the desk. "And here are the papers ..."

"The pilot will take care of the papers," said Josh over his shoulder as he went through the front door.

"But you'll need a copy," said the genial, coffee-stained man ineffectually, as he heard the unmistakable sound of gravel-spitting departure.

Chapter Fifteen

Sgt. John Armstrong was a very tenacious man. That was written in the way he walked, in the set of his jaw. It was a part of his personality that the twenty years he had spent in the military had nurtured. Since he had come to the C.I.D. he had, like the Canadian Mountie, always got his man. And this one was going to be no exception. Not if Sgt. John Armstrong of the United States Army could help it.

The major had been only too glad, at the end of a terrible afternoon, to be rid of him. In fact, he didn't like to think of how glad the officer had been to say good-bye. He hadn't even quibbled about letting him use the military police sedan as they left the police station. How could the major have failed to fathom the vast importance of securing the U.S. Army against the plots that these spies were right now perpetrating?

But he was not going to give up. It wouldn't do for a man who saw his duty to shirk. No, he would stand, alone if need be, against the enemy horde from outer space. And one day, when the war was over and its history was written, it could just be that his name would figure large in the accounts of those great days. He would have struck the first, perhaps the deciding, blows. He would have been able to see what was happening long before anyone else did; his ability to grasp situations would be unquestioned. Perhaps he would be cast in bronze, and be set with statues of other American patriots who had given their lives, their loyalties, their intelligence in the service of their country.

He, Sgt. John Armstrong, would do this, by himself. And, to begin with, he was going to follow the two spies to their lair. Beard the alien in his den, so to speak. His aggressively clean, stubby fingers flexed on the steering wheel. He would do what he could. That he vowed.

He followed the lawyer's car with professional ease. The Padeyevsky estate was quite easy to infiltrate. Although there was open country in back of the mansion, the acreage on each side of the house was dense, uncut forest land. There was a front lawn, but it was modest, and both sides of the house were very close to the heavy woods. He had no trouble getting next to one of the side windows of the front parlor, where the front of the house went back for half a room before spreading out into the additional width of the screened-in porch.

Armstrong heard Padeyevsky's telephone conversation with Josh at the airport. Josh and Theodore were apparently headed for Fort Lauderdale.

Now there was a decision to make. His future as a patriot depended upon this! Should he watch the man from space, who was at present not twenty feet from him, on the porch, or should he go off after Joshua and Theodore, and find the space girl with them?

It was a hard decision. A bird in the hand seemed worth two in the bush. And yet, the major had had the man from space, but the importance hadn't seemed to register. Perhaps he could get more evidence by following Joshua. There wasn't any more evidence here.

And how could he get to Florida before Joshua did? Joshua was already in the air. The Sergeant spent some minutes in thought and decided that, in addition to laying his life on the line for his country, he was going to have to lay his finances at its disposal as well. It was a hard blow. But he could see no way out. And perhaps, if he kept careful accounts of all that he had spent in its service, his country would see fit to reimburse him after the holocaust had been averted.

He was going to have to call a detective agency, the same as Joshua had. Because he had to have them followed, until he could get there and take over himself.

His decision made, he moved his broad, strong back away from the wall, pulled his shoulders back rather painfully, and was up on stiff legs. The car took him to another of those public telephones; grimacing slightly with distaste he picked up the receiver of this one, deposited the coin that was doubtless at least as filthy as the receiver was, and called Miami Information to ask for the name of the first detective agency in the book. He didn't care. Any one would do.

He was soon speaking to the Acme Detective Agency. When they discovered that they were talking to a man connected with the Army C.I.D., they were most anxious to accept his business. "We're a little understaffed, right now," said the man in Miami. "But we'll make a special effort in your case, Sgt. Armstrong."

They were commissioned to put a tail on two men who fitted the descriptions of Joshua and Theodore, who would be arriving in Fort Lauderdale in a chartered jet. "Yes, Sgt. Armstrong," said the man. "We'll certainly do that. And how shall we report back to you.

"I'll call back later and let you know."

"Yes, Sgt. Armstrong. That'll be fine." The detective hung up feeling rather lightheaded. Two good jobs in one day. The agency was sizeable, but a day when one guy said, "spare no expense," and another had the financial resources of the United States behind him was still a great day.

The only difficulty was that he had men staked out at every airport around here already; he'd already had to call in every part-time agent he had on the books. He called around, and could find no one else to put on the case. There was only one thing to do: double up the assignments. Put the same men on both cases, and when one broke, then he could reshuffle his agents to fill in. He had a contact in Miami Air Traffic Control Center that should help in the chartered jet case. He'd lost one man just this afternoon, in one of those freak accidents. Damn rich snobs, too busy spending their money to watch out for a pedestrian. It was terrible. This was a rich man's city, all right. The chauffeur probably wouldn't even go to jail.

But that, which was neither here nor there as far as the business went, had lost him a very good operative. One that he'd had to replace, since this Mr. Padeyevsky had said that the subject he wanted found would most likely be coming into Miami International. He sighed, and pulled his phone over to him. He was out of ulcer medicine, too. Well.

He called the number reported in by Ernesto Lopez, the part-time operative who had been covering the Ft. Lauderdale Airport for Padeyevsky. Lopez was a good man, although too fat and too old to be of full-time caliber. He was also too fat and too old to be hired as a policeman. Which was a shame. Because in his native country Lopez had been a policeman, and a good one, for Battista, until Castro's government had finally made him feel it would be better for him and his family to leave. And he had left with all possible haste, in fear for his wife and his children. In fear that his children would grow up in a country they could no longer love. And in fear for his wife, if she were left a widow. He had decided that Miami was a better port of entry than New York City. The trip was cheaper; the ghettos were not as bad.

But it had been bad enough here. He was not trained for any but police work. When he couldn't get that, there were two possible roads left open to him. He could become a criminal, which he was well suited to do, having studied criminal techniques for many years, and being possessed of a quick, shrewd mind. Or he could search for other honest work.

Ernesto Lopez was an innately good man. He did not become a criminal. To feed his wife and children, whom he loved deeply, he discovered it would be necessary to work as a dishwasher in a restaurant, or as a pumper of gasoline for cars. He liked the outdoors. He pumped gasoline. No one else would hire him, a short, powerfully muscled man whose body looked weak and ungainly in its heaviness of girth. His face was always oily; he looked as though he never washed; his beard was heavy; his hair was black and straight. He looked all too much like what he was, an immigrant. There were so many immigrants in Miami. All looking like him, all wanting jobs, and mostly younger and cleaner looking.

He supposed he had been lucky to find work at all. And it was not too bad, pumping the gas in the pleasant neighborhood in Ft. Lauderdale. Even though it paid very little, so that he had difficulty giving his family what they needed. They had to live far away, in north Miami, and he had trouble even coaxing his ancient car to make the trips to and from his employment. It was difficult. And he had been glad to discover part-time employment with the Acme Detective Agency. For they paid much more, by the hour, than did the gasoline station. And he could do the work. It challenged him a little, more than the gasoline pumping did. But more, it soothed him. He was used to doing this kind of work. He could feel, evanescently, that he belonged to his new country when he was on these assignments.

But perhaps, more than anything, he was simply happy to be earning money for his family. And he had grabbed this assignment eagerly and without thought, even though he had already worked a shift and a half at the gasoline pumping, and his hands were dark with grease still, and smelling of the gasoline. He had gone to the Ft. Lauderdale Airport, had placed himself in a strategic location so that he could see all of the active runways, and had placed an out-of-order sign on the nearby pay phone, after calling its number in to the detective agency.

He nearly went over backwards in his tilted chair when the telephone in the booth rang. His bulk moved quickly to the telephone; he had picked up the receiver by the end of the second ring. "Lopez," he said into it.

"Lopez," said the agency man, "You've got another case now, as well as the blonde girl. You are also watching for two men in a chartered jet." He gave Lopez Joshua Starr's and Theodore Behr's descriptions. "If you spot the girl, just call in and report. The client didn't ask us to follow her. But if you spot the two men, follow them if you can, as long as they are in the area. If you can't, call in and report the direction they were last seen going, and then get back and watch for the girl again. Got that?"

"Yes, si, amigo," said Lopez. "I will watch for them all three. And I will call you if I find anything to report."

He hung up, went back to his chair, and began thinking. How could he get from here to his car fast enough to follow the two men if they did come in here? The field was huge; maybe five miles of road stood between the most widely separated of the hangars. Which one would they go to? He couldn't possibly get to some of them in time to catch the two men, if he had to watch them land and taxi to their destination first. And yet he couldn't leave here to try to find out from the tower, unless he knew when they were coming in. And, too, he mustn't neglect his watch for the beautiful blonde. Although that, most unfortunately for him, was surely a hopeless task. To find one beautiful blonde girl at the Ft. Lauderdale Airport. As though they had said, Lopez, we want the sweet stalk in this field of sugar cane.

The telephone in the booth rang again; again Lopez moved his ponderous bulk to it. The call solved his difficulties, and set his heart racing. How much money might he make this night! The man at the agency had told him. "Listen, Lopez. Miami Center has just received a hand-off from Jacksonville on a chartered jet. It's supposed to land in Ft. Lauderdale a few minutes from now. Sounds like what we're looking for. Be on your toes, and if they fit the descriptions, try to tail them. Forget about the blonde girl. I'm sending a man out now to cover that. Got it?"

"Yes, si, I have it. And I will keep up with them. And report back later, yes?"

"Right. Just keep them in sight, Lopez. Now, the number on the airplane is four seven two eight alpha. Got that? That's what you're looking for."

"OK," said Lopez, anxious to hang up and get ready. "Thank you. Good-bye, amigo."

He hung up. The first thing would be to go to the Control Tower. He had to find out what flight service they were going to. He had some experience in this sort of investigation. He had been a policeman for a long time, in Cuba.

He sat for a minute, and formulated his plan, rehearsed his speech. Then he ran up the steps to the Control Tower. This time of the evening, there was very little air traffic, and the Federal Aviation Agency employees welcomed any visitors. He launched immediately into his speech, the company chauffeur speech. He was hoping that they'd heard many variants of it, over the years, and it looked as though they had, for they nodded as he told them that his employers were coming in on a chartered jet, four seven two eight alpha, and that they had been here before, but had been dissatisfied with the service they'd gotten at the hangar they'd used then, and were going to change to another one. They'd told him which one, explained Lopez, looking very Latin, very unhappy, but he couldn't remember which one. They were due in at any moment. Could he just stay here until they landed, and find out where they were going to go?"

"Sure, Mr. Lopez," said one of the men. "They'll radio us where they wish to taxi as soon as they land. Just have a seat. You say they'll be in soon?"

Lopez nodded, thanked the man profusely, and sat down to wait. When the airplane was on the ground, and had switched to ground control and advised the tower of its destination, Lopez moved towards the door and said, "Thank you so much."

And so he was in his moving car, and close enough to identify Joshua's shaggy mop of hair as he and Theodore spat gravel away from their rear wheels and took the bumpy side road away from the south end of the field, He was able, barely able, to keep behind them as they drove recklessly, in irresponsible abandon, towards the ocean. Lopez kept a wary eye on the needle which quivered at the right end of his temperature gauge; he watched droplets of brownish water spray back onto his windshield as the radiator cap strained against its fitting. It had been clear that these two were bent upon their own destruction. But the speed also made it clear that these were his prey. And he was not going to lose them. This was the job he could do; the pumping of gasoline was no job! He felt no exhilaration at the chase; the emotion that swept through him was utter fear, that he should be going this quickly, in a vehicle which had previously been nursed just to move at all. It was making noises, and moaning in its bones with every jolt of the suspension; the bald tires were beyond trusting. But he would not lose them. There could be a full night's employment here, perhaps more than that. Perhaps the agency would keep him on this case, since he had so successfully begun it. And if he showed the agency what he could do, might they not use him more? He bent over the steering wheel and clung grimly to the road in front of him, slowing when they did, and finally parking his ancient automobile under overhanging palm branches when they did. He began to make his way after them in the moonlight.

Joshua had become aware that they were being followed before they were off the airport road, but he had been completely unable to figure out who had sent the tail. The obvious person to follow them was Trostrick, or Trostrick's agent, but there seemed little possibility that anyone connected with Trostrick would drive the dying pile of junk that was behind them. It amazed him that the vehicle had been able to keep up with their new rental car. As he neared the Trostrick estate, he dismissed the man from his mind altogether. The only important thing at this point was to move in as quickly as possible, and try to retrieve the girl from space before she was an imprisoned spirit. For once Trostrick had succeeded in completely subjugating her mental body, there was no hope of saving her. No hope at all, as far as Joshua knew.

Because of the urgency of Joshua's mission, he had not taken the time to prepare protections against the various spiritual dangers that might be waiting for anyone who crossed Trostrick's property line. The black magician could have done many things, all of them most detrimental to trespassers' continued health and well-being. But there was no time to lessen the risks. He turned to Theodore.

"Listen, Ted. This is the most dangerous thing I've ever done. Or you've ever done. I don't know what's waiting for us, and I don't have the time to find out. But the best chance of coming through this is for you to take my hand and don't let go, whatever you do. I don't expect any physical danger; the danger we face is much greater than physical death. Do you understand me?"

Theodore had watched Joshua closely ever since he had met him. He had seen that Josh was never completely serious; that he used the language lightly, never trying to say too much with it.

And this last sentence or two of Joshua's was different. It was not lightly said. If Joshua said there was danger here, there was indeed. Theodore took the magician's hand, and felt the beginning of strong apprehension move across his back, and down his spine. "I won't let go for anything," said Theodore. "But what do you expect will happen?"

"I don't know." Joshua's face was baffled. "It would take me quite some time to shield us from all the things that Trostrick might have done. There are so many magical techniques for people like him to make use of. I do expect something, because there are no fences around his property, which would lead one to look for protection of his place by non-physical means. I am just hoping that whatever he has set up, I can counter by what I know. I want you to hold on to me for two reasons; first, your light will help me. And second, I can protect you only if I have contact with you. Now, don't let go."

The two men wriggled out of the rented car, clasped hands, and began to run in step across the palm-studded lawn towards Trostrick's side yard. Lopez, getting out of his car to follow, shook his head. He had seen a lot of things in his day, but two young men holding hands in the moonlight-that was a new one! He followed them to the side yard, and watched them run in step across the long, curving driveway, and onto a stone patio. He saw them disappear inside a wide glass door, the slightly taller of the two men pushing the door open without letting go of the other man's hand. Now what should he do? He decided to wait here for a few minutes, and go inside only if they did not come out again.

Ted and Josh had made very little noise as they moved lightly and carefully across the patio and into the house itself. Joshua had his spirit braced for any assault, and was astonished as he stepped inside the door to discover that not one trace of threat had been placed in their way. It seemed arrogance to Joshua, that a man with so much at his command would not bother to use any of it for his protection. But it was a relief, and a help to them now. Joshua realized that since he was in the house, and could still sense no assaults upon his mental or physical senses, he could go to work unhindered.

He stopped in the darkened living room, looking about him. There were no lights showing. There had been one small lamp shining out a window above the garage; Joshua had decided that must be where the chauffeur slept. It was a small light, and the window was small and opaque; Josh had deduced, correctly, that it was a bathroom light, and that the chauffeur was probably in bed for the night.

Josh waited until he had become aware of a tiny sliver of light down the hall that led off the living room. The source of the radiation was at the very end of the long passageway, and he and Theodore walked down the hall to it, pulled aside the red curtains that covered the doorway, and discovered the same scene that had greeted the girl from space. The unclothed body of Trostrick lay on the black table; the thick tapers flickered lower in their sconces.

And Theodore's apprehension grew to cutting awareness of the danger of which Joshua had spoken. For the room was alive with evil; it could be felt, palpable on the skin. The baseness which he sensed made him feel a degradation of the spirit which went far beyond the intellectual awareness of degradation, and the chill of the room's aura pulled at Theodore's very soul, and made him press his hand even more tightly into Joshua's, putting all his faith in the man of light.

Joshua had been standing next to the body for some few seconds, his eyes closed in concentration. He opened them now, and whispered to Theodore. "We're in real luck. He's not with his body. I think we can handle things now. Once we gain control of Trostrick's physical body, we should be able to get the girl from space away from him. After all, a black magician would be seriously handicapped without a physical body, far more so than a white magus."

Joshua turned towards the velvet curtain, checking to be sure that they were still safely alone, and saw two green eyes about six inches past his shoulder, and about six inches higher. He barely had time to take in the rest of the manservant's huge proportions before the heavy fist had crunched into his face, tearing him off his feet and away from the altar.

Theodore had closed his hand upon Joshua's in the spasmodic grip of a frightened man, and he was carried with Josh, but he did not fall, until the enormous fist found the whole side of Theodore's face. The welded grip was broken, and through shock-clouded eyes, Joshua saw Theodore sprawl and lie quite still. He struggled against the demands of his pain to get up, and had pulled himself as far as his knees when the leather-covered iron of the man's heavy boot caught him solidly in the right side of the chest and tossed him, still conscious, into a now immobile heap.

The huge man's green eyes turned to the velvet door, and he moved with slow grace, reaching behind its outer folds bringing out a curved sword. The scimitar was easily recognizable to Joshua, even as he lay paralyzed with loss of breath. It was of ceremonial value in certain magical rituals. With every ounce of his will, Joshua tried to rise to ward off this attack, but he found himself totally helpless. He prepared his spirit for physical death, and watched the great blade rise into the air above the huge manservant's head, and poise for the downward blow.

And then, without warning, going inexplicably out of character, the large man pitched uncontrollably forward. The scimitar missed Joshua and clanged loudly but harmlessly against the floor. Behind the manservant stood the still, tensed figure of Ernesto Lopez, who had come into the house, entering as he had seen the two ahead of him do, who had seen the enormous man go through the velvet curtain, and who had watched what happened thereafter until he could no longer remain neutral. For he was a good man, and it was quite impossible for him to stand by and allow a murder to be accomplished.

The huge man apparently decided that three opponents, including one strong enough to send him to his knees with a single well-placed blow, were too many to handle comfortably. He picked up Joshua and Theodore and threw them clumsily through the curtain, strong-arming Lopez after them. They heard the sound of a heavy door swinging on its hinges, and there was a concussive thud as it was closed behind the curtain. It would appear that their assailant had locked himself and his master in the ceremonial chamber.

Lopez frisked the unconscious Theodore, and bent over Joshua to do the same. "I would not attack me, if I were you," he said, "for I have much skill in fighting, and I am armed with a knife."

"No, man," spoke Josh haltingly, painfully. "We're not going to bug you. Go ahead. Search me." The swarthy Lopez did so. "We just want to thank you for saving our lives."

Lopez's broad face broke into a smile. "It was no trouble."

"Is there a locked door there now?" asked Joshua, inclining his sore neck and head towards the chamber.

Lopez got up, satisfied that neither Theodore nor Joshua had any weapons, and put his shoulder to the curtain. Wood behind it creaked slightly. "A sturdy door, with a sturdy lock," said the Cuban.

There was a sudden vibration in the floor upon which Joshua sat, fighting for breath. The vibration grew greater, and they could hear the muffled, close sound of a power boat almost directly under them.

"Go outside and see what that is," said Joshua. "Please, man. I just can't make it yet."

Lopez looked quickly from Josh to Theodore. He could hardly see how the man could be lying. And the other man was obviously still unconscious. He nodded, and ran back through the living room, and out across the patio, just in time to see a boat with an enormous hulk of a man at the wheel go out of sight around the curve of the shoreline. He turned, his eye caught by a motionless form on the beach. He moved closer to it. It was a girl's body, stiff on the sand. She was obviously dead. Well, he could come back to look at her in a minute. She would keep. Right now the important thing was to discover where the boat had come from.

He ran on the beach towards the far side of the house, and found the neat parking place for the boat, right under the house, the water lapping on its foundations. There were steps to a walkway under the house from the patio; he ran down them and on to a little pier. Here was a door into the interior of the house. It was unlocked. Lopez went through it and ascended steep stairs into the magical chamber from which they had just been evicted. There was no longer a body on the black marble table. The servant must have the body with him in that boat.

This was most puzzling, most peculiar. Lopez walked through the chamber, ignoring a slight feeling of unease, and unlocked the bolted door. It swung back and he secured it beneath the velvet curtain, and again confronted Joshua and Theodore.

The unconscious one had regained his senses. His eyes were open, and one hand was touching his bruised face. The other man was in the same position in which he had been left; his hands were also exploring his hurts, feeling his ribs, very gingerly, for breakage. These two hadn't put up much resistance to the big man, that was sure. Maybe they shouldn't have been so eager to hold hands. They might have been able to use them for fighting if they had been free. Lopez shook his head again.

What was he going to do with them? They were a meal ticket now; he had been given orders to spot and follow them, and he couldn't have carried his orders out more thoroughly. They were here now, right under his thumb. Perhaps he could enhance this good fortune by discovering some information in excess of his assignment. There was such an air of strangeness to this whole case, this sequence of events, that he didn't know whether he should assume that these men were honest or criminal, sane or insane. That room, so full of an unnamable dark force, was like the movies of horror he had so enjoyed when he was a child. He did not enjoy them in real life. The hand holding. That too was extraordinary. The body on the table, the one on the beach. Extraordinary, and very evil.

He decided that the best policy in this case would be straightforward honesty. He could perhaps find out something while these men were still in shock from their recent beating. If he could just intimidate them a little. He addressed Starr, the older of the two men.

"My name is Ernesto Lopez. I am a private detective from the Acme Detective Agency."

Joshua looked distinctly puzzled, an unusual reaction.

"I will shortly be calling my agency, and the police in the city. But first, if you have anything to tell me, I would be happy to hear of it."

"Joshua Starr," said Josh, "and this is Theodore Behr. I'm the one that hired you, man."

Lopez's eyes lost their focus as he tried to unravel that statement. Why would Joshua Starr employ him to find Joshua Starr?

"I am sorry, Mr. Starr, but I was hired to find you. You could not have hired me."

"I hired the Acme Agency in Miami to find a blonde girl that was coming into the area by plane. Weren't you looking for her?" Lopez nodded. "I was looking for her, and also for you. Her I did not find. You, I did."

Starr was still checking. "She was tall, and blonde, and very beautiful ..."

Lopez made a halting motion with both hands. "Yes, yes, I was watching for her. But I did not see her."

Well, thought Starr, another little mystery. Who could have known that he and Behr were coming here? It didn't seem to matter, any more than the fact that Lopez was following them had seemed to matter. Things all paled before the main point: to find the girl from space.

He withdrew into his painful body for a moment, and looked carefully at the aura of the private detective. It seemed quite light, and free from the heavy, baser matter of the lower mental planes. Joshua decided that it might be a good risk to be honest with the man, despite the fact that he had been telling their predicament to too many people. "It doesn't matter about who hired you," he said. "This is a matter of life and death that Mr. Behr and I are concerned with. The blond girl that you were assigned to spot was kidnapped, and we suspect the man who owns this house of being the kidnapper. That's why we came here. He's the one lying in that room, on the table." Joshua turned with painful slowness to look into the chamber, and saw for the first time that Trostrick's body was gone.

"I saw the big man drive away in a motorboat," said Lopez in explanation. "I think perhaps he has taken the man of whom you speak with him, for there was no one in the chamber when I came through it, and there are steps directly down from the room to the place where the boat is kept." His mind went over his run down to the boat, and suddenly he thought more carefully of the body he had briefly but professionally examined on the beach. A tall, blonde body. She had had a blindfold on her eyes, and she had been tied. Was this not the obvious victim of a kidnapping?

Lopez looked keenly at Starr. He would not have the man going down on the beach and destroying evidence, trampling around in the surrounding sand, perhaps even moving the body. This was a matter for the police. But the man should be told that his search had ended. He spoke slowly, watching Starr carefully. "There is a body that fits the description you have given very well, out on the beach. No, no, she is dead," he said louder, as Starr attempted to rise to his feet, gasping audibly with the pain that knifed through his body at the movement.

"I've got to look at her," said Starr.

"No, there is no need," said the Cuban. "She is dead. I am sure of that. I have seen many dead. We shall call the police."

He moved slowly down the hall, looking for the telephone, and wondering if Starr had anything more to tell him.

"Wait," said Starr, finally managing to stand on both feet and balance. "There is no hurry to do that, is there? Let me tell you something first."

Lopez smiled a little. His plan of intimidation seemed to be working; perhaps he would be able to get quite a lot of information this way. "Let us go into the living room," he said, "and there you can sit more comfortably. And also this one, he can rest there better than here."

He helped Theodore to his feet. The boy had come dazedly awake now, still barely in reality. "You warned me of danger," he said to Joshua as he stumbled, held by Lopez's arms, "but you said it wasn't going to be physical."

"Man," said Joshua, "I never dreamed that an Ipsissimus, with the whole lower astral plane at his fingertips, would ignore the whole thing and hire a goon. I'm sorry. I would have expected anything before getting mauled by King Kong!"

Lopez deposited Theodore on a sofa, and sat down in a chair next to Joshua. "And what was it that you wished to tell me?" he asked.

Joshua looked very deeply into Lopez's dark, soft eyes. "I have strong reason to believe that the girl on the beach is not dead, but merely deeply asleep," he said.

"She was dead," said Lopez, noticing the steadiness of Starr's gaze, finding it unexpectedly pleasant.

"No, she was merely given a very strong drug to make her sleep. This is a new drug, an experimental drug, and it produces drowsiness. It is a drug that brings on sleep. It is a drug that suggests sleep. It produces such a deep sleep that it approaches very closely the condition of death, but it is only sleep, a very comfortable, deep sleep. A very, very deep sleep." Starr's voice became slower as he gazed intently into the Cuban's eyes, and continued to talk about sleep. He discussed deep sleep for a full five minutes, until Lopez was in a deep trance, and then suggested to the detective that he lie down on the sofa. He suggested that he would sleep there until morning. Lopez lay down on the couch obediently. He was fully relaxed.

Joshua grinned at Theodore, who grinned back, uncertainly, through the damage. They both looked considerably the worse for wear. Joshua made the sign of victory with his thumb and forefinger, and then waggled the fingers at Theodore. They quietly walked out the patio door, and towards the still figure which lay so stiffly upon the gentle, yielding sand.

CHAPTER SIXTEEN

Joshua and Theodore turned from the sleeping Lopez and ran out across the patio and onto Trostrick's private beach. They found the girl they had come to find. She was lying still as a corpse.

Joshua regarded her in the moonlight, then shut his eyes and released his close bonds with his physical being. Theodore stood by, feeling that his most helpful attitude would be one of calm support. In a few minutes, Joshua's eyes were open again. He picked up the girl's body, his lean strength making the awkward bundle manageable. "Let's get out of here. Trostrick may come back any minute." He started towards the driveway.

"Is she dead?"

"No. She's left her physical body, but the body isn't harmed in any way."

"Can we get her back, like you did the man from space?"

"No." Joshua let it go at that until they were in the rental car. "You wait here a minute. I want to make some calls."

He walked back into the house and dialed the phone, looking at the pilots' card he took from his wallet; they were just beginning to settle for the night, and were immediately available for the trip back to Washington. He called Pablo next, and told him to meet the plane.

"We've got her physical body, Pablo," said Josh. "That's not what you'd call a complete victory."

"Well, Josh, it'll all work out. See you soon."

"Yeah," said Josh. He was out to the car and in the driver's seat at a run, and began the drive back to the Ft. Lauderdale Airport. Theodore swallowed his fear at the excessive speed which seemed to be becoming a habit with Joshua, and sat with the girl in the back seat.

"You say we can't bring her back, Josh?"

"No. It looks like she left the physical of own free will. At least, there was no sign of trauma from the outside. Until we can contact her spirit, there is no way we can hope to retrieve her."

"Where do you think she is?"

Joshua sighed, as though the events of the last twenty four hours were finally catching up with his energies. "I can guess. In the lower of the astral planes, there are many places of such strong negativity that research on them has been impossible. Trostrick would try to put her in a place from which there could be no escape, any more than our physical bodies could escape from prison. I was not able to contact her." Starr sat up a little in his seat. "But we'll keep trying."

He was slowing down now for the turns into the parking area in front of the flying service which had hangared their plane. Leaving the rental car where they had found it, they walked into the office of the place, and found their red-haired pilot, ready for them this time. "Flight plan's filed. We're set to go right now."

The pilot accepted Joshua's story about the reason for the condition of the girl much more easily than he had hoped, seeming quite willing to believe that she had been a kidnapping victim who had been drugged. He replied only that he was glad Joshua had rescued her, and that he wished he could have been part of the action.

The conversation dwindled as Joshua finished making the girl comfortable on one of the couches in the airplane's cabin. He walked back down the air stairs. "I'll see you in a little while, Ted."

Theodore watched him go across the ramp and back inside the office, as the air stairs were retracted. His feelings were divided between intense curiosity and desire to be, as the red-haired pilot had said, part of the action, and an overwhelming flood of relief at being out of the storm for a moment, safe with his prize in hand. He was tired, and home sounded good. He was asleep before the jet had climbed far from Miami's air.

Joshua was tired too, but tired in a deeper sense; his spirit ached in anticipation of the battle it would soon be asked to join. Joshua disliked talking; he knew it was a white magician's weakest weapon, and that he could only hold his own against Trostrick by means of exercises of will he regretted in advance. He regretted them because he knew that he was almost certainly going to use his strength in vain. And yet, he could not go back to the group at the farm until he had tried everything.

His ribs were sore, but it did not seem that any of them had been broken. Joshua's breathing was not as painful as it had been, although he was stiff. The energy that had kept him going for nearly twenty-four hours stood him up and made him alert and quick, but the sour malaise that comes from not having attended to the physical needs of food and rest weighed upon him. He stopped the rented car in plain sight in Trostrick's driveway and was not at all surprised to see Trostrick walk out across the stone patio to greet him. The man's smooth, quiet voice sounded genuinely pleased. "A pleasure, Mr. Starr," he said. He extended his hand courteously.

Joshua looked at the hand a split second, and nodded inwardly. His mind was set more grimly. He accepted the hand. "How do you do, Mr. Trostrick."

"Mr. Lopez has been having some trouble recounting the events of the evening. How unfortunate that there was a misunderstanding! If only I had been expecting you! But tell me, what can I do for you, Mr. Starr?"

Joshua stood in stolid quiet, staring at Trostrick.

"Now then, my dear fellow. Come inside. You do look tired. Do sit down."

Lopez watched Starr move his fingers together and press against his trouser as he sat, composedly and slowly. "Mr. Starr, I will go now. I have the report to make to my employers."

Trostrick's expression showed moderate traces of embarrassment. "Mr. Lopez! Please remain here a little longer. I am sure that we owe you a few more minutes of comfort. To repay you for your moments of discomfort, which I regret. Here. Another drink."

Lopez felt compelled to stay, and he sat next to the finely groomed black magician on the sofa, his round, oily face registering the frustration of entrapment.

"Let him go, Trostrick."

"My dear fellow, he can leave when you do. He has no effect upon our business, does he? Could we not speak of any matter we wished in front of him? He is only the neutral counter of our planet, the man who resembles the powerless men who make up the masses. The powerless masses. Should we who are strong remove ourselves one step for him who is weak? Nonsense! Let him stay. Perhaps he can learn. And you will wish to speak with him before he goes, will you not?"

Joshua realized that Trostrick had arranged the situation so that this exchange of thought could be aired. It gave Trostrick the advantage of attack. He made the only counter-attack left on him. "Trostrick, I have come for the girl that you kidnapped."

"Kidnapped? Such a criminal act? How could you think it of me?"

"I'll change the language then. You have control of the spiritual body of our guest. We have her physical body. We want her spirit back."

"My dear fellow!" Trostrick seemed somewhat disturbed. "You do misunderstand my actions. This girl of whom you speak has made several choices, quite freely. And at this point, her spirit is some way from here, in this illusion we call space and time."

"I want her back now," said Starr.

There was silence in the room and the two men looked steadily at each other. When Trostrick spoke, it was without a flicker of his gaze.

"She will return to you whenever she decides to, my dear fellow. There are certain changes she would have to make in order to come back to you just now, and it would seem that, for the time being, she has decided that she prefers to stay where she is."

Joshua regarded the black magician silently. Trostrick continued.

"Let us say that she is learning a great deal about certain configurations of mind in the mental planes that your program of instruction omitted. Could we allow her education in the ways of this planet to be completed without showing her a full picture? My dear fellow, I sometimes think that you look down on part of our Creator's universe."

"Well, Trostrick, I admit I do look down on conjuring up demons and using them against innocent people like Pablo, when your influence caused him to start the mix-up with the syndicate, or like that deputy's wife, or the Sergeant. You managed to have both of them kill for you. No, I don't approve of that, or of talking an innocent child into a corner from which she can never return without total loss of-what? Her innocence, at least; probably her identity. I don't approve of evil, Trostrick, and I don't approve of you."

Trostrick's eyes softened, and a look of regret crossed his face. "I cannot understand why you think that way. My dear fellow, I do admit to experimentation with demonic forces. I have, in fact, always tried never to miss any opportunity to expand my knowledge and abilities. In fact, I have little time for anything else, no time for physical pleasures. You, I notice, seem to have taken a good deal of time out for such pleasures, through the years."

Implying, thought Joshua, that his power was less because of his lack of total concentration. He had to admit that the black magician was right. His art was not perfect. And Trostrick's seemed to be approaching perfection.

Trostrick was continuing. "And further, something that you said reminds me of one of my main interests. I cannot see why you insist upon saying that our interests differ. Why cannot we unify, and blend our power together? We both want the same thing, do we not?"

"Namely?"

"We both want power, my dear fellow. Power to use for the aid of the masses who are like Mr. Lopez-unwashed, unlearned, undisciplined. We want power to help these people become what they might be, what they have the potential to be. We want power to guide, always remembering that each man must make his own choices. For the Creator made free will a tenet of His universe, and you will find it is the first rule of my magic, as well as it is of yours."

Joshua knew that by "free will," Trostrick meant only the will to choose "freely" between carefully pre-set circumstances. It was the use of black force reduced to the most civilized of garb, and the worst of it was that it made the man so very difficult to fight, using the white arts. For the positive portion of the planetary mind could not recognize this as evil until after it was done, and so its indignation could not be used as a unifying factor. It was a cold war, and Trostrick was the acknowledged master of it. "Our magic is opposite, Trostrick. Our power is opposite. You have polarized towards the negative; I have chosen the positive. We are at opposite ends of the creation. We have no affinity. You have chosen to take the power which you have gained and use it to usurp what you can of what I have attempted to do for the good. Don't call me an ally."

Trostrick shook his head. "Please do not be angry. I think you exaggerate, warp things. I really do, my dear fellow. You say we have no affinity, but how can two things in the same creation be separate? We are simply two sides of a sheet of paper; different, yes, for we face opposite ways. But close, too, for we touch each other at all points, and are made of the same material. Negativity and positivity. Yes, we have chosen these different poles. But what makes one better than the other? They are both provided for in our Creator's universe. The Creator gave us the will to choose one pole or the other. As far as I can see, and I've been an earnest student, my dear fellow, the problem basically is that all of this planet's people haven't really quite chosen between them yet. The consensus leans rather heavily towards negativity. You'll grant me that. But it hasn't identified with it completely. And so it is denied the power that it could receive if only it could completely make the choice. I see it as our job to help the masses find the purity and the power of total polarization. And, really Mr. Starr, isn't it more reasonable to move the short way to the negative pole than to try wrenching the collective consciousness of the planet all the way back to neutral and then all the way over to positivity? That's quite a lot of wasted effort, isn't it? We can guide these poor souls, Mr. Starr, we can help them find the security and stability of total identification with wisdom."

Starr had nothing to say. The man was the culmination of the black magical arts. And he was winning this battle.

"Mr. Starr? Do you not agree? Would you perhaps be willing to help me educate the people of this planet? We could do so much for them. We could give them material security, leave their minds and bodies free from physical trouble, so that they might live out a comfortable life, spending all their time, if they wished, in spiritual seeking. This planet's network of security is constantly growing, and one day we shall have a total and complete system of security for all people. We shall direct the wise hands of the government, which shall in turn remove each problem for each citizen, so that he may lead a life quite free from any worry."

Joshua stood up. "I do not want power over people, Mr. Trostrick. You have a girl trapped outside her physical body. You have the power to bring her back to it. I ask you to do so. I am willing to repay you by taking her place. My mind for hers."

"My dear fellow! What would I do with your mind? It is a good one. A pity, I think, that you have let it wander for the past few years, for it has fallen into error, and chosen the wrong path, the wrong pole, on a planet that has to all intents already chosen the other one. But I have no wish for your subjugation to me. The Creator has willed that each of his creatures shall be free. I assure you, the girl you seek is free. Free to choose."

Starr did not reply; there was nothing to say. He went over to Lopez and put a hand behind his shoulder. "Come on. I'll take you back to your car."

Lopez jumped uncontrollably at the touch, and pulled himself up from the deep cushions.

"Come back again," said Trostrick. "And stay longer next time. There are so many interesting experiences and thoughts we could discuss, if we had the time."

"Thank you," said Starr equably. "Perhaps we'll be in touch again."

"Soon, I hope." Trostrick stood by the glass door, holding the portieres back with a courteous hand.

"I hope so too."

Joshua took Lopez to his car and told him to follow him to the Ft. Lauderdale Airport. When Lopez had nursed the old vehicle to a stop outside the terminal, Joshua leaned into his car window on his elbows. "Listen, Lopez. You have to turn in some kind of report for your other client, don't you? And one for the case I hired you for as well, for the agency's records?"

"Yes, si, Senor. But I am not crazy. If I told them the truth, they would fire me. I will make up something. This much I know. I am glad to be done with the thing!"

"Listen, Go ahead and report things exactly the way you saw them. They won't fire you. Forget the part about being hypnotized. What were your orders for the other case?"

Lopez thought it over. He could see no breach of ethics in telling the man that. "To tail you while you were in the area."

Starr nodded, chin propped on the elbows. "Well, I'm on the next plane back to Washington, either out of here or Miami. You tailed me as far as the airport. OK?"

"Thank you. Yes. That will be fine." It would look good on the report. And he could give a very full report, except for the corpse that he had seen. The blonde corpse, that had disappeared. But that was for Mr. Starr's case anyway, not the other one. He would not have to report that. This Senor Starr was a very helpful person.

"And, listen, Lopez. You probably won't get much for your work tonight. And there's the chance that you may be in for trouble because of it. Take this." He handed the man some bills from his wallet. "And if anything goes wrong at home, or you have bad luck on the job-just anything-you call me collect at this number." He gave Lopez his card. "OK?"

"Why are you worried about me? You don't know me."

"I just am. You call me, all right?"

"Sure. Any problems, I call you."

Starr was satisfied, and walked back to the main terminal building. It was a strange man, thought Lopez as he watched the shaggy-haired, poorly dressed man with the fat wallet. He left to go home and show the $500 the man had given him to his wife. Perhaps this was enough money to go somewhere where a person like him could get a better job. He could look for advertisements. Maybe, somewhere out west, someone would need a policeman. He carefully put the money away.

Starr's body was pulling at his consciousness with the bruises he had sustained in the one-sided fight, but his mind was filled with such a greater pain, as he waited for the trip to be over, that he was not even aware of the hurt ribs. His spirit ached with the traveler's cramp of the defeated; he had had to endure in silence rude injury that he would have liked to avenge by the most extravagant action. By schooling himself to silence and seeming acquiescence he had saved himself to fight another day, for had he fought with the better equipped Trostrick on Trostrick's home ground, he wouldn't have been in one piece, spiritually, for long. He knew he had been shrewd to garner his forces, but there is no medicine for the acid ache of losing. The weight of the whole episode felt its heaviest to him, for he had assumed its onus, and in his own mind he was responsible for the present danger to the girl from space. As he drove the Miura down the narrow road to Pablo's farm, dejection settled into the lines of his face like grime.

Esmerelda's response to the look of hopelessness was a cup of coffee; Pablo's was commiseration. "Well, Josh, at least her body's upstairs, safe and sound. But we can't keep her indefinitely. Church keeps calling, wanting to know the outcome. He says the Sergeant that was with him at the deputy's house has made things a bit hot, calling up people and telling them about men from space. All very difficult. No one believes him, but the Colonel says he doesn't think he can keep it quiet much longer. We're all going to be subpoenaed for the Captain Crouse inquest. How did your business come out? Did you see Trostrick?"

Joshua nodded his head from behind the mug of coffee. "Yes. I talked with him. Trostrick's got her, and he's put her where we thought he would. He admitted it by inference."

"The lower astral?" asked Esmerelda.

Joshua nodded. At Theodore's look of enquiry, he went on. "The lowest of the mental planes are completely negative. I didn't have the time or the inclination to tell you earlier, Ted. But remember I said there were places of maximum negativity? In order for the space girl voluntarily to leave the place she is now, she probably would have to become one with the vibrations of that plane, which would mean that she would release all of her positivity, all of her intelligence, all of her personality, and become as dark as the abyss. Trostrick is waiting for her to do that-of her own free will, of course-and then he will have all the power that her spirit held released into his use."

"How in the world did he do it? I mean, the whole thing?" Theodore was dumbfounded.

Joshua gritted his teeth slightly, and shook his head. "He has been underestimated. For years, apparently, he's had the power to accompany our rituals, and he knew about everything. At least, that's what he inferred. And the fact that he was able to get the girl from space to Miami without our being able to find her would suggest to me that he's not just boasting about being able to mask astral presence. So he just conjured up a slew of minor demons and set them to work, assigning one to Pablo, several years ago and having the others hover around, waiting for targets of opportunity like the deputy's wife and Sgt. Armstrong. He used you, Pablo, instead of the rest of us because we're alien to this planet's mental planes, and far less likely to be affected by one of the demons than a person whose spirit is of this planet. Although, perhaps the whole idea was inspired by the demons!"

"Hush, Josh," said Esmerelda. That's just not so. Demons are too stupid to do more than one thing at a time. So you say he knew all about us, and has been watching us ever since the ritual. Why didn't he come and get the girl himself, instead of going through all the twists and turns? Sheer love of complication?"

"No. From what he said, I gathered that the way he's been working lately, he likes to get people into situations where they can, quote, freely, end quote, choose to do negative things. Apparently this free choice bit is why it's so difficult for us to fight him. He doesn't disturb the positively polarized astral community. Meanwhile, he keeps trapping people by his manipulations, and they do things like betting on horses and shooting people. Anyway, I think the way he got the space girl was by encouraging chaotic situations to develop. He also probably used his act of rescuing the space girl from her kidnappers to influence positive astral thought. Astrals have no more intellect than we do here on Earth, and are certainly as easily fooled by metaphysical politicians. And this Trostrick is a master politician. So Trostrick got her, and then, before he could be recognized as a negative Karcist, he put a shield around her, and she was beyond reach of any of us."

"So Trostrick's just a vote-getter in heaven?" Theodore was frowning at the thought.

Joshua shrugged, with a hint of his usual carelessness. "Sure. All magicians are, for that matter. The heaven world, and the other mental planes, are all peopled to a large extent by human entities that have at one time or another been incarnate on the physical planes of this planet. Many of them will eventually incarnate again. They come in all types and polarities, and together they make up the collective mind of the planet. Some of the entities are positively oriented. Some are negative. I might point out that there is much more negative than positive power. That's obvious. What Trostrick did was trick the positive segment into ignoring him until it was too late to shield the space girl from evil."

"Then what we have to do is get more votes than he has?"

"That's right, Theodore. But I don't think we can. The place that he has taken her has almost never been penetrated by the forces of light. The negativity is simply too strong there. One thing that might comfort you a little, Ted. The girl will not be able to see the ugliness of what she faces. It will look like sheer blackness to her, for she does not, at this time anyway, have a spiritual body that can see such dense matter. So she will be spared viewing the citizens of that plane."

"I'm comforted," said Theodore.

Esmerelda was sitting back into her seat. "Well I'm not. Even though she can't see what is outside her prison, she will know that it is a prison. And that will be terrible for her."

Joshua lowered his head into cupped hands, placing the empty mug on the floor by him. "I know, I know. That man's aura stank like a sewer." He raised his head. "Where's the man from space?"

Esmerelda pointed upstairs. "We left him with his sister's physical body. He and our teacher have been searching for her spirit all night. No luck."

Theodore was doggedly pursuing his train of thought. "Well, then, what do we have to beat? What percentage of the astral consciousness can our most powerful ritual command?"

"I don't know. A very small percent," said Joshua. "Of course, thought's powerful stuff. You don't need much."

"Well, how much can Trostrick command?"

"It's hard to say. He might have as much as ten times what we have focused on this placement of the space girl. The reason for the difference isn't that his magic is stronger, per se. Black magic just takes the white rituals and debases them. It's just that it's more popular. There are just more negatively oriented souls in the voting population than there are positive."

"But we would have to beat his tally?"

"That's right. But the positive population on this planet has been so fragmented by different religions, and sects within the religions, and bad blood between all of them, that there aren't many rituals that are general enough to command that many eyes."

Theodore pushed his lips together, put both palms on his knees, in a gesture of collapse. "So there's nothing we can do?"

Joshua was heavily silent, his mind turning over the events that had brought them from the birth of their hopeful plans to this moment.

Pablo felt that the situation was his fault, just as Joshua felt that it was his. His instinct was towards a sort of helpless belligerence.

"What does Trostrick want, Josh? The end of the world?"

Josh rocked his head from side to side, deathly weary now. "Oh, no. He's very, very fond of things just the way they are. After all, his side is winning. He wants power. Total subjugation of all people here in the physical plane, with their wills dependent completely upon the wills of those he calls their leaders and protectors. He looks for uniformity, control. The ordered society."

Pablo considered. "He's got things working out very nicely for him then, doesn't he? The regimentation is enough to gag you now! You can hardly sneeze without filling out a form! Give the man some time and he should do very well for himself."

Josh nodded. "Yeah. Beautiful little planet, isn't it?" Esmerelda had been silent for a long time, and seemed calmer than any of them as she sat, her head turned out towards the front yard, her forehead furrowed with thought. Pablo noticed her withdrawn look. "Do you have an idea, Esmerelda?"

Esmerelda turned her gaze towards Joshua and contemplated him. After a time, she nodded. "I might, What do you think, Josh, of trying some of the experimental maneuvers that we've discussed before? Summoning a higher power than Trostrick on the negative side?"

Josh raised his head from his hands and narrowed his eyes, thinking about the idea. "Well, I don't know. At least it's a thought."

"What's she talking about?" asked Pablo.

"Black magicians often summon demons and make bargains with them. There are many formulas for calling various demons which we've come across and recorded in our research, and we could make use of one of them, and summon one."

"What could you possibly gain by that?"

"It depends upon the bargain we can strike with him, and the protection we have during the ritual. You see, it's a black magical technique, and white magicians using it are in great jeopardy."

"What bargain could you strike? You don't have anything that's worth more than the girl, do you?"

"Probably not. But it's better to try this than just to sit around and do nothing. Besides, maybe we could just make a bargain to contact the girl, and then we would at least know where she is, for sure. We'd be in a better position to rescue her then."

"That sounds weak." Pablo was beginning to worry about their safety. "Why endanger yourselves when it might not even do any good?"

Joshua's mouth twisted a little in exasperation. "There's nothing else that's even possible. And we can't just do nothing. Doing anything is better than doing nothing! Besides, Pablo, we'll use the best protection we can devise. It won't be too dangerous."

"We could use that old barn for the summoning, Uncle Pablo," said Esmerelda. "We wouldn't want to use the temple for this sort of thing; it would lower the positivity too much. We need a place that's not been used for a while, a neutral ground. The barn would be perfect. We never use it."

That was true. The building had originally been a cattle barn, but its stalls had been removed by the movie company when they had been filming on the property. They had housed their equipment there. It now stood, sound enough, though weathered, filled with a glut of big old things that had been deposited there through the years when they overflowed the house. It was a quarter of a mile past the house along the access road, and cut off from sight by a hill between.

Pablo conceded defeat in his objection-making. "All right. All right. Use the barn. We'll burn it down afterwards. What else do you need?"

"Some wooden crosses, for us to wear for protection." Josh was feeling much more fit now that there was a problem at hand to deal with.

"Yes, that would be the logical thing to do," said Esmerelda. "What else do you suggest?"

"Well, we'll draw the circles and inscriptions very carefully, and be rested before the ceremony. We can clean and disinfect the barn. We'll have the crosses to wear, and I have some other materials at my place."

Esmerelda looked a bit tense. "I was thinking about those crosses, and I remembered something we could use, perhaps, if you think it's a good idea. You know that old hitching post back behind where the old kitchen used to be? I never had it removed, but we certainly never use it, and it's sound enough wood. We could use that wood to make a really large cross, maybe ten feet tall or so, and put it in the center of the barn. Wouldn't that give us more protection?"

"Excellent suggestion," said Joshua. "You don't mind losing the wood? It's probably valuable as an antique."

Esmerelda made a face at him. "I think Pablo and I can live without it."

Theodore was working on the implications of the plan, and asked, "Can you really use black magic without losing your own positivity?"

Joshua tried to explain. "Summoning spirits is not either positive or negative, per se. It's just that most of the spirits that can do you any good are negative. The negativity comes in there. It's usually black magicians who want something done for them on the lower planes. White magicians usually don't have any interests there. But in this case, since we can't penetrate those lower planes alone, we need help. Esmerelda and I have talked about this theory before, and we feel that it's quite possible that, if we summon the spirit for a purpose that is not negative, then we will not be negative by requesting it. Of course, since the spirit itself will be negative, we'll have to go to all these elaborate precautions to protect ourselves against it. As I told you at Trostrick's house, the dangers are far worse than physical death. In fact, it might be better if you and Pablo didn't take part in this."

Looks from both Pablo and Theodore informed Joshua that he wouldn't be able to talk them into that.

"All right," said Esmerelda. "We need Mathpart, don't we, to help with the heavy work. I'll call him."

Josh got up. "I'll go into the city and get enough Lysol to wash down the place after we've gotten all the junk out of it."

They all worked steadily through the afternoon, and by suppertime it was clear that they would need a whole day more to complete their preparations. Accordingly, the next morning they were all down at the barn. Even the girl from space had been brought there, as well as her brother, since Joshua wanted to take no chances by leaving them unguarded a quarter mile away.

Mathpart, Theodore and Joshua completed the Lysol washing of the empty barn's walls by lunchtime, and after feeding Mathpart, they sent him home, leaving him to wonder why they wanted the old building cleaned out so thoroughly. After the meal, Josh and Theodore set to work erecting the big cross. The heavy wooden rail had made an imposing cross almost eight feet high, with a crossbeam of commanding width. Then Joshua pulled out a loose-leaf notebook for reference, and he and Esmerelda spent the rest of the afternoon constructing the circles, a large one and four smaller ones, and drawing the intricate symbols for summoning the demon with whom they had decided to bargain.

When Joshua had put the last detail into the symbols, and Esmerelda had checked his work, evening was upon them. They were all very tired.

"What do you say we set the ritual for tomorrow night, instead of tonight," suggested Esmerelda. "We all need the rest, and this summoning might take most of the night."

Josh reluctantly decided she was right, although he wanted very much to get the thing done with. They didn't want to fail just because they were too tired to do it right. They would need all their strength against the demon they were going to call among them. Even with all their forces firmed against the summoned spirit, Joshua could not see how they would be able fully to control it. But at least it was something to try. In the face of his increasing torment of mind, action was the only release from the gnawing doubt and self-recrimination, and he didn't want to stop moving.

And so he prepared himself for the night's sleep, trusting it to heal his physical energies, even if it could not touch his troubled mind.

Chapter Seventeen

The danger that the U. S. Army and planet Earth were in preyed on Sgt. Armstrong's mind in the days following the kidnapping, and he tried repeatedly to talk to people about it. No one would listen, and with each rebuff his emotional balance became less sturdy. Major Harris had suggested that he take a leave, and had told him to rest up, to pull himself back together. He had tried to talk to Col. Church, but the Colonel would admit nothing of what they had witnessed together, and told him to forget the entire incident. He had contacted an old friend of his from early Army days; he was an officer with some rank now, and might be able to help. The friend had gently suggested psychiatric care. It was, he had pointed out helpfully, very easy to get, in the military. Nothing to be ashamed of, and free.

Pull himself together! Forget the whole incident! Go to a psychiatrist! This was all that his friends and superiors could say to him? Didn't they know? Couldn't they see? There was an interplanetary war about to break loose, and no one would listen.

Armstrong had formed a loyalty to the Army that was as strong as any family tie; the organization had been parent and brother to him through the years; he had found his place in its service. And now it was he alone who could defend it. Defend the uniform! That was it. Do not disgrace the uniform!

He'd gotten the detective's report from Miami over the telephone. Thirty minutes, long distance. That was going to cost! The detective fees would probably wipe him out financially. And the report. The mystical room and the candles. And the body on the table. And no one to understand it all but him, the only one.

He poured himself another drink, and looked at his hand. Steady as a rock, even after half a bottle. That was the only way. Tough, hard, fighting trim. And clean. Precise. Defend the uniform! He was at a motel close to the Padeyevsky farm. A day and a half had passed since Starr's return from Miami. His watches had been long. He had seen much. Now was the time for action.

He was ready. It was dark now, and he went out to his car and removed a duffel bag and a garment bag from its trunk. His best green uniform. Defend the uniform! Careful inspection of the combat boots. Not one fleck to mar their round-toed shine. He fitted his steel helmet over its helmet liner, careful not to scratch it. He looked with pride on his old unit insignia, which was painted in its warm colors on the left side of the helmet. A place in this world. A place where there was order to things. Black stripes on the front of the helmet, because he was a Sergeant First Class. That was who he was. Sergeant First Class John Armstrong. His name. His whole name! Defend the uniform! He carefully put the decorations above the left breast pocket, and snapped the combat infantry badge above them, his blood tingling in his veins. His uniform!

He hung the coat where it wouldn't wrinkle and opened the duffel bag. His U. S. Army carbine had been bought and paid for; he wasn't one to appropriate U. S. Army material. But it had been an M-1 when he got it; it was now an M-2. He'd made the conversion himself, using parts that an ordnance sergeant friend of his had slipped him. A fully automatic weapon! A man was only as good as his weapon. He had 15-round magazines for the carbine; he cursed himself for not having obtained 30-round magazines long ago. The moment was coming! He was ready! The time was near!

What are my orders? He put the short bayonet into position at the muzzle of his carbine. It seemed a ridiculous appendage to such a short weapon, but he was dealing with aliens. They might withstand bullets. But the bayonet? He was fit and ready. He could tear them limb from limb! He carefully set the selector to full automatic. One bullet might not stop the alien, but fifteen would!

He knotted his tie, looking into the mirror. Oh! Was there a smudge from the bayonet's scabbard on his finger? A disgrace to the uniform! He rubbed until the bit of oil was off. Cleanliness! Precision! Order! What are my orders, sir? There was a spring device to stiffen the collar of his shirt; he inserted it. The helmet's rim was two finger's width from the bridge of his nose. Just so. Regulations, soldier. That's the Army way! His keen eyes spotted a speck of dust on one of his boots. He bent stiff legged and wiped it off. The coat went on. The webbed belt that held his .45 went on. The full canteen balanced the weight of the pistol. The poncho went in back. No, wait! It was a night mission. Ponchos at night? Leave the poncho. Full uniform without the poncho. The folded ponchos spoiled the looks of the uniform.

He picked up the carbine, slung it across his right shoulder, and assumed the position of attention in front of the mirror. There was something. What? He saluted. The image saluted back, the shiny image. But the ribbons! That was proof! The ribbons were on the wrong side! That was what the aliens would do! What are my orders?

He knew his orders. Words were inappropriate. He did a precisely correct about-face, walked out to the car, unslung his carbine and put it across the back seat, got in, and started down the highway towards Padeyevsky's farm.

CHAPTER EIGHTEEN

Joshua was in Pablo's best guest room, but he was nowhere near sleep. When the knock came on his door, he was up to open it immediately.

Esmerelda came through the doorway, her expression one of regal calm. It struck him how different from his own emotions hers must be. She smoothed back the tossed covers of the bed and sat down at its foot.

He tried to wait for her to break the silence. "Well?" he said at last.

She turned her face full to him, and again he noticed the particular sweetness of her gaze. "Tell me, Josh. Do you think there is any hope that we will succeed in getting the girl from space back using the summoning of this spirit?"

Josh broke the glance and looked out the window, his eyes shadowed. "No, not really," he said, after a painful pause.

"I don't either," she said. "But I do know how to get her back." Josh pulled his eyes back to her face. "How?"

She looked at him, her gaze moving over his features, watching his reactions carefully. "Our usual rituals all fail to attract enough power because positivity here is fragmented and difficult to align."

"So?"

"So we need a ritual that is capable of alerting and then aligning a larger percentage of the discarnate mind."

"We need one. But we don't have one."

"I have made one up," said Esmerelda. "And it will work."

"How could a new ritual work?" asked Josh. "The ones that we use now only work because certain segments have accepted them, through the centuries, as symbols of goodness. Without repetition, how could your ritual be any use?"

"This particular ritual," said Esmerelda, "would not lend itself to repetition. But I believe it would alert a very large part of the positively oriented mind. The emotion it engenders is powerful enough to do what we need to do. Joshua, I want you to crucify me."

He stared at her.

She went on. "It's very simple, Josh. If we make this sacrifice, the positive force that I will be able to use will be more than we have ever gotten before. And I think that with it, we can penetrate the lower astral planes and make a path of light, so that the spirit of the girl from space can use it to rejoin my spirit. I think that if we could focus that much power on those planes, there would be a great possibility that our consciousnesses would seek each other out instinctively, since we are parts of the same segment of total consciousness.

"No." Josh uttered the single word, gripping her shoulders. He looked at her, realizing much about his feelings for her that he had never before admitted to his waking consciousness. Esmerelda might be right; her crucifixion might be able to alert enough astral power to rescue the space girl. But, although he had never claimed her, Esmerelda was his. He would not lose her. He could not give her up.

"No," he repeated.

Esmerelda knew him too well to argue with his decision. His mind was set. He sat, eyes blank as rock, staring after her as she closed the door behind her.

She paused a few moments as though gathering her strength, then went down the hall to Theodore's room and let herself in. She leaned over the soundly sleeping boy, and took one of his hands. Theodore came awake quickly, saw who it was, and pulled her head down to his to give her a kiss of greeting. "What is it?" he asked.

"Get dressed," said Esmerelda. "There's something we have to do.

Theodore was used to following her lead, and although he had no idea what he wanted, he found his pants and a shirt and was quickly dressed. Esmerelda took off her dressing robe, and Theodore was surprised to see that she had a white robe on under it, not embroidered with gold like the one she had worn for the previous ritual that he had witnessed, but pure white.

"Come," she said. She led him through the door, down the stairs, and out of the house. They walked down the wagon road to the barn. The large barn door creaked open as Theodore pushed it back for them to pass through. Esmerelda took some matches and walked around the four walls of the clean-smelling, empty barn, lighting candles that she and Josh had carefully placed earlier in the day. As each candle added its feeble, flickering light to the vastness of the empty barn, Theodore became more and more aware of a feeling of subtle chill. When he had been part of the ritual in Joshua's temple he had felt nothing but goodness and purity of light in the air; here there was something slightly wrong, something out of phase with the positivity they had wished to create. As the last candle was lit, Theodore thought he saw a vague shape move at the back door of the barn. His eyes strained to penetrate the darkness, but there did not seem to be anything there.

Esmerelda was staring down at the illumined patterns Joshua had drawn on the floor. She turned to face Theodore squarely in the moving shadows that the candles cast, and told him of her plan. She explained it to him just as she had to Joshua, but there was a great difference in her presentation of the idea. Josh had been requested to help; it was assumed that Theodore would help.

Half a dozen times, Theodore was on the verge of walking out of the barn, and yet he could no more leave her than stay. The most rational objection that he could think of was that he could see no real difference between having the genuine willingness to make the sacrifice, and actually doing it, as far as the world of thought was concerned. It seemed to him that the positive mind would unify behind the thought as well as the act.

"That's not really so," said Esmerelda. "It just doesn't work that way. The only difference between discarnate mind and mind incarnate here is that minds on the mental planes don't dwell within physical bodies. The biases and emotions of the minds remain pretty much as they were while they were incarnate, and high intellect is as rarely found there as it is here. Look at it this way, Ted. If I got up in front of a group of people and told them I was willing to die for what I believed, how many of them would care? Not many. But if I made a symbol of myself, and actually made the sacrifice in front of them, then I would have stirred their emotions. Isn't that right?"

Theodore could only nod dumbly, as he watched the leaping shadows fall across her face.

"That's why the actual physical crucifixion is necessary. There isn't any other way to generate enough positive interest to rescue the space girl. Do you see?"

Theodore saw in her eyes the clear gleam of purpose, and knew beyond any doubt that she was determined. He felt the pressure of her will in his mind too, and in the end stood straight, and held out his hands to her. "OK. I'll do what you want."

Esmerelda took his hands, softly sure of the correctness of this plan. "If there were any other alternative, I would not ask it of myself, or of you."

Theodore felt her mind's certainty becoming one with his mind, smoothing his doubts.

Esmerelda broke the touch of their hands to bend over the intricate circles of design that Joshua had drawn to invoke the spirit. "Can we erase this?"

Theodore wanted it gone too; it seemed that the slight feeling of dead chill in the air came from there, as though the symbol of the spirit, not yet conjured, still brought evil into the place.

"I don't want this here, Theodore," said Esmerelda.

Theodore looked around. There was nothing in the barn at all to use; it was spotlessly bare. He rubbed at the paint with his foot; it smudged, but was wedded to the earthen floor, and would not be removed entirely. Esmerelda tried too, but to no avail.

"It doesn't matter," she said. "It will not stand in my way." She went outside the double barn doors and returned with a heavy hammer, huge nails, and an empty wooden soft drink case. She must have hidden them some time ago, thought Theodore. She handed them to him, and he set himself to do her bidding.

It took Esmerelda a full fifteen minutes to complete the ritual she had created. Theodore was swept up in the luminous beauty of her words and movements. At its end, he felt no longer like an executioner. Her will had become his own.

Esmerelda stepped up onto the small case, and leaned against the vertical member of the cross. She extended her arms until they were flush against the strongly bolted crosspiece. Theodore looked at her; she was nearly in silhouette in the dim candlelight, the flying shadows picking out light in her golden hair, licking along the bones of her finely drawn face. The wind outside was enough to stir the hair against Esmerelda's shoulders, and strands of it blew across Theodore's face. He felt immersed in her, and her will was his. He raised the hammer above his head for the stroke, and placed the nail against her cupped palm. But then he looked up at the long-shanked nail, accepted so easily by Esmerelda's yielding skin, and he broke away from the cross, lowering the hammer and backing away from her.

"I can't," he said.

He dropped the hammer and put his arms around her, and held her tightly to him for a long time. She was still and calm in his arms, and when Theodore had regained control of himself, she kissed him, and put her hands to his cheeks. Moving her fingers gently along his face, looking at him again with her purpose shining quietly in her eyes, she spoke. "I know. I know what your pain must be. And I know my own. But you know that we are losing. And we cannot lose."

"Why can't we lose? Let the planet go. We don't belong here, anyway."

"When this is all over," said Esmerelda, "we will find each other again. The time will come, and we will be together again."

She put her arms around Theodore, and they stood close for a long time, until her will was Theodore's again, and they both had accepted the leave-taking, and had said good-bye.

Esmerelda walked back to the cross and placed herself against its vertical member once again, while Theodore tried to bring himself to walk the few steps to her side, and fulfill his part of the hard task. His thoughts worked to quiet his spirit, to make him accept Esmerelda's sacrifice and become one with its purpose, and only a sudden noise made him look up.

Through his tears, he could see a figure coming through the door, holding a short rifle. Theodore had only a second to see the intruder before he was hit. It was impossible to tell whether Armstrong had intended to kill him instantly, or whether a glint from the hammer in Theodore's hand caused the reflex action on the trigger. The carbine spurted fire. The stocky Sergeant controlled the gun with the ease of long practice, pressing down hard on the hand guard as it attempted to rise. He emptied the full magazine in one burst, spraying Theodore and the wall behind him. Death was almost instantaneous, and Esmerelda was able to see Theodore's spirit separate from his riddled, torn physical body.

Then the Sergeant turned to her, his eyes hard and bright as he looked at her. He pointed the carbine at her and pressed the trigger, but the weapon was empty. He lunged, driving the bayonet through her and deep into the heavy wooden post. His thrusting lunge was professional, and the bayonet was imbedded in the wood of the cross. He tugged at it. It would not yield.

The sergeant put a heavy boot against the bottom of the cross and, as the life slipped from the girl, worked frantically to free the blade of the bayonet. As he wrenched the weapon up and down, blood began to run down the short barrel and onto his hands. He jumped back in horror, and carefully inspected his immaculate uniform. He was able to work his handkerchief out, and wiped his hands meticulously. The weapon was now slimy with blood. He could never hope to clean it. It was no longer an acceptable part of the uniform. He would leave it there. He opened the flap of his holster and took out the Match .45. His stubby thumb cocked the hammer. He walked out of the barn and started up the road towards the house.

As he approached the top of the rather steep rise that hid the house from the barn's view, he suddenly saw headlights and heard the clever whine of a finely-tuned engine. Joshua had heard the shots, and had come to investigate. Armstrong leveled his pistol at the lights, and as soon as he saw the windshield of the car, he squeezed off a shot. Glass splinters sprayed past Joshua's face, temporarily blinding him, so that he never saw the man that his car bumped harshly over as he started to brake. The car came to a lurching stop, and he was out of it and running back to the road from which it had veered. In the dim, red glow of the tail lights, Joshua could see a body. He took a closer look. It was Sgt. Armstrong, his face contorted, his eyes wide and fixed in death. The .45 automatic was still gripped tightly in his right hand.

Joshua straightened up. He looked towards the barn and saw for the first time its dim, dancing lights. His body grew cold, and he ran towards it. Inside the big room, the blowing candles tossed their little lights into long, fantastic shadows. The smudged diagrams on the floor had drops of blood on them, and Joshua saw that both Theodore and Esmerelda were dead. Theodore's body lay near the foot of the cross; Esmerelda was pinned to the cross like a grotesque doll, held crazily half-vertical by the blade that had crucified her.

Joshua stumbled over to the wall of the barn and circled it, putting out the candles. He walked back to the big house. Pablo was on the porch. Joshua sat down, heavily.

Pablo seemed unable to move. "What happened?"

Joshua told him, as well as he could.

"We'll have to call the police," said Pablo.

"Yeah," said Josh.

"The space man and the space girl have disappeared," said Pablo. They're nowhere in the house. Everyone's gone."

"Esmerelda succeeded, then."

"You mean the space girl came back to her body?"

"Yeah."

"Where'd they go, then?"

"They went home."

Joshua and Pablo sat there until the sun came up, listening to the branches brush their sides together, watching the wind blow a few remaining leaves past them on the porch.

Postlogue

Night has fallen on the planet of light, and the air is crisp with the winter cold. Two youthful figures walk under the vaults of the high-domed ceiling, into the hall of white marble. As they clasp hands, they offer their experience and their confusion to the teachers of this temple, for they wish to understand what they have seen. And they listen to the wisdom of their teacher:

"In the depths of the cavern burns a candle, but this candle is not straight. Its flame flutters in the breeze, and wafts its way through the cavern, moving gently, constantly moving, its wax dripping upon the floor, for the candle is not straight.

"Off of the ceiling of the cavern come droplets of water. They fall about the candle, but they do not put it out.

"Into the cavern comes a creature, and this creature has a mind. And the mind is aware of the candle, which it does not understand. Water droplets fall upon this creature, and this the creature understands. But it does not understand.

"It looks into the cavern, and sees the candle, and hesitates. The gentle breeze wafts the creature and the candle, and the flame flutters in the cavern. And with this fluttering, shadows dance across the walls.

"Out of the floor of the cavern comes life, in the form of moss, which grows in very slight profusion. And the creature has trodden upon this, and felt it under its footpads. And it understands, but it does not understand.

"But into its environment has come the alien, and this alien burns with its bright flame, and its wax drops upon the cavern floor, falling upon the moss, coating it with its waxen surface.

"But courage builds within the creature, and it creeps forward, trying now to determine the essence of the intruder. But it does not understand. And yet it does not seek to understand. For its mind is transfixed by the flame burning brightly in the darkness.

"And closer comes the creature to the alien, out of the darkness, out of the dancing shadows, out of the wetness, across the mossy surface. It approaches the alien, and it looks into the flame, and the flame is all of newness, and has depth and meaning.

"But yet the creature does not understand, for it is not accustomed to such an intrusion. And it holds fear within its heart, for it does not understand.

"And while the creature is transfixed by the flame that holds it immobile, into the cavern comes the beast. This beast falls upon the creature and brings it *death. And the candle flickers, and the images dance across the walls, and the creature is devoured. And yet it did not understand.*

"*The beast stands erect, the life-blood of the creature dripping from his jowls. He looks steadfastly into the candle, and he laughs aloud, his laughter echoing through the cavern, causing droplets to fall from the roof and wet his fur. He walks over with his red eyes fixed upon the candle, and with one quick motion snuffs it out.*

"*For he understands. And he laughs his laughter, which echoes once more through the great cavern. For he is wise. For, once more, he has used the Creator's light to serve him. And it has served him well. For the substance of his prey now acts to give him strength and life. And he is fat of belly and satisfied, his task and trickery complete.*"

The two bright beings gaze long into the golden light that hides their teachers' forms, eyes held in an inward, searching look as they absorb their teachers' parable.

The delft white girl moves first, kneeling softly upon the temple floor, "We have gone, and attempted to serve," she says, and pauses, gathering her thoughts. "My own self, the one known as Esmerelda Sweetwater, has brought me back from a place I think might have been like the cave of which you spoke. Or, beloved ones who offer your wisdom, do you mean to suggest that my friend's planet is like the cave?" Again she pauses.

Golden swirls the light as one of the teachers moves towards her. "My child, learn well that all may use the light, both those of love for others and those whose love is for power over others. We leave our lesson for your learning, and would not take that opportunity from you, for you have seen much. We ask you now our question: Is the power of the beast stronger, or is the power of the one who uses light to save the victim of the beast stronger?"

The man kneels before the teacher too, again grasping the girl's hand. "We know the light of Esmerelda's love for my sister was greater than all that held my sister in thrall. We know that the universe is full of love. But in that place—on that planet—"

"*It is an unusual planet," agrees the teacher.*

"*But have we served, then?" asks the girl, her eyes almost gray with concern.*

The teacher rests a hand upon each blonde head. "In love and light were you sent forth, and in the same love and light you have returned. Yet you have been touched. Think you then that you have not touched others? Now rest, and heal yourselves, and learn, my children."

The two bright beings walk slowly outside the temple and find again the garden which they had visited what seemed a long age ago. Still clasping hands, they sit upon the soft, living grass, and begin to meditate.

APPENDIX

THE PROPHETIC QUALITIES OF *The Crucifixion of Esmerelda Sweetwater*

Don Elkins and Carla L. Rueckert wrote *The Crucifixion of Esmerelda Sweetwater* in 1968, the first year of working together as the L/L Company, which would later become L/L Research. It was also their first shared writing effort.

The writing of the book came easily because they didn't have to conceive of the story or the characters—it came *to them*. They were able to see it playing out upon the inner stage of their blended minds. It was more like taking dictation than writing. They draw from this shared vision in different, complementing ways. With Carla's head resting in Don's lap, Don dictated the plot of the story into a cassette recorder. Carla, seeing the same story unfold in her own mind, then filled in the plot with character and dialogue.[1]

That is, except for the ending. When it came to the ending, they knew that at least one of the three major characters would have to die in order for the book to make sense, but they didn't get the same clear image for who would die as they had gotten for the rest of the book. Ra spoke about this unique experience 13 years later:

> When the commitment was made between two of this group to work for the betterment of the planetary sphere, this commitment activated a possibility/probability vortex of some strength. The experience of generating this volume [*The Crucifixion of Esmerelda Sweetwater*] was unusual in that it was visualized as if watching the moving picture.
>
> Time had become available in its present-moment form. The scenario of the volume went smoothly until the ending of the volume. You could not end the volume, and the **ending was not visualized** as [was] the entire body of the material, **but was written or authored.** This is **due to** the action of **free will** in all of the creation. – Ra, 68.14

Here Ra indicated to us that the ending wasn't visualized (as the rest of the book had been) because the ending was unknown, it would be determined only by free will itself.

---

[1] This and a sprinkling of material elsewhere in this essay were transposed from L/L's publication, *The Quixotic Quest*.

Why is that important? Because—though Don and Carla had no idea at the time they were writing the book—much of the book's content would come true in their lives and my own. In other words, they were writing about their own future. Ra speaks to this in the same quote:

> However, the volume contains a view of significant events, both symbolically and specifically, which you saw under the influence of the magnetic attraction which was released when the commitment was made [between Carla and Don] and full memory of the dedication of this, what you may call, mission restored. – Ra, 68.14

Their first inkling of the book's prophetic nature occurred in 1974 after they read the book *Uri,* by Dr. Andrija Puharich. As they read this book they realized that Dr. Puharich had an amazing similarity to one of the main characters in their book, Dr. Pablo Padeyevsky.

Don reached out to Dr. Puharich who later called and invited Don and Carla to visit him at his home in upstate New York. The parallels between the real-life Puharich and the fictional Padeyevsky began to grow. In that conversation they discovered that Puharich was also known by his friends as "the good doctor," which was the way Dr. Padeyevski was also known by his friends in their book. Upon arriving at his estate they noticed that his house was built just like the house that Dr. Padeyevsky owned in their book. Except for one thing: the circle driveway in front of Dr. Puharich's house did not have a ring of peonies around it as did Dr. Padeyevski's in the book. When they mentioned this to Dr. Puharich, he laughed and told them that he had the peonies cut down two years before. Meaning that at the time Don and Carla had written the book, the driveway was, indeed, ringed by peonies as they had seen it in their minds.

The next curious similarity between their book and reality was their description of a character in the book named Theodore Behr, whom I represented in real life as the third member of L/L Research. In the book, he had the role of the third person in the magical rituals used to summon the two beings of light from a distant planet of light. When I read their description of Theodore's face in the book, I thought that I was looking into a mirror: "slender, pale face, with its high cheekbones, its wide-spaced, rather deep-set eyes, the high forehead, the carefully molded, almost arrogant discipline of the nose and mouth."

Then there was the parallel to the "appurtenances" used during the Ra Contact. In the *Crucifixion of Esmerelda Sweetwater* is a temple in which Joshua Starr and Esmerelda Sweetwater practiced their white magical rituals. The temple contained an altar that held a gold cloth, candle, and open Bible. This was quite similar to the table that held the accoutrement for the Ra Contact: white cloth with green, gold, and red flowers painted around its circular edge, Carla's Bible opened to John 1:1, a candle, incense in a holder, and a chalice of water.

In both the book and the room in which the Ra Contact was held, the Banishing Ritual of the Lesser Pentagram was used to cleanse each room of negative influences. We changed one line to read "Yod-Heh-Shin-Vah-Heh" instead of "Yod-Heh-Vah-Heh" because the addition of "Shin" renders the word to mean "Jesus," and Carla was devoted to Jesus Christ for all of her life.

In *The Crucifixion of Esmerelda Sweetwater,* the black magician's name was Trostrick. He energized various violent situations in which people were magically directed to kill others to promote his ends. During the Ra Contact, we didn't receive that particular type of energization, but we were monitored by a negatively oriented discarnate entity. This entity would greatly intensify any freely chosen disharmonious choices that we might make in an attempt to stop the Ra Contact from producing information and inspiration, or light.

In one such instance during the Ra Contact years, we had moved into a new house in Atlanta, and we encountered the extraordinarily mundane situation of a dirty carpet. Carla wanted the rug clean, Don didn't and indicated that he wanted to talk no further of the matter. Carla subsequently withheld communication that was important to her and our negative friend took the opportunity to energize her inability to clearly use her throat chakra. As a result she almost died of suffocation the next day on a walk that she was taking with me. A good deal of simply talking about the situation of the house solved this problem.

Due to these "psychic attacks"—or "psychic greetings" as we came to call them—Carla's faith in the goodness of all things was tested. Esmerelda Sweetwater's faith was similarly tested when she saw the negativity that her uncle, Pablo Padeyevsky had been involved in. An even greater test of Carla's faith came with the death of Don Elkins by his own hand. Her faith in real life almost did not survive that outcome.

As mentioned at the beginning of this essay, the one thing that the visionary book did not disclose to Carla and Don, and thus could not fully predict, was the ending. All they knew was that either Esmerelda (the idealized version of Carla) or Joshua (the idealized version of Don) must die, but they don't quite know who. About how they arrived at the decision of which character would die, Carla said in the *Tilting at Windmills* interview:

Carla: Well, it didn't make any sense; it wasn't logical, and we were both very logical people. Don was preternaturally healthy. His vision was 20/10. When he was in the Army he could run rings around his unit all day while he was running them on a ten-mile hike and never run out of breath. He was just so healthy, he was incredibly healthy, never been sick. He'd never. been. sick. He'd never had a cold.

I was very, very frail. There was no question about it. I accepted that much myself although I didn't accept anything more. I was normal. It just took a little bit of skill to stay normal. There was this way and that way I could screw up, and then I would be having a problem because of earlier sickness—kidney problems, rheumatoid problems, that kind of thing. But just seeing that I wasn't long for this world, I was just frail. So it made sense that this person most like me in the book would die, whereas Don's character would not. And we worked with that and worked with that and worked with that, and that's the way we wrote it: the space girl, or Esmeralda, dies at the end.

And for reasons just stated, they allot to Esmerelda the role of dying at the story's conclusion. Esmerelda loses her life through the choice of martyrdom in the book, which, also in parallel, Carla came close to doing in the events of the Ra Contact. But that was not to be Carla's fate in our world. "This is due to the action of free will in all of creation," as Ra said.

As you the reader are probably already aware, it was, in the end, not Carla but Don Elkins who died.

Don felt financially responsible for the three of us and for L/L Research. But in the early '80s, his employer, Eastern Airlines, was suffering financial problems, and it didn't look like the airline would survive much longer. Both Joshua Starr (Don's character correlation in the book) and Don felt that they had "dropped the ball" and were failing in their chosen duties.

In addition, further psychic greetings from our negative friend had threatened Carla's life and also threatened to gain control of Carla's spirit while she was in trance for a Ra session, attempting to lead her into what Ra called "negative time/space," a very undesirable scenario when you understand the metaphysics of the situation. Had that outcome transpired, it would have stopped the Ra Contact and given the negative entity Carla's power through her physical death and spiritual imprisonment, again repeating the basic scenario of the book.

In the book, Joshua Starr tries to make a deal with the black magician Trostrick. He offers to trade his own life for Esmerelda's spirit, which

Trostrick has imprisoned in negative time/space. At one point near the end of the Ra Contact, when Don was obviously declining in his own mental and physical health, he asked me what I thought of him making a similar deal with our negative friend. I told him that I thought that it was a bad idea because we could not trust our negative friend to do anything that we wanted him to do.

Whether he attempted such a deal, Carla and I never knew. But given the way Don began to decline that final year and a half, his death seemed just as inevitable as Esmerelda's and Theodore's in the book. In the last session that we had with those of Ra, Don asked Ra about his own deteriorating mental and physical conditions. Ra described the various elements that had gone into making it one of grave concern. Ra's suggestion to Don was that he concentrate on praise and thanksgiving as a means to find his way out of his mind and body dilemma. But Don could not give praise or thanksgiving because he was convinced that he was not long for this world.

In a happier ending to Don's life than for the characters that died in *Esmerelda,* Carla was able to see Don on two occasions in waking visions after his death. In these visions Don told Carla that all had turned out as it was supposed to. He said that she and I would not know how this could be until we too passed through death's door.

Now Carla knows, and only I am left to wonder.

Jim McCarty
Louisville, KY
April 1, 2016

Made in the USA
Las Vegas, NV
29 March 2021